*7 Figure Publications presents . . .*

# Beautifully Ruthless

## by

# Belle Ahosi

7 Figure Publications
PO Box 9334
Augusta, GA 30916
http://7figurepublications.com

(Paperback)

ISBN-10: 1-7329145-0-8
ISBN-13: 978-1-7329145-0-6

Library of Congress Cataloging-In-Publication Data:
LCCN 2018961413

Editor, Linda Wilson

Cover design by Davida of Oddball Designs

Published October 2018

## Dedication

*Isaiah Amir and Elijah Malik, my love for you will forever be misunderstood.*

*To my mother, the strongest woman I know, and to my father, you are truly forgiven. I love you all with everything in me.*

# Acknowledgments

Yahweh, your love, mercy, and forgiveness has shaped me. And without it, none of this would be possible.

My great uncle, Ronnie Gross, you're more than great. He truly blessed me when he blessed you. No words can express my gratitude. My brother, The Mister, I love you and thank you for never giving up on me when everyone else did. My sister, Shannon Lenora, thanks for all of your lines of love and encouragement.

RT, my love, my friend, I can never repay the love you've shown. I love you for so many reasons, for teaching me how to survive in this concrete jungle. My warrior, Ashley, Jordan Gray, your prayers and strength have pushed me to be a better woman. Renee Harris, my best friend, I love you and never thought I'd meet another woman who felt the depths of my pain or mirrored my soul. Nikita Moore, this journey has been long and hard, but this too shall pass, and even when things don't seem right, trust HIM and know that I'll be here. I love you forever. The Liz, my dog, I love you and your laugh, like you, is unforgettable. Zhioukellia Brown, you've taught me so much and don't even know it. My love for you is that of a sister. Angela Mercer, I love your life. You touched me, and even though a tear never fell, you were my shoulder. B. Sullivan, you told me that I was going to make it, and I believed you. Tiffany Gonzalez, the prettiest woman I know, stay focused. You got this!

Sereniti Hall and Linda Wilson, the whole 7-Figure Publications Team, thank you all for your belief in me. Made my blood, sweat, and tears relevant. Everyone stay tuned for more. I'm just getting started.

*The Beautiful Warrior*

# PROLOGUE

"Stop . . . Please!" Harmony's body cringed as Mr. Pratt's calloused hands fondled her most private parts.

"Shut up!" Mr. Pratt grabbed her by the throat. "You already know the drill!" he whispered harshly, kissing down Harmony's neck, his lips reeking of cheap vodka. She refused her tears as they pooled in her chestnut-brown eyes. Nobody cared. They never had. Almost every night for the past three years, Mr. Pratt had snuck into her room to carry out his sick fantasies. No one ever heard her cries, or pleas for help and probably never would. Cursed by her beauty, she felt trapped. Alone. The baggy clothes and plain appearance Harmony took on didn't even deter Mr. Pratt. Nothing did. He was relentless, and she was his every night. Her body belonged to him.

Mr. Pratt slid on a condom, forced Harmony onto her stomach, and gripped her honey-blonde curls while viciously pumping into her. The pillow stifled her pleas for the torture to end. Tears involuntarily burned down her face. What have I done so wrong to deserve this? Harmony wondered. Yeah, she had stolen a few meals out of the grocery store, sold and smoked a little weed, but it was all in the name of survival. She tried anything to suppress the pain and imagined herself back at home with her brother. It had been almost three years since the pretty brunette with a bright smile from Child Protective Services came to her doorstep. That was the day she felt she had been snatched away from her older brother, Peezy and the safety of their home after their mother had been sentenced to prison.

Mr. Pratt's heavy grunting and sweating forced her into the present. He pumped hard and fast, still ripping into her. Finally reaching his peak, he slid off her, then shoved her head into the

i

pillow. "Don't move," he said through crooked teeth. Harmony wasn't stupid; she knew the drill just as he had said. She was well aware of the consequences for moving before he made it out of her room.

For another hour, Harmony lay stiffly still, as if her body was ice cold in a casket. She hated her beauty, her curves, and anything else that made him seek her out every night. Once the house was quiet, she crept down the hall into the bathroom where she attempted to rid herself of his scent. It was all over her, in her hair, in her clothes, even her pores reeked of his cheap cologne. Hot tears slid down the sides of her cheeks. "It's almost over. Just one more year and I'll be free," she said, suppressing her anger.

# CHAPTER 1

Aria awoke early in the morning instinctively glancing at the floor. She grabbed the pink envelope, unsure of who could have written her. Everyone that was important to her, which was pretty much no one, knew that she would be released today. She had less than an hour and it would all be over. Sighing, Aria peeled open the letter. Her mouth dropped open when she read the bold words written across the pretty stationary:

> Everything can be bought with a price and I have the means to see to it that my promise is kept. See you in the streets.
> Nat

Aria smacked her lips. She had other things to worry about than her late girlfriend's cousin Natalie's idle threats. She ripped the fancy stationary up and flushed it down the toilet. Her nightmare was over. She was one step closer to freedom. Aria gathered her belongings, wrapped up her linen, and headed down the long hall where Officer Jackson waited to escort her to the holding cell.

"Good luck," Officer Jackson said.

"Same to you." Aria sat in the cell and allowed her thoughts to intrude.

Damn! I can't believe Momma died of cancer just two weeks before my release. Aria slid out of her juvenile state-issued uniform and into the pair of jeans and plain white T-shirt her social worker brought for her. She checked her reflection in the stainless steel mirror and fixed her unruly hair. It seemed like yesterday her mom was just here visiting, making an attempt to mend their strained

1

relationship. Her mom's drug abuse and failure to believe that her uncle had violated her in the worst way, stripping Aria of her innocence, had caused their family so much turmoil. Aria didn't have a real plan for once she was out of state custody, but she was more than sure that she would be able to survive.

The wounds were still fresh, and the unexpected death of her mother and nonexistent father left her feeling lost. The three years that she'd spent in the detention facility for murder had sharpened her mentally and allowed her to stuff every emotion behind her mask. If all else failed, she planned to link up with her cousin Envy, who had voluntarily given her over twenty grand for her defense attorney. They had always been close and it showed when it mattered most. It hurt to know that so many bridges had been burned by her mother that nobody felt the need to come to Aria's aid when the state contacted them about seeking custody. The sad part was only eleven months of what the state considered her childhood were left. Aria's anger boiled over, spilling out onto anyone who she felt deserved it, which was everyone. So this is what it feels like to be alone, huh? Aria thought, smoothing her hair over one last time.

"You ready yet, Aria?" the redheaded social worker said through the door.

"As ready as I'll ever be," Aria said, sarcastically. She had no clue what to expect, but whatever it was would only be temporary, because in eleven months she would no longer be a ward of the state.

The ride to meet her temporary foster family was quiet but long. Especially as she made her way to their front door and waited for someone to answer.

Meeting the Pratts was like meeting Mr. and Mrs. Frankenstein, only Mr. Pratt was severely obese and the knockoff pearls Mrs. Pratt wore looked more like a dog collar than a necklace. They seemed nice enough, though it mattered none because Aria had little to no intentions on getting acquainted, or to like them very much. The moment she was released from the detention facility and into the state's custody, she had begun counting down the days until she was finally going to be free. Her social worker, Ms. Wynn, patted her on the shoulder reassuringly, letting her know all that she could do, which wasn't much.

"You will be enrolled in school in a few days. Mrs. Pratt will be taking you shopping to get all you need, and I will be stopping by regularly to check on you. Just try to relax, hopefully things will get easier."

They probably won't, Aria thought. "Thanks, I um have to use the restroom," Aria said, looking at the Pratts.

"Uh, yes. It's down the hall, last door on the right," Mr. Pratt said.

Once in the bathroom, Aria suddenly felt nauseous; her nerves formed a knot in her stomach. She leaned over the toilet. Nothing but dry heaving. She splashed water on her face, then stared at her reflection. Chill, Aria. You have survived worse.

She came down the hall wiping her hands on her jeans as she returned to the living room and stood. Mrs. Pratt and Ms. Wynn were conversing. Her eyes just happened to meet with the pretty chick rocking the low Caesar haircut that complemented her oval, toffee-colored face. The hairstyle only projected the beauty she was trying to hide, amplifying it in a sexy, dominant kind of way.

Mrs. Pratt's eyes bucked at the girl who'd just entered the room, her gaze oozing with disapproval. Yet Aria peeped her putting on a fake smile that she seemed to have mastered. "Harmony, sweetheart. Meet Ms. Wynn."

"It's nice to meet you, Harmony," the redheaded woman said softly, then extended her hand.

"Nice to meet you, too . . . ma'am."

Damn, she is beautiful, Aria thought as Harmony's radiant eyes locked with hers. She could see the pain hidden beneath them. Oh, I'm definitely fuckin' her. Her bad boy swag was sexy, alluring, and it had Aria intrigued. She read people well and could sense Harmony's uncertainty, but she was sure the girl's face flushed when their attraction registered. Breaking down peoples' walls and gaining their trust was like taking candy from a baby, so Harmony's uncertainty posed very little threat to Aria, and knowing that she would be here, eased Aria's nerves a little.

The Pratts showed Ms. Wynn out, and Aria roamed about her new home. She opened the patio door and breathed in the fresh scent of flowers and earth. It had been a long three years in the detention facility, and now that she was free, she would take advantage of every opportunity that presented itself. She now understood what they meant when they said "dog eat dog world." Aria would live or die by it.

Walking down the path, Aria smiled at the garden of vegetables and flowers. "This is Tammy's favorite spot in the entire world," Mr. Pratt said, startling her. Aria quickly recovered from the brief fright, then smiled. Mr. Pratt was sloppy and ashy looking. He creeped her out, but because she promised to give this place a shot, she wouldn't flip on him about sneaking up on her. She shook off the eerie feeling.

"My grandmother had some of these same vegetables in her garden. I used to help her when I was younger," Aria said.

Mr. Pratt grinned, showing crooked, yellow teeth.

"Tammy sure could use some help."

Aria didn't know how to place the feelings that suddenly overwhelmed her, so she stuffed them deep within the layers of her heart.

\* \* \* \* \* \*

A few minutes earlier, Harmony had climbed off the bus dreading the walk to the hellhole the Pratts called home. She figured Mrs. Pratt was more than likely going to flip and probably try to kill her once she saw her new haircut. It didn't really matter though. She had already mentally prepared herself for the mayhem. But once she entered the house and saw a redheaded woman dressed in a black business skirt and jacket standing there, inside she rejoiced.

Is she here to take me home? Has she found Peezy? Is my mom out of prison? For a split second, Harmony had allowed her emotions to dominate her and carry her to a place far from here.

"Harmony, meet Aria. Aria, Harmony. Welcome to our family!" Mrs. Pratt exclaimed, proudly as she guided Aria forward into view.

Family? What family? Harmony thought.

"And this is her social worker, Ms. Wynn." Harmony's first mind told her to tell Ms. Wynn to take them both far away from this place. This was no place for a child, especially a teenage girl. Her eyes locked with Aria again, and an instant attraction sparked. Her face flushed, and her heart thumped wildly against her chest. She was unsure of the feelings dwelling within her. Aria's flawless skin was the same rich color as a Hershey's bar. Her voluminous jet-black hair was pulled high into a bun on top of her head, and her dark, almond-shaped eyes summoned her the moment she peered into them.

"Hey," she said softly.

"Hey," Harmony said, waving. Her eyes fell on Mr. Pratt, who couldn't keep his eyes off Aria. Every chance he got, he managed to sneak a glimpse of her beauty.

Sorrow filled Harmony's heart for the girl who knew nothing of the torture being condoned in this house during the wee hours of the night. Harmony knew that Mrs. Pratt only wanted the check that came, along with the very little responsibility of caring for a foster child, who was almost in adulthood. And Mr. Pratt wanted nothing more than to get his dick wet. Sick bastard, Harmony thought.

"Well, I have tons of homework to do," Harmony said, excusing herself. She turned to Ms. Wynn. "It was nice meeting you." She stole one last look at the beauty, then ran up the stairs two at a time, closing her bedroom door behind her. She scoffed at the new comforters. "Wow! Mrs. Pratt is laying it on thick, ain't she?" Harmony said to the empty room. Her heart suddenly sped up, and visions of her torture flashed in her mind. "I have to do something about this, about them. They can't keep getting away with this." Harmony got up and snatched open her room door.

WHAP!

"Who the fuck told you that it was all right to cut your hair?" Mrs. Pratt asked, calmly knocking Harmony back into the bedroom door. Harmony grabbed her face and steadied herself. "Oh, so you don't hear me talking?" Mrs. Pratt asked, striking the other side of her face, sending her stumbling back into the door.

"I cut my hair because—"

WHAP!

"There is no reason, is there? You did it just to piss me off, didn't you?"

WHAP!

Mrs. Pratt knocked Harmony against the door, harder this time. She was no fool; she knew what went on between Harmony and her husband at night. Tammy Pratt also knew that Harmony was the reason he refused her sexual advances and need for love, leaving her bitter, hurt, and scorned. Every chance she got she took her pain out on Harmony, reprimanding her for the smallest offenses with no mercy.

Harmony's anger was rising, and her tolerance had dropped. She had, had enough and knew that if she didn't remain calm, she was going to end up hurting Mrs. Pratt. She firmly planted her feet on the ground.

"I'm sick of your disrespectful ass!" Mrs. Pratt said, raising her hand to strike her again. Harmony grabbed her wrist in midair.

"Stop fucking hittin' me! It's my damn hair, and I can cut it if I want!" Harmony stated, coldly.

Mrs. Pratt froze at the sound of her voice. It seemed as if she had grown in size as she pierced Mrs. Pratt with her eyes.

"Look, I don't like you, and we both know why you don't like me, but if it's any consolation, I would much rather he fucked you every night and not me. The best news is that I will be eighteen in less than a year, and then there isn't anything you or he can do to me." Footsteps on the stairs silenced them both.

"You're grounded, you little bitch!" Mrs. Pratt whispered harshly, snatching her hand away and walking down the hall.

Harmony rushed to the bathroom trying to calm down. She felt as if she was about to lose it. She had suppressed the pain and anger that lie dormant in her long enough, and it was becoming impossible to continue to do so.

* * * * * *

Aria had heard how harshly Mrs. Pratt had spoken to Harmony. She was far from naïve, so the smile she gave Aria on the way down the stairs didn't sway her. Aria went into her room and sat on the bed. Boredom was beginning to set in, and her mind was on overload. The ridiculous nine o'clock curfew Mr. Pratt spoke about would never be met if she had to travel by bus and trolley. She was determined to figure out how to set her feet back in her old stomping grounds and get up with a few of her old friends.

Harmony came into the room breaking Aria's train of thought. "I uh, I wasn't sure which bed was yours, so I just picked one," Aria said.

"It doesn't matter," Harmony answered nonchalantly, sitting down on the adjacent bed.

"What time is dinner?"

"Every night at eight o'clock except for Sundays. It's at seven-thirty." Harmony wasn't even looking at her. Usually, Aria's presence commanded everyone's attention, and the fact that she seemed uninterested made Aria demand it. Harmony lay across the bed, pulled out her calculus work book, and began working on her homework.

"Um, excuse me," Aria said. Harmony looked over at Aria, not in the mood for small talk.

"Yeah?"

"Can I have something comfortable to change into? I own absolutely nothing."

"Sure, look in the top drawer over there. There are some basketball shorts and tank tops you can choose from. Get whatever you need."

Aria grabbed something to wear, then stripped naked. "Oh, one more thing. Can I wear your robe?" Harmony turned around, irritated.

"I—" Her eyes scanned Aria's thick, curvaceous frame. "Uh yeah. I don't care. The towels are in the hall closet." Aria smirked.

"Thanks," she said, smiling at Harmony stammering over her words. Nobody ignores me. I am that bitch, and I see I'm going to have to let her know it, Aria thought.

# CHAPTER 2

The dinner table was quiet as usual. Occasionally, Aria eyed Harmony, sending a wave of butterflies flying every which way inside of her. Aria had shocked her when she dropped her clothes in the middle of the room. Girls had flaunted around the locker room every day, but Aria was built like a stallion. She didn't know those type of bodies existed outside of magazines and couldn't explain why she was turned on by it, or why there was an attraction. The way Aria licked her lips, slightly biting the bottom one, left Harmony sorting out just what was going on inside of her. Why her heart beat sped up, or why her mouth went dry, she didn't know.

"Harmony!" Mr. Pratt said loudly, snapping her out of her thoughts.

"Yes!" she answered, her tone dripping with irritation.

"Would you or would you not like some dessert?"

"No thank you. I'm actually done. Can I be excused?" Harmony looked from Mrs. Pratt and back to his dark stare. Mr. Pratt nodded, excusing her. Whenever she was in their presence for too long, her blood would begin to boil, making it hard to pretend that everything was okay.

Harmony went upstairs and prepared herself for school. She had saved up her weekly allowance for months to pay for her transformation into a tomboy, and now that she was grounded, those new Jordan's she was supposed to cop this month would have to wait. Mrs. Pratt didn't approve of Harmony's new wardrobe. *But fuck her!* is how she felt, and even though it didn't deter her perverted ass husband from sneaking into her room at night, she had begun to like the baggy jeans and plaid button ups. It had become a part of her,

9

fitting the personality that she didn't know existed. Harmony showered, and then dressed in a pair of basketball shorts and a white T-shirt, then climbed in bed. She said a silent prayer, mentally preparing herself for another night of torture. She could not help but wonder if Aria would be welcomed into her world, or would Mr. Pratt spare her? The way Harmony was feeling, this wouldn't be any ordinary night. She would not submit. Mr. Pratt had no idea that Harmony's dreams placed murder on her mind and malice in her heart.

Thankful for Friday, Harmony headed home with her thoughts weighing heavily on her mind. Life had not been all that bad at the Pratt's residence. Unfortunately, all Harmony could think about was when everything ceased what would follow? She noticed a change in the Pratts and how they took to Aria, praising her for the smallest achievement. Then she realized the pattern; it was the same one she had gone through before the late night visits and unwarranted punishment began. Harmony remained hidden, steering clear of the Pratts and their deception, avoiding Aria as much as possible, even though she made it hard to do. Mr. Pratt had not snuck into her bedroom in weeks, and she was grateful. She knew that once he got his chance, he would be rough and vicious. As much as she tried to mentally prepare for it, she couldn't.

Welcoming the silence, Harmony unlocked the front door and stepped inside her home. A strange feeling crept over her once she reached the top of the steps. He's here, she thought, storming into her room, praying that Aria had made it home before her. She hadn't. Harmony closed the door, quietly backing right into Mr. Pratt's arms. She gasped. He gripped her butt through her baggy jeans. She moved away.

"Come on, baby girl. Don't act like that. It's been so long since you gave me some of—"

"I never gave you anything!" she yelled, snatching away from him. Mr. Pratt smiled tightly and pressed her against the wall.

"Well, you're going to give me some today," he said calmly, with a crazed look in his eyes. Mr. Pratt was pissed when he found out they would be taking in another bastard child, until he saw how beautiful Aria was, but his instincts told him that Aria was off limits and would do more than reveal his dirty little secret if he dared. So he was forced to restrain his urge to sneak into Harmony's room at night. He was aching for her youth, and now that this small window of opportunity had presented itself, he had to have her. Mr. Pratt cocked his head to the side. "Okay, how about a little head then?" he reasoned.

"No!" Harmony screamed. Mr. Pratt dropped his slacks to the floor and gripped her jaw tightly.

"I'm not asking, you little bitch. I'm telling you!" he said, shoving her to her knees. Harmony looked up at him.

"And I'm telling you that I'm not doing it." He smashed Harmony's face into his manhood. Harmony opened her mouth.

"There you go . . . that's it." Mr. Pratt relaxed. She grabbed a handful of his balls and squeezed hard.

"Aaahhhh! You little bitch!" he yelled. Harmony climbed to her feet, but Mr. Pratt shoved her hard, sending her crashing back down to the floor.

"Ah!" she screamed. Mr. Pratt climbed on top of her and wrapped his hands around her neck. "Get off of me!" Harmony yelled at the top of her lungs. "Stop it!" she screamed and continued fighting. The sound of the garage door closing sent him scuffling down the hall. Harmony sat up and smiled; she had fought back and won. He will never touch me again, she thought. Ever.

\* \* \* \* \* \*

11

Aria walked past Mr. Pratt, who appeared disheveled, and went straight up to her room. She had heard a muffled scream over Mrs. Pratt's telephone conversation. Harmony was wiping blood from her mouth when she entered the room.

"What the fuck happen to you?" she asked.

"Nothing, I'm good." Aria took the towel from her and patted away the flowing blood.

"Did he do this to you?" Aria asked. Harmony said nothing. "Did he try to touch you or something? Is he—"

"Look! Mind your damn business, Aria!" Harmony snapped, snatching the towel from her. "You have no idea what's going—"

"I heard you screaming, Harmony. I have a good idea of what is going on. I see the way he looks at you . . . the way Mrs. Pratt is towards you. Has he touched you before?" Tears formed in Harmony's eyes. She nodded.

"Yes, every night . . . until you got here." Aria wrapped her arms around Harmony and consoled her. Many nights her own uncle had climbed into her bed, but unlike Harmony, she had fought, forcing a steak knife through his stomach and leaving him to explain why he was in her room at three in the morning covered in blood.

"Listen, we will take care of this. I will help you, I promise," Aria said, snatching the towel back. "But there is only one way to handle this. We—" Harmony grabbed Aria's arm.

"Nobody is going to believe us. We can't tell anyone!"

"Of course not, who said anything about telling?" Aria smiled, leaving Harmony with mixed emotions. She decided she wouldn't get excited. Nobody had ever attempted to liberate her from the hell she was living in, not even his wife. Every morning Mrs. Pratt sat across from Harmony with hatred in her eyes, knowingly condoning her husband's sick behavior.

"I'm going to need one thing from you." Aria stepped closer.

"W-what's that?" Harmony's body became weak as a rush of heat swept over her.

"I'm going to need you to trust me," Aria whispered, placing a soft kiss on her lips. Harmony's body turned to liquid. "And know that I got you," Aria said convincingly.

# CHAPTER 3

Aria tried to plot on a way to get out of the house and into the streets, but it seemed as if ditching school was the only way. She snatched her tie off and balled up her skirt, shoving them into her backpack. She loved her new school, but today she had plans. She boarded the bus headed to downtown San Diego, excitement and fear filling her. It had been almost three years since she'd seen anybody from around her way. Aria glanced down at her cell phone and checked the time. The two-hour commute was wrecking her nerves. As Aria neared her destination, her palms began to sweat. She didn't really know what to expect. The hood had been shocked and heartbroken behind the tragedy of her being carted away and her girlfriend Emily losing her life.

The trolley came to a slow stop, and Aria exited one step at a time, her heart racing the whole while as she moved through the crowded trolley station.

"Ay, isn't that Aria?" a girl said within Aria's hearing range.

"Hell nah! You trippin'. That bitch ain't dumb enough to show her face 'round here after what she did. I—" Aria turned to the two girls and smirked

"Yeah, it's me. I see much hasn't changed; you two bum bitches still sack chasing?" Aria said to the twins, Mia and Tia Overbee. *Are these the same tricks who once loved and respected me? They've got a lot of nerve. They've sucked and fucked nearly every nigga in the hood. Up here talkin' shit about me. Hmph!*

"Mia, I don't know why this 'ho smiling. Biggs got a hefty price on her pretty little head, and if I had a pistol, I'd shoot this 'ho myself," Tia said, sarcastically.

"Well, you don't, bitch. But when you find one, make sure to do the world a favor and off yourself," Aria said, pushing past them. A shiver went up her spine as she sorted through the twins' words. *Biggs has a price on my head?*

Biggs was the uncle of Aria's ex-girlfriend, Emily. He ran the city with an iron fist. He knew the ins and outs of her and Emily's relationship—the lies, the infidelity. Aria's mind went to his hot-headed daughter Natalie, who was sick about her cousin's murder, and she promised to take Aria's life in return for Emily's. Aria had received several threatening letters, which to her were frivolous, but apparently they weren't.

A commotion in the crowd made Aria look up from her phone. Her feet carried her down the ramp and through the Food 4 Less parking lot and into traffic before the first shot rang off. Aria jumped into the path of a Mercedes station wagon, startling an older black woman.

"What the hell!" the woman screamed as she slammed on brakes.

"Please help me! They're trying to kill me!" Aria pleaded, out of breath as she raced around to the passenger door and raised the handle. The doors were locked.

"What? Who is?" the woman asked, looking around.

"Please, ma'am!" Aria pleaded, frantically lifting on the handle.

Uncertain, the woman unlocked the door and Aria hopped in. The sound of gunshots made her step on the gas. Aria looked back and saw her childhood friend Edwin chasing after the car, his dread locks swinging wildly. *What the . . . Edwin . . .* Shock overwhelmed her, and then pain settled in her heart. It hurt her to know that he would try to off her, especially when he knew all of the intimate details of her and Emily's relationship. Aria and Edwin went way back to the sand box, but money made people do strange things, and a lot had probably changed in the three years since she had been away. The woman sped up Euclid Avenue and got on the expressway.

"I don't know what you did, or who you pissed off, but you better be careful," the older woman advised.

"Yes, ma'am."

"Well, where do you want me to take you?"

"I live in Mira Mesa," Aria said, digging for some gas money.

"Oh no, honey, keep it. I don't live too far from there."

"Thank you," Aria said, allowing her tears to fall. Silence filled the car as her thoughts raced. *There's a price on my head. I have to get out of this city before Biggs finds me.*

Once she returned home without any bullet wounds, she felt relieved. Aria tipped up the stairs and went to the bedroom, breathing out her relief. Harmony was sitting there, as if she had been waiting.

"You ditched school?" Harmony asked.

"Yeah. I had to go pick up a few things and handle some business," Aria said, distracted from her thoughts.

"You do know that the school has probably called, right?"

Aria shrugged. She had bigger issues on her hands. Natalie was definitely trying to make good on her threat. Her father Biggs was dangerous, powerful, and rich and because he had promised her the world, Aria's head would be nothing but proof that he would do anything for his baby girl. As far as Aria knew, niggas were still hungry, and Biggs would feed them if they bodied her, which made her a breathing target. *It's just a matter of time before one of his hounds sniff me out. I gotta get out of here,* she thought. Even though she was up against a very powerful man, she still had no remorse for killing Emily, who played with her heart like an X-Box console. Toying with her emotions came with a hefty price, and Emily paid with her life!

Harmony came and sat next to Aria. She moved a strand of hair from her face. "What's the matter?" Harmony asked.

"They're going to find me, and when they do . . . I'm dead." Tears filled Aria's dark, fearful eyes.

"Dead! W-wait . . . what? Aria, who's going to find you? What are you talking about?" Aria turned toward her.

"I have some serious shit going on. I have to leave this place— leave San Diego. I can't—" Harmony stood to her feet.

"Leave? I thought you said—"

"Nothing I said has changed. It's just . . ."

"Aria, if you want me to trust you, then you're going to have to start by trusting me. It goes both ways," Harmony said, sitting back down.

"There's a time for everything, and right now isn't the time, trust me." Aria smiled sadly.

Their eyes lingered on each other's for a few seconds, then Aria leaned in and kissed Harmony. "I don't want to lose you because of my past mistakes," Aria said.

"I don't care about your past. I want to know the good, the bad, the ugly and beautiful," Harmony responded.

*Gotcha!* Aria thought, kissing down her neck gently. Harmony couldn't place the feelings, but they felt like nothing she had ever experienced. They began undressing each other, their bodies on fire. Chills formed up Harmony's back as Aria kissed it softly, then up around her neck. Their tongues explored each other's, hardly breaking contact as moans escaped the deepest parts of them. Aria climbed on top of her and stared her in the eyes. "Listen, I know you've been hurt, but I'm asking you to let me love you," Aria said. Harmony kissed her softly, giving Aria the okay. Aria slid her tongue inside her mouth and slid her fingers up and down Harmony's slippery slope. Her moans were like music to Aria's ears as she strategically gave Harmony everything her body unknowingly craved. She knew that the more lines she pushed Harmony past her apprehension and fears, there'd be no turning back. Feelings would grow like weeds in a garden, and the overwhelming need to feel wanted and loved would give Aria the control she needed. Because once she had Harmony's heart, her loyalty would follow, which was exactly what she wanted. Loyalty.

\* \* \* \* \* \*

"I am not going to ask you again, Aria. Where were you?" Mrs. Prat asked.

Harmony eyed Mrs. Pratt. She knew what was coming next. It was clear that Mrs. Pratt had lost her patience. Aria sat at the table nonchalantly and smirked before she answered. "I told you already. I was out handling some personal business, and to be quite honest, I don't feel the need to explain my—"

*WHAP!*

"Do *not* tell me what you feel the need to do or not do, little girl," Mrs. Pratt said. Harmony forced herself not to lunge over the island and attack Mrs. Pratt.

*WHAP!*

"I'm the only woman in this house, and the sooner you two figure that out, things will be a lot easier around here," Mrs. Pratt said, cutting her eyes at Harmony. Aria smiled, touched her lip, and looked down at the blood, then up at Mrs. Pratt, who was towering over her.

"I want you to understand me, and hear me clearly when I say this, Mrs. Tammy Ann Pratt. You have allowed your ego and pride to cause you to make quite probably the *worst* mistake of your miserable, pathetic ass *life*," Aria spat coldly. "See, I was going to spare your weak, spineless ass, but fuck it." Aria pierced Mrs. Pratt with her icy gaze. Mrs. Pratt finally sat down looking stunned by her words.

"Watch your mouth. Are you threatening me?" she scoffed, crossing her arm.

"No, Mrs. Pratt. That was a promise. May I be excused?" she asked, her tone patronizing.

"Both of you, get out of my face!" Mrs. Pratt ordered.

Aria slid her chair back and stood. Mr. Pratt came into the kitchen eyeing her then Harmony. "What the fuck is your perverted-ass looking at?" Aria barked.

"Come on," Harmony said, pushing Aria into the hall. "Chill, or you will become their target."

"Fuck them! They have become *my* targets!" Aria snapped. "I'll let it go for now, but I'm a woman of my word, and I never break my promises. *Ever.*"

The girls went to their room to prepare for school the following day, but discussed the problems they knew they would have with the Pratts and what to do about them. At some point their conversation eventually went silent and they hugged each other for comfort. Their comforting became sensual touching that grew into lust.

Aria had put her sex game down, giving Harmony more than her body could handle, leaving her in a trance-like state. Right where she needed her. She had not only been fucking her physically, but mentally as well. Feelings had grown seemingly overnight, something Aria was well aware of. She was always good at hiding her emotions and was beating herself up because she had not intended on actually liking Harmony so much. She seemed like a frail, vulnerable, scared child who needed her to come to her aid, but in the midst of their desperation to break free, an alliance was formed. Harmony was falling for her, and the loyalty that followed was worth more than gold. Aria bent down and kissed Harmony, who was in a deep sleep, on her forehead. "Sleep tight, baby," she said.

As Aria crept down the steps, she listened to the wind assault the old townhouse. She had been studying the Pratts' every move over the past few weeks and knew that Mrs. Pratt could not start her worthless day without a fresh cup of coffee. Aria opened up the refrigerator, her eyes scanning the shelves trying to find what she needed. Her eyes fell on the carton of creamer. She smiled and grabbed the carton. *Gotcha, bitch!* she thought.

\* \* \* \* \* \*

"Spare the rod, spoil the child," Mrs. Pratt said aloud, but eyed Aria and Harmony, who quickly grabbed eggs, toast, and turkey bacon. They sat at the table in silence.

"Good morning, Mrs. Pratt," Harmony said in a flat tone. Aria remained silent. The girls ate quickly, only looking at each other.

"You girls need to get going. Time is of the essence," Mrs. Pratt said, looking at the kitchen clock. She caught their sneaky stares. "Aria, is there a problem? You haven't said much of anything in weeks?"

Aria looked down at her watch, then smiled. "Gotta run. Time is of the essence," she mocked. She then tugged on Harmony's arm. They left the table, then Aria slammed the door behind her.

The next morning, Aria sat across from Mrs. Pratt as she drank her second cup of coffee and nibbled on her toast.

"Aria! We are going to be late if you don't come on," Harmony said, oblivious to the importance of Aria's procrastination.

"Have a nice day, Mrs. Pratt," Aria said coldly.

\* \* \* \* \* \*

Mrs. Pratt climbed inside her Mercedes and pulled out of her driveway. She had a long drive ahead of her and wished that Frank would do something with his sorry ass life besides pretend to fix cars and stay drunk. "He didn't even have the decency to drive with me. Just *no good!*" Mrs. Pratt mumbled as she pulled onto the interstate. She hated taking these monthly trips to Riverside to visit her father. *I wish he'd die already so that I can have what's owed to me,* she thought. Her father's life insurance policy, including his assets would make Mrs. Pratt a very rich woman. Just thinking about what she could do with almost ten million dollars is what compelled her to make the drive to the nursing home every month. Deep within the secret places of her heart she resented him for the pain he had caused her and her mother over the years.

An hour and a half into the drive, Mrs. Pratt's stomach began to erupt and burn with pain. A hot flash swept over her body followed by chills, alerting her senses. Slowly she began to breathe in and out of her nose. Mrs. Pratt felt sick. Checking her watch, she decided not to exit the freeway. She hated stopping, and because she only had a forty-five minute drive left, she pressed on. She shut her eyes tightly and shook her head from side to side as her vision began to blur, no matter what, she couldn't stop the uneasiness. Her mouth became dry almost instantly. *What the hell is going on?* she thought, looking in the mirror. She did a double take at the red blotches on her face. Panicking, Mrs. Pratt flipped on her signal and fought to get through traffic and over to the shoulder of the road. She wasn't sure where the nearest hospital was but knew she couldn't keep driving in her condition. *I just need some air,* she thought as she parked and climbed out. A sharp pain shot through her abdomen, leaving her gasping for air. "Ahhh!" she cried out. Suddenly, her breakfast was spilling out onto her pants leg, leaving her throat and mouth aflame. "Ahh!" The swift wind that surrounded her from the passing cars made her more nauseous. She bent over as her body forced up the poisonous lining in her stomach until she began to dry heave. Tears slid down her face from the agony she was in. *I need some water!* She fumbled toward the backseat where she always kept a bottle of water. Mrs. Pratt struggled with the door, only to find the box filled with empty water bottles. Fear jolted through her. The sound of her phone ringing calmed her racing thoughts.

"Hello?" she answered, ignoring the caller ID.

"I thought that you would've been dead by now," Aria said coldly.

Mrs. Pratt gasped. "You little . . . *bitch*! What . . . what did you do to me?"

"How easily we forget. I made good on my promise," Aria said, matter-of-factly. "Oh, and tell Satan I said hello."

"Why you little bi—"

*CLICK*

Mrs. Pratt's phone beeped. She looked down at the screen, her vision now blurry: LOW BATTERY. *I could've sworn I left it on the charger last night.* Shooting pain attacked her insides, doubling her over. She coughed hard, and the taste of copper left her panic-stricken. She touched her tongue, and a trace of blood was left on her finger. "Oh my God!" she cried. Mrs. Pratt fumbled with her phone, but before she could dial 911, her phone rang. "Frank," she answered, frantically. "Frank, I'm in tr—"

"Nope. Your perverted ass husband is going to need some help himself, and even if you call the police, they won't make it in time," Aria said, laughing hysterically. Then she hung up. Mrs. Pratt looked down at her phone. Her mind began to cloud. She squeezed her eyes shut, wiped the sweat from her face, and then dialed 911.

"Nine-one-one. What's your emergency?" the operator said.

*BEEP! BEEP!*

LOW BATTERY showed on the screen, and then the screen went blank. "No, no!" Mrs. Pratt cried. Almost instantly, the pain became unbearable, crippling her. *Just calm down, Tammy, and find something to drink*, she thought, coaching herself. Mrs. Pratt eased down into the front seat and grabbed her coffee mug. Unscrewing it, she took another gulp of poison. It only momentarily calmed her beating heart. She searched her glove compartment for her charger. "Got it!" she said, panting triumphantly, but was quickly sent back into panic mode when she realized the wires had been clipped. Something was very wrong and she knew it. Tears spilled down her face as pain wracked her body. Her mind screamed at her to get help. The pain momentarily eased up. Mrs. Pratt bolted out of the car.

"HELP! PLEASE!" she began screaming frantically, clutching her stomach. Mrs. Pratt waved at cars passing at dangerous speeds. "HELP!" she yelled again. Cars began to honk, warning her of how close she was to oncoming traffic. Coughs shook her body, sending her stumbling out onto the interstate. Her eyes locked with the driver of the Tahoe.

"God forgive me," Mrs. Pratt said.

# CHAPTER 4

Harmony smiled down at Aria who was resting in her lap. She gave her a sense of importance. Nobody had ever really been there for her besides her brother Phillip, and even he was snatched away by Child Protective Services without a good-bye. She was shipped to the Pratts, and he went to a group home for troubled teens. Her brother Phillip wasn't troubled, just misunderstood. She missed him, yet blamed him at the same time. Once their father was killed in a car accident, Phillip was supposed to be her protector when her mother couldn't. Harmony closed her eyes and mind to the thoughts of her brother. She hadn't seen him in years. That was the past, Aria was her future. She was smart, funny, recklessly beautiful, and Harmony was infatuated with her. So much so that just a few hours earlier she felt desperate the moment she looked out the window and spotted Aria crying and bleeding from her arm.

"What's the matter?" Harmony asked, looking back at Aria who had burst into their room.

"They've found me! Oh my God . . . I'm dead!" Aria said hysterically, looking around.

"Who's here?" Harmony asked, grabbing Aria's arm. "Why are you bleeding? What happened?"

"Biggs! He sent his men after me. I have to go. We have—"

"Biggs?"

"Listen, I can't explain . . . I don't want you to get hurt, but I have to go."

"You have to go . . . Wait . . . Aria, what?" Harmony said, hurt and confused.

"Come with me!"

"Come with you—where?"

"Anywhere!"

"Aria?"

"Look, I'm asking you to come with me because—"

"Because what?" Aria searched her brain for the words that would leave Harmony no choice but to leave with her.

"Because I'm in love with you," Aria said. "Please don't make me leave without you. I can't stay, and I can't tell you why. I just can't," she cried. Harmony weighed her options quickly, then grabbed Aria's hand.

"But what about Mr. Pratt?" Harmony asked.

"Forget him! I've gotta go now!" Aria grabbed a few things.

"Come on. I know another way out," Harmony said, sliding open the window and stepping onto the roof. Aria followed as Harmony shimmied down the tree and jogged out of the backyard gate. She was unsure of what lie ahead, but for once she had found someone who loved her because they wanted to, not because they had to, and she wasn't giving that up for anything or anybody in the world.

The Greyhound bus hit a bump in the road as it exited the freeway into downtown Los Angeles, stirring Aria from her memory of leaving the Pratt's home. She smiled up at Harmony, remembering how she had so gently patched up her arm.

"Are we close?" Aria asked the man sitting across from them.

"Uh yeah. We're down the street," he said.

Aria smiled at him, but his smile was returned with a mug from Harmony. She now knew what men were capable of and vowed to never trust one.

They exited the bus in search of an easy target. Aria searched the faces of bystanders who looked as if they were familiar with the city. "Excuse me, can you tell me where a motel is around here?" she asked. The short, buff man nodded.

"Yeah, there's one for pretty cheap about two blocks from here," he slurred.

Harmony stood by watching Aria "work her magic," as she called it. She didn't object when told to watch and learn. She figured Aria had far more knowledge about these streets than she did.

"Well, do you mind renting us one? Neither of us have any identification. I will definitely make it worth your troubles," Aria said, rubbing her thumb and fingers together.

"Sure, toots. No problem. Follow me," he said, stumbling forward.

"My name's Yvonne," Aria lied. "And this is my friend Brittany."

"I'm Jeffrey," the man said, taking a second look at Harmony. She mugged him hard.

"*Brittany*, be nice," Aria said, sweetly.

Harmony cut her eyes at them, then fell in step behind Aria. Her brain was in overdrive. She was wondering if the police were already looking for them and what Mr. and Mrs. Pratt were going to say once they realized they had run away. Harmony had never not come home, let alone skipped town. She knew nothing about the life she had just jumped head first into, but would soon find out.

Aria took the key from the drunken man and smiled. "I would appreciate it if you kept this between us," she said, handing Jeffrey fifty dollars. He winked in assurance, then disappeared into the sea of faces. Harmony and Aria climbed the steps, then settled into their hotel room. It reeked of stale cigarettes and old linen.

"So, what now?" Harmony blurted. The question had been weighing heavily on her mind for the past two and a half hours.

"First, we are going to get fresh linen," Aria said, snatching the sheets off the full-size bed. "Then, we are going to grab a bite to eat."

"And then?" Harmony asked, letting Aria know she wasn't

talking about what they were going to do in the next few hours, but in the next few months.

"Let me worry about all that. You just chill and be my king. I'll handle everything else," Aria said, a little too slick for Harmony's liking. Her eyebrows shot up.

"Your *king*? I'm not a man!"

"No, you're not, but you're *my* man," Aria explained. "My dominant. I need you to be my strength and play your part. Be a king to this queen. I mean, somebody has to wear the pants because I prefer skirts and pumps," Aria said, stepping close and looking deep into Harmony's eyes.

She chuckled at Aria's intensity. "I got you, but understand that I only took on the appearance of a man because I was searching for anything I could to deter Mr. Pratt's perverted ass from being turned on in any kind of way, and even though it didn't work, I kind of like it. But in no way am I confused about who or what I am." Harmony shrugged. "It's just me."

"And it fits you to perfection," Aria praised, placing her lips on hers. Harmony kissed her back, then pulled away.

"I'm going to tell you now. I've never been the type to sit on my ass. I want to be a part of every move you make, so I'll know what's going on and what to expect. Tell me what successful king you know laid around and chilled, leaving his queen to handle everything?" she asked. Harmony wasn't the fool that Aria pegged her to be. She had a good idea of what it took to survive from watching her brother over the years, something Aria wasn't aware of.

"There isn't one I can think of," Aria said. "I just don't want these streets to overwhelm you."

"Oh, they won't. I adapt fast and well, and I'm confident you will teach me all there is to know."

"Harmony, we can't afford the smallest mistake. This world,"

Aria said, waving her hand over the room, "is nothing like you've experienced."

"Don't count me out just yet." Harmony frowned. "I left nothing but torturous memories in San Diego. You and I are in the same boat, and I don't mind helping you paddle. We'll make a great team."

"But—"

"No buts . . . just trust me," Harmony said, smiling.

Aria smiled and nodded. "I'm usually not in the business of trusting anybody. That's why I always make my own plans."

"I'm not just anybody, Aria, and you will learn to trust me in time. You'll see."

Aria mumbled something.

"I'll show you better than I can tell you," Harmony said.

"Good. Then I really will see," Aria said in a smug tone that left Harmony wondering if she should have given Aria her full loyalty so instantly. She wondered if she'd jumped the gun a little too soon.

* * * * * *

Harmony took in her surroundings as they made their way back to the room. Hustlers hugged the block awaiting the fiends to come searching for the vice they served. A few girls stood on the corners dressed in close to nothing, beckoning johns to buy their goods, while their pimps looked on, and the homeless winos roamed the streets endlessly. *In nine months we'll be eighteen, then we can roam these streets without fear*, Harmony thought. *But our environment will definitely be different.* She could feel her mind snap into survival mode; she figured that hustlin' was more than likely going to be the easiest way to flip the money Aria had bragged about stealing from Mr. Pratt's stash. Thankfully it was enough to put them up for a while, but Harmony was eager to solidify their security. She quickly remembered the steps and revenue Peezy acquired from flipping bags of kush and decided to start there.

"You straight?" Aria asked, breaking through her thoughts.

"Yeah, I'm good. Just ready to shower and rest up," Harmony responded. Aria knew when she was being lied to.

"No you're not. I can see the worry in your eyes, but I know exactly what to do to temporarily set our minds free of our current circumstances." Aria smiled and so did Harmony.

\* \* \* \* \* \*

Harmony lay next to Aria's naked frame and watched the news. She was surprised she hadn't seen their faces plastered across the television. It had been a little over two months since they'd left the Pratts. It was ironic that not a word had been spoken about their absence. Harmony's nerves had calmed, but were now becoming antsy. She watched the traffic and drama that surrounded the powder blue two-story motel. A few dudes had set up shop a couple doors down selling just about everything. She figured she'd be able to fish out a connect in this environment, if she could get away from Aria long enough. Easing away from Aria's sleeping body, Harmony slid into her baggy jeans, then pulled her white tee over her head. Aria had praised and stroked her ego, giving her the confidence she unknowingly needed. Harmony checked her reflection in the mirror, brushing the honey-blonde waves that had formed in her low fade that she maintained. After admiring herself for a moment, she slipped out the door and walked down the hall. She took a deep breath, then knocked on the door. A tall, dark-skinned man answered the door in a pair of jeans and no shirt.

"Ay, lock that behind you," he said. She did as she was told and did a quick head count of the sleeping bodies stretched out around the motel room.

"Let me get a dub of that shit I smell seeping into the hall," Harmony asked, pulling a twenty dollar bill from her pocket.

"What's ya name, lil nigga?" the man asked, placing a few forest green buds on a scale.

"Jane," Harmony answered with a straight face.

"Jane, as in Mary Jane?"

"Nah, as in Jane Doe." Harmony smirked. The man chuckled. Harmony didn't.

"All right then, Jane Doe. Enjoy ya fruit. I'm Betta, and if you need anything, come holla at me." Harmony handed him the money, then left.

Every other day afterward, she made a trip to Betta's. Eventually, they built a business relationship, and then a friendship followed. She had a feeling this friendship would lead to greater things.

# CHAPTER 5

"Can I have a box of regular swisher sweets too?" Aria asked the Indian cashier sweetly, in hopes that he wouldn't ask her for an ID that she didn't have. He smiled at her flirtatiously, then placed the cigars on the counter. She paid him by returning his flirtatious smile. "Have a nice day," Aria said, stepping into the sun. It felt so good on her skin, and in that moment she was thankful she no longer had to look over her shoulder for Biggs' goons.

"Ay, ay, lil mama. Slow down." Aria rolled her eyes at the man who was hanging out of his car window.

"Shit!" she said aloud when she realized he was turning his Cadillac around. Aria quickened her pace, walking as fast as she could. She hated when men harassed her, assuming her no meant: "Yes, I'm just a little shy."

The dark-skinned man pulled alongside her, riding slowly. "Ay, lil mama. You fine as hell. Come roll wit' a real nigga for a while, smoke a lil somethin'," he boasted, holding up a Ziploc bag full of weed.

"No thanks," she said, without breaking her stride, or bothering to look his way. It only caused him to press and be more aggressive.

"For real, ma? I see them swishers in ya bag."

"Thanks again, but I'm engaged," Aria lied.

"Damn, that nigga got you out here walkin'? If you was Chi's bitch, you wouldn't have to do nothing but me," he responded, laughing at his own joke. "Well, let me give you a ride then."

"No thanks. I'm just down the street," Aria replied, walking past the motel entrance, hoping he would get the picture and drive off.

"Well, give me your number then. Come on, ma. Let me be everything that nigga ain't."

She cut into the alley, then into the back of the motel's entrance, willing her feet to make it to the back door. The man pulled in quickly, cutting Aria off. She clenched her chest, feeling her heart rate speed up. His long legs strode across the parking lot. Aria looked around. She was trapped between him and his Cadillac. He grabbed her arm.

"Bitch, I said give me ya' number. I wasn't fuckin' playin'!" he snapped.

"Stop it! Get your hands off me!" Aria screamed.

"Bitch, shut up before I teach your little sexy ass a lesson."

Aria had been in this situation before and knew what defiance could bring. "Six-one-nine. Three-eight-one . . ." Suddenly the man's body stiffened. He grabbed his chest, dropping to his knees.

Harmony stood behind him with malice in her eyes. Aria moved out of the way as his body fell to the ground.

"Are you okay?" Harmony asked. Aria nodded. "I heard you screaming."

"I'm fine," Aria said, bending down, then pulling the knife from his back. "Search his car," Aria ordered. "Quickly."

Harmony bounced into action, ransacking the car, and searching his glove compartment. A chrome glock stared back at her. Grabbing it quickly, she searched the backseat, looking for something to conceal it in. She chose a large camper's backpack and dropped it inside, then checked the trunk in haste. Her gaze met with Aria's.

"It's empty. Come on! Let's go!"

"Here," she said, handing Harmony the stack of rubber banded bills she found in his pocket. "Wipe everything you touched," she urged, then lifted his head by his afro and slit his throat. *No witness, no suspect, no murder,* she thought as she back peddled away from the body. *Now who's being taught a lesson? Bitch!* Aria thought as she glared down at the unmoving corpse.

\* \* \* \* \* \*

In silence, Harmony sat at the round table in front of a key of cocaine, a few pounds of kush, and $11,000. It turned out that the backpack had a whole lot more to offer than the concealment of the weapon. Aria came out of the bathroom from a quick shower; she had to rid herself of any traces of blood. She had taken another life and realized that it became easier with every breath she took. She knew that Harmony had hit a vital organ by the way he was bleeding out, but the urge to cease his breath was too great. It was personal. Nobody put their hands on her without consequences.

Aria noticed a malicious look remained in Harmony's eyes. The fact that Harmony would kill for her turned her on.

"Baby, you okay?" Aria asked.

"Yeah, I'm good," Harmony responded.

"What's all that?"

"This," Harmony said, holding up the key of cocaine, "is what we are going to build our foundation on."

"Well, let's pack everything up and get out of here. This place is going to be crawling with cops in an hour," she said calmly. Harmony admired Aria's ability to remain calm and never show any signs of panic.

Within minutes, the duo was climbing into a cab. "Can you take us to a hotel not too far from this area?" Aria asked the Hispanic cab driver.

"Do you plan on staying for a while?" he asked.

"Yes, we're staying." Aria laced her fingers in Harmony's and smiled.

Within fifteen minutes, they were in a new room at The Extended Stay, which wasn't so bad. It didn't have nearly as much traffic, but the same things were going on here as the first motel they stayed in. It didn't take Harmony long to spot the drug dealers and dope fiends and pimps and prostitutes that came and went all hours of the day. It only made it easier for her to set up shop.

Harmony climbed into the shower. Tense. She felt like a different person, but guessed she would be after helping to murder someone. The way she let her anger guide her replayed in her mind; how Aria had so ruthlessly slit his throat for violating her brought a smile to Harmony's face. In her mind, she had killed a thousand people, but once her vision came to life, it was like pure euphoria. She had no idea that deep down within her lay an alter ego who wanted out and was ready to take over. All the hurt and betrayal from those whom she had trusted caused Harmony great pain. Pain that she had stuffed so deep inside her that a monster was slowly created, one that Aria saw no need to suppress any longer. Harmony loved Aria even more for allowing her to be exactly who she was, but was there a motive to Aria's madness?

The sound of the shower curtain sliding back grabbed her attention, and she turned to face Aria as she squeezed in behind her. Aria wrapped her arms around her small waist and kissed her neck.

"Harmony," Aria said in a seductive whisper.

"Yes?" she answered as chills spread over her entire body. Aria gave her everything she could have ever thought to ask for, being that it was her first relationship. It felt good to know that she wasn't alone, that she had someone there for her mentally and emotionally. Where even the physical relationship was consensual and completely orgasmic. The love that Harmony had for her was undeniable, and anyone who saw them together could see they were deeply in love.

Harmony turned to Aria. "Nobody can know what we did the other day," Aria finally said.

"What did we do?" Harmony answered with a straight face.

Aria pulled Harmony's face to hers and kissed her intensely. As the water fell over them, they tasted each other's lips as if it was their last time. Aria kissed down her body, dropping to her knees, seductively sucking and kissing Harmony's treasure. Aria was addicted to the taste of her petals; she fiend for it fervently. Harmony's eye's rolled into her head as the overwhelming feeling creeped up her walls. Aria pleased her with ease, giving her something she never knew existed.

"Damn, baby!" Harmony moaned as she released her sweet nectar. Aria swallowed her warm juices.

"I love you, Harmony, and together nobody will ever hurt us again. It's us. Fuck them," Aria said as hot tears ran down her cheeks, mixing with the water. Harmony's mind was gone, and she didn't even know it, refused to acknowledge it.

\* \* \* \* \* \*

Furious, Aria cleared her throat. "Uhhh, it doesn't take that fuckin' long to buy a sack of damn weed!" Aria snapped as Harmony spoke to one of the many attention-deprived women that stayed on their floor. Harmony counted through the bills and handed the woman two bags of kush. She didn't understand how jealousy could so quickly set in Aria's heart. True, it had been a solid month of Harmony constant hustling. Maybe Aria was growing tired of the late nights and early mornings.

"All right, Money. I'll holla at you," the needy woman said, cutting her eyes at Aria, who stood there with her arms folded.

Harmony nodded and walked off, making a mental note to check Aria about her attitude. She loved her to death, but it had not been more than thirty days and her jealousy and controlling ways were beginning to be a bit overwhelming and crazy. Even though it stroked her ego more than it got on her nerves, it still wasn't becoming of her. "No, it doesn't take that long, but a little conversation doesn't hurt either," Harmony tried to reason, sliding the key through the door.

"Yes it does, Harmony. I don't want these bitches around here thinking they can converse with my nigga, or have a chance at anything that's mine. Conversation rules the nation, so cut that shit short," Aria argued.

"Babe, these 'hos around here know it's nothin', you know it's nothin'."

"Easy for you to say. What bothers me most is when some of these chicks be throwing themselves at you, disregarding my presence like I'm invisible."

"Do you not know that I don't want anybody but Aria?" Aria nodded. "Okay, so don't be doing all that psycho shit, embarrassing me when I'm dealing with a customer, man or woman. Respect my hustle."

"I'm sorry," Aria said, setting her bags and purse down. "It's just that I can see the thirst in her eyes and body language. And I'm sick and tired of all these women in your face."

Harmony went over to the couch and kissed her forehead softly. "Order us a pizza. Pablo should be here in a minute to show me the car."

"What car?"

"The Chevy I showed you a few days ago."

"Oh, that's what's up," Aria said, forcing herself to stay calm.

"I know we need a car bad," Harmony said, scrolling through her contacts. "I also need to invest our money as best as I can. The kush is almost gone, and I have yet to find a connect that has consistent quality and prices, so my next move has to be my best; our survival depends on it."

Aria took in a deep breath and held her words. For now.

At 2:17 p.m., Pablo texted that he was in the parking lot waiting with the car. Harmony kissed Aria's cheek. "I'm about to go check this car out. You coming?"

"No, I'm going to wait on the pizza," Aria said, trying to hide her irritation. She could feel the power that Harmony had over her emotions and mood. Even though Harmony included her in every final decision, she still felt the lack of control. Because of Harmony's need to survive in the world that Aria dragged her into, seemingly without a plan, forced her to make moves and stay one step ahead to keep them financially stable. It made Harmony aspire to reach levels that would secure their future. Harmony texted Aria pictures of the car from different angles.

*2:39 p.m.*
**Harmony:** *I got it. I'll be up in a minute.*

*Knock. Knock. Knock.*

The knock at the door broke Aria's thoughts. She answered the door, paid for their dinner, fixed Harmony a plate, then smiled. *I'll control her emotions if nothing else*, she thought. And control them she would.

\* \* \* \* \* \*

"Jane Doe!" a familiar voice yelled from across the parking lot. "What's up, little nigga?"

"Betta?" Harmony asked in shock. She had not seen him since the day she checked out of the Harvey two months ago. He strode across the parking lot and embraced her.

"What's been up with you? You lookin' good."

"Thanks. Not much of nothin', trying to get this money. What are you doing over here?"

"Man, the police got super-hot around that way after my homeboy Chi got stabbed up by some niggas, so I'm making a few plays. I told

39

him about fucking with them off brand muthafuckas. The streets been real dry since he been gone," Betta said, shaking his head.

"Damn, that's fucked up."

"Yeah, but when you live in the streets, nine times out of ten you die in them. Ay, you still with the pretty chocolate girl?" Harmony smiled at the thought of Aria.

"Yeah, we holding it down. I want to holla at you real quick though," Harmony said, inviting him to her car. She passed him a bag of kush and a swisher as they chatted.

"This you?" Betta asked, referring to the black 2005 Chevy Impala.

"Yeah, for now. I came into some money and I want to invest, flip it wisely." Harmony thought about the key of cocaine she had stashed. She couldn't really trust anybody, not enough to let them know that she was sitting on a key. Flipping it would be so much harder than she had originally planned. "My family up North might be able to shoot me a key." She had to mix a lie with the truth.

"A what?" he asked, looking shocked.

"You heard me," Harmony said, laughing at his reaction.

"Jane D—"

"My name's Money," Harmony said. Betta smiled.

"Money, why do you want to get in the dope game? It's nothing like selling these bags of kush," he said, holding up the empty bag.

"Look, all of that is irrelevant. I asked you because I figured, out of everybody you would keep shit real with me."

"Okay, first let me say like any other drug it depends on quality. I would say anywhere from twenty-one to twenty-four grand, depending on who you are."

"I was thinking about buying one," she lied. "I need to make some extra money fast." Betta pulled on the blunt and looked over at her.

"Money, why do you want to sell dope?" he asked again.

"Are you going to help me or not?"

"My cousin, he'll—"

"No, I don't want no nigga thinking I owe him anything. The only help I am asking for is yours, and even that was hard," Harmony expressed truthfully, her pride standing firmly in her way. Betta smiled at Harmony's honesty. She and Betta got along great. They had this unspoken respect between them; his spirit put her at ease.

"Trust me when I say this is help I doubt you'll regret asking for. 'Cause those other niggas around my way only going to make shit hard for you, or try to take advantage. This I know. So . . . quick question, do you know how to whip work?"

"Whip? What's that?"

"Once you buy your key, who is going to help you break it down and cook it?" Harmony sighed, realizing there were more aspects to this venture.

"Here, take my number." Betta smiled. "Call me when you're ready. I got you." She shook his hand.

"I'll be in touch."

* * * * * *

Lately Aria had been acting strange and moody, sending Harmony on an emotional ride day in and out. She had so much on her plate that she tried to ignore her attitudes and slick comments, but today she had reached her limit. She was sick of the random attitudes and silent treatment.

Aria sat in the passenger seat fuming and the tension was at its peak. Harmony placed her hand on Aria's thigh. "Babe, what's the matter?" she asked, gently.

"Nothing!" Aria snapped, moving her leg and returning to her iPhone.

Harmony pulled the car over into the emergency lane and slammed on the brakes sliding the car into park and jumped out. "Get out!" she yelled, stomping around to the passenger side. She snatched Aria's door open. "Now!"

Aria jumped, trying to suppress her smirk. She loved that without much effort she could control Harmony's emotions with a stroke of a button. Aria climbed out of the car and folded her arms in front of her.

"What's your problem? We are not doing this again."

"Doing what?" she snapped.

"What are you so damn mad about?" Harmony snapped back. "What did I do?"

Aria couldn't tell her the real reason she was pissed; she didn't want to seem petty or childish. She had to remain in control and keep up the bad bitch persona. Aria needed Harmony to know that she wasn't weak or shallow.

"We never get to spend any time together. *Ever!* You are always out, *hustlin'!*" she said, putting emphasis on the word. "That's all you seem to care about. That's all you do," Aria whined.

"Baby!" Harmony said, realizing how needy Aria had suddenly become. Her initial plan was to insure their survival, which seemed to not come easy, leaving her to do the one thing that came natural. Hustle. "I have to hustle, or else we will be out here fucked up. Didn't you say that I was your king?" Aria turned on the water works.

"Yes!" she cried, letting tears spill over her cheeks.

"And kings provide for their queens, right?" Harmony said, stepping closer to console her.

"Right," Aria said, burying her head in Harmony's chest.

"So let me provide until things get better. I promise it won't be like this forever."

"Okay," Aria said, but inside she was boiling over the fact that the strings she once pulled from behind the scenes had been cut. Bad bitches didn't take the backseat to anyone, not even the streets.

# CHAPTER 6

Harmony's nerves were getting the best of her. Betta was supposed to have met her ten minutes ago. She waited almost three weeks before she called Betta about their arrangement. She needed everything to be in order, and because Aria would be eighteen in a few more months, she needed to make this flip so they could move out of the hotel and into a nice place. Harmony wanted to do something special for her.

Betta climbed into the passenger seat. "My bad, Money. My baby moms is up there straight trippin'!"

"I was about to pull off on your ass," Harmony said with a straight face. "My paranoia started kicking in," she said, truthfully.

"Nah, man. I would never bring no harm your way. For whatever reason, I like your dyke ass." Harmony looked over at Betta. "No disrespect," he said, holding his hands in the air.

"None taken," she said, pulling off into traffic.

"How's the wife?" Betta asked.

"She good. We good, but she been trippin' lately. There is a part of her I can't reach."

"Just give her time, all things come with time. She is probably just used to you guys laying up all day, and now is a little shook about you being in the streets all day with these vulture ass 'hos." Harmony never looked at it that way because the only woman that Harmony wanted or desired was Aria. She never gave her any reason to think otherwise, or be insecure.

"Make a left at this stop sign and park next to the red minivan. I already called him and told him to be ready. We are about to cook at his mom's house." Harmony pulled over and double parked. A

45

short, brown-skinned man walked down the street clutching a red backpack. He was buff like a bodybuilder, but had a soft face resembling Larenz Tate, only he had a beard that was razor sharp. Harmony eyed him. "Don't worry, Money. He's straight," Betta said as he climbed in the backseat.

"What's good? I'm Woo." He stretched out his hand.

"And I'm paranoid, so don't give me a reason not to trust you." Woo looked over at Betta and shook his head.

Forty-five minutes later, Harmony stood in the kitchen listening intently as Woo schooled her step by step. "You have some grade-A cocaine? Where in the fuck did you get this shit from?" Woo asked. "This that shit like Chi had floating around for a minute." Harmony's hairs stood up on the back of her neck. She cleared her throat.

"My fam got it from someone up north. Ain't no telling," she replied as Woo nodded excitedly.

"See, niggas' work is stepped on, two—maybe three times before they get it. Then they try and stretch it, but this, this is the truth and you're going to make a lot of money. The way we about to whip this shit, I *promise* you all the fiends will walk a green mile to get what you got," Woo said with so much assurance. Harmony took a mental note of the ingredients, tools, and technique he used to make the dope.

"Now it's your turn," Woo said, catching her off guard.

Harmony mixed and measured, mimicking Woo's every move. She was nervous, but wouldn't dare let these niggas see her sweat. She was about to make thousands of dollars, and they all knew it. Harmony turned the Pyrex dish over in her hand, then held the cookie up for them both to see.

"Damn, Money, you sure learn fast, don't you?" Betta said.

Harmony winked at him and smiled. "Now that that's out of the way, tell me about the block."

Woo looked over at Betta, confused. "First, we need a tester," Woo said, stalling.

"A what?" Harmony asked. Woo laughed at her innocent ignorance.

"A tester is going to make sure your dope is as good as mine."

Betta went down the hall and returned with an older lady that probably had seen better days. Her eyes bucked and mouth watered at the sight of all the slabs lying on the kitchen counter. She fiddled with her pipe.

"Here, Ma. Try this one, then this one, and tell me which one is better," Woo said, breaking off a piece from each cookie and handing it to her. They both turned their head as she sampled them, but Harmony didn't. This was the same drug that her mother abandoned her for, and she needed to see this. The woman smoked Woo's then Harmony's, smacking her lips. She smiled a satisfying smile.

"Oh, you guys got some good shit there. They both are very good. You can't hardly tell the difference."

"Good!" Woo said proudly.

Harmony smiled at her accomplishment, knowing that everything she had planned was going to flourish.

"Let me get a fifty," the woman asked.

"Here is your first customer, Money, and personally, I don't think that you should be out on the block," Betta said.

"It's just too risky," Woo added.

"Well, if not the block, then where?" she asked.

"I got a spot, but you have to pay thirty-five dollars a day, and I promise the fiends will come straight to us." Harmony shook Betta's hand, then Woo's.

"Good lookin'." Harmony smiled, knowing it was up from here. Her hard work and well thought-out plans had paid off. She was almost sure she was about to make more money than she ever had. But she knew nothing in life was ever certain.

* * * * * *

Harmony slid the electronic key inside the door to the hotel suite. The sound of Aria laughing made her smile. She pushed the door open and rounded the corner of the kitchen and entered the living room. The dozen tulips she held for Aria dropped to the floor. Her smile quickly turned into a scowl. Aria sat on the couch, legs crossed and glistening from under her robe. She held a blunt in her hand, smiling at her company seductively.

"Aria, what the fuck are you doing!" Harmony barked.

"I'm chillin' with Yae. What's up?" Harmony's eyes met with the female who sat on the opposite end of the couch. "Yae, this is Money. Money, Yae." The female stood.

"All right, lil mama. I'm gon' holla at you later," she said flirtatiously, looking Harmony up and down, then scoffing. Yae was beautiful, with her bronze complexion and flawless dreads that touched her True Religion T-shirt. It enraged Harmony to see Aria entertaining another woman.

Aria placed the blunt in the ashtray and stood to her feet. Harmony blocked her path. "She can let herself out," Harmony snapped, stopping Aria in her tracks.

"You trippin'!" Aria said, slickly.

"Nah, I ain't trippin'. You are. I should never come home and find my woman in the company of another nigga. Who is she anyway? And what the fuck made you think it was all right to bring that nigga in here where I lay my head at?" Harmony said, raising her voice. "You disrespectful."

"You weren't here so . . ."

"So what. You decided to chill with a—"

"I decided to chill with a friend that could be!" Aria barked harshly. She knew that comment would hurt her, but what she didn't know was that Harmony didn't take disloyalty lightly. So many had already betrayed her. She was tired of trying to break through the walls that Aria had built around her heart, only to be shut out again.

Harmony charged toward Aria and got in her face. "Well, I hope that nigga can be here for you when you need her the most, 'cause I'm out." Aria grabbed her arm.

"Wait, Harmony. It—"

"Man, watch out!" Harmony said, snatching her arm away and storming out. The door slammed and Aria jumped. She stood there in shock, and had not expected Harmony to react that way and knew instantly that she fucked up. Aria could see the murderous look Harmony held.

"Well, damn!" Aria said.

Harmony had to put some distance between them, or she would hurt her and that was the last thing she wanted to do. She climbed inside her Chevy and fought the tears that wanted out. *Is this what heartache feels like?* she thought. As Harmony tried to sift through her feelings, she sent her ringing phone to voicemail; she didn't want to talk. Didn't want to hear her excuses or lies. It had almost been a year since Aria came into her life and rescued her from the deep, dark hopelessness she lived in. They had experienced so much, and she thought their bond was unbreakable. She loved Aria with everything she had. All she wanted to do was be her king and give her everything, but Aria was making it seem impossible. She needed some space; maybe it would help Aria to see what she stood to lose.

\* \* \* \* \* \*

Overnight, Harmony's money seemed to stack. Once Betta spread the word and Woo's mom vouched for quality, fiends were beating down her door coming from as far away as Watts. She had not talked to Aria in almost three weeks, but every night became lonelier than the next.

"You look like a sick puppy over there. I see Aria got yo' ass pussy whipped," Betta said, taking a pull of kush and passing it to Woo, who was laughing.

"I am not ashamed of it," Harmony said smartly.

"Man, go handle your business. We'll hold down the fort," Woo said.

Harmony thought about it for a split second, then grabbed her keys and bolted out the hotel room. She pulled into the Shell gas station and filled up her tank, then bought a single tulip. *Hopefully she got her mind right.* Harmony looked down at her missed call. *I would rather speak to her in person*, she thought, pulling into traffic.

The drive was brief and Harmony was glad about that. She parked and hopped out, nearly rushing into the hotel. "What's good, handsome?" the front desk clerk said, her green Extended Stay Hotel shirt clashing with her pink hair.

"Handsome? I am not a man. I'm just comfortable in baggy jeans," Harmony said, checking her.

"Well, your girl is over by the pool if you want to know."

Harmony walked off toward the pool, shaking her head at the clerk who made it her business to flirt with her every chance she got. Harmony wasn't prepared for what she saw. Yae was bent down openly flirting with Aria, who was smiling from ear to ear. Yae stood abruptly and headed her way. Yae's eyes locked with hers, and she gave Harmony that familiar grin, chuckling loudly as she passed, adding insult to injury. *I know this bitch is not blatantly disrespecting me. She still hanging with this nigga?* Harmony went against her first mind, which was to drown Aria right in front of everybody. Instead she turned and walked to her car. She had to get far away from Aria, or she was going to kill her. *The nerve of this 'ho.* She threw the tulip out of the window and it sailed into oncoming traffic.

# CHAPTER 7

Harmony looked over the balcony and smiled at the view. The sun was high in the clear blue sky, spotlighting the rooftops of her soon to be neighbors. She had accomplished so much since she'd left the Pratts. The only thing missing was her better half. Every day that passed without Aria got harder. Nothing was easy about not spending her life with her, not even the thought of it was. It had been a little over a month, and she needed to see her. She needed to look in Aria's eyes and see if she still loved her. All the women that Woo and Betta brought around were just groupies, pocket watchers, and freak 'hos that wanted everything Harmony couldn't give them. With Aria it was different. She knew her inside out. She knew her deep dark secrets, what made her laugh, and why she refused to cry. Harmony turned toward the petite blonde and smiled.

"Mrs. Copeland, I think I'll take you up on your offer," she said, referring to the two-bedroom, two-bath townhome.

"Great, if you wouldn't mind following me to my office to fill out the appropriate paperwork." Harmony smiled and followed the lady out.

Mrs. Copeland gave her the rundown of what she expected from her tenants, and Harmony gave her a duffle bag full of money along with false information to keep their little arrangement a secret. She clutched the keys in her hand and smiled. It amazed her how a little money could make any situation lean in your favor.

Twenty-five minutes later, a proud Harmony pulled up to the Desert Eagle Inn and hopped out. Her gemmed-out True Religion get-up caught the attention of a rare beauty. Her chocolate skin tone was flawless, and her cheekbones sat high on her face like Mount

Everest. The way her legs elegantly strode across the parking lot toward the fire red Mercedes made Harmony swallow hard with guilt. Normally she wasn't moved by these women, but the confidence in her stride made her want to know her name. She clutched the envelope and forced herself to climb the steps to the room she and Betta were making thousands in.

"What's good, Money!" Betta said, embracing her.

"Shit, I can't call it. I do need a favor though."

"What's up, my nigga?"

"I need you to go check on Aria and drop this off. I think it's time we talked."

"I got you. I did want to ask when you planned on copping some more of that? We good right now. I just don't want to run out, and I know you want to flip some of that money you made."

"Right, I need to get at my folks. Give me a minute, and I'll get with you."

"Bet," Betta said, grabbing his keys and heading out. Harmony rubbed her hand over her face. Now she had a problem. She needed a connect.

* * * * * *

It had been a little over a month since Aria had heard from Harmony. The only thing keeping her from spazzing out and tearing up the city was the fact that she knew very little about it. The contact information she had for her cousin Envy had changed, and her Facebook, Twitter, and Instagram search had come up empty. It was if Envy had disappeared from the face of the earth. Aria was truly alone. Her plans had gone to shit. If it wasn't for Harmony keeping the room paid and sending her spending money, she would be broke and homeless. Her life had come to a screeching halt when Harmony walked out. She needed to hear her voice, see her face, anything to let her know that she still loved her. No matter how hard she tried to shake these feelings, she couldn't. Aria was in love, and because she hadn't plan on it and didn't want to be; it seemed as though it was even harder to recoup. Their separation was consuming every part of her, consuming her every thought. The knock on the door broke through Aria's misery.

"Who is it?" she asked, hoping it would be Harmony, but the deep baritone of Betta's voice shot down the little hope the knock brought.

"It's Betta." Aria opened the door. She knew he was here to check on her and drop off some money.

"What is it?"

Betta looked into Aria's chinky, chestnut eyes, mesmerized by her flawlessness, quickly scolding himself for admiring his boy's broad. He cleared his throat.

"Money sent me over here to check on you and—" Aria broke down into tears.

"Betta, please. You gotta talk to her; it wasn't even like that with Yae. I swear. I need her." She sobbed. "Please!"

"I don't know what to tell you, Aria. That's between y'all."

Aria told Betta how frustrated she felt when she kept hearing Harmony's voicemail pick up every time she called her. "It's been almost three weeks, and she still refused my calls. But she gon' send you over here with some money and to pay for the room for another month. And that's it?" Tears welled up in Aria's eyes unexpectedly.

"Well, at least you know she cares about you," he responded. She nodded from left to right.

"*I'm* the one that send 'hos to voicemail! Bitches chase *me*. I don't chase them!" Aria yelled. Betta stood quietly with his arms folded and an unreadable expression.

"Anyway, after I called for the tenth time and got Harmony's voicemail again, I just started tearing shit up. The way she's ignoring me is ridiculous. Hell, I tired myself out turning over everything in our room. After a while, I knew I needed some air, so I changed into my bathing suit and grabbed my shades, hoping a few laps around the pool would calm my temper and clear my head."

"And lemme guess. That's when Yae entered the picture, right?" Betta asked.

"Right. So this is what happened . . ."

*Aria sat by the pool in her white Prada bikini with her feet in the water. She figured a little fresh air would aid in her attempt to get past the pain.*

*"What's good, lil mama? You lookin' damn good today." Aria looked over at Yae and rolled her eyes.*

*"What's up?" Aria asked with an attitude.*

*"Shit. Let's go grab us a bite to eat or something. I hit you up a few times, but you ain't hit me back. I thought—"*

*"You thought wrong. I'm good," Aria said, waving her hand dismissively. Yae frowned.*

*"Fuck you then, bitch." Yae was in no way used to rejection.*

*"Nah, fuck with me, bitch." Aria flipped her Prada shades up on her forehead.*

*"Oh, I most definitely will. I got something for yo' ass since you want to stunt."*

*"Don't threaten me with a good time." Aria smiled.*

*"Fuck you!" Yae barked, walking away.*

"I knew she was pissed off, but—" Aria started to say.

Betta cut her off. "Aria, as much as I want to believe your story, I know the games that some females play. When the dog's away the cat's gon' stray almost every time."

"That's not me at all, Betta. You got me fucked up. It's her being in the streets and not spending enough time with—"

"Listen, Money is my potna, and as I said before, I'm not getting in you guys' business."

"I'm just sorry I picked Yae to be the pawn that made Harmony tick. Yes, I was attracted to her, but I only wanted her to serve one purpose," Aria said. "To make Harmony jealous."

"Yeah, but now that Yae fell into your lil game, it's obvious she's not done playing," Betta stated firmly.

"But I am. And that's all that matters. So please tell Harmony to come home."

"It's not my place, Aria, but I will say that she's hurting just as much as you, if not more. Here." Betta handed her the envelope, then turned to leave.

Aria closed the door behind him, then slid to the floor. She opened the envelope.

> *Aria,*
> *I love you and have come to realize that a life without you isn't living. So go buy yourself something nice and be ready by seven sharp.*
> *Love,*
> *Harmony*

Tears rolled down her face, but a smile spread across her lips as relief sank in. The steam and hot beads relaxed Aria. She was so nervous. She had no idea what she would say to Harmony. She guessed the truth would have to do. In an effort to control Harmony's emotions and make her jealous, she had hurt her and torn apart their relationship. Control didn't seem so important anymore, all she wanted was for Harmony to forgive her, to hold her. For once she could admit she was wrong and admitting her faults was nothing Aria was used to. Aria turned off the water and stepped out onto the cold tile floor. She paused, hearing the sound of a lighter flicking on and off.

"Harmony?" she called out.

Aria went into her room and frozen. The sight of Yae stretched out on her bed smoking a blunt enraged her. Harmony would be here any minute.

"Nope, it's me, baby." Aria's eyes fell on her phone, and then at the bed where the pistol was tucked between the mattress and box spring. The phone would alert Harmony, but the pistol would protect her.

"How in the fuck did you get in here?" Aria barked.

"You naive little girl," Yae said, shaking her head, holding up the key to Aria's room. She had only paid the clerk a small fee for it.

"Naive? Bitch, please. You might as well get your psychotic ass up out of my room." Yae pulled her pistol out and pointed it at Aria. She scratched her head with it.

"I'm not going anywhere. It's obvious you don't know who I am, 'cause—"

"I don't give a *damn* who you are!"

Yae jumped to her feet. "I've had enough of your smart ass mouth for one day." She removed her belt, then shook her head again. "Your mother must not have taught you any manners?"

"No, she didn't. She let her brother sneak into my room and fuck me," Aria snapped. Her response caught Yae off guard. Aria lunged for her phone, managing to hit the call button. In seconds, Yae was across the room. She gabbed Aria's arm, bending it, and forcing her to drop the phone. Then she slapped her.

"I'm going to teach your pretty ass a lesson, and the consequences when you play with a nigga like me." Yae snatched Aria's towel off her body, then pressed her damp body against hers.

"Get off me, Yae!"

"Make me!" Yae taunted.

"Bitch, fuck you! Yeah, I used you to make my girl jealous. It was nothing more, nothing less. I used you as a pawn. That's all you will ever be to me."

*WHAP!*

Yae struck Aria's damp body with the belt. Aria screamed loud, but screams and pleas to stop were nothing uncommon amongst these walls. "It's a shame," Yae said, pausing to breathe. "We could've been an item." Aria laughed hysterically, despite the pain she was in.

"An item? Only in your thoughts, you psycho bitch!" Aria knew that Yae was probably going to beat her ass, but she didn't care. She had been abused mentally, sexually, and emotionally almost all her life. The physical was just a fraction of what she had endured.

\* \* \* \* \* \*

Seven rolled around quickly. Harmony changed into a pair of Diesel jeans and matched a red and gray button up. Her Jordans were as fresh as her low Caesar cut, and the potent smell of Usher drifted from her presence. It had been a month and a half since she looked in Aria's eyes. The last time she saw her she wanted to kill her, but she couldn't stay away any longer. Everything in her life was falling in line, and she felt like Aria should fall in line too. They had to make things right between them; her heart wouldn't let it be any other way. Harmony climbed out her car and walked into the lobby, her mind racing. The clerk's eyes bucked when she saw her strolling past.

"Hey, uhh." Harmony gave the flirtatious woman a nod but kept moving, and then boarded the elevator. Her palms grew sweaty, and knots formed in her stomach. Her pride wasn't strong enough to keep her away from Aria.

As the elevator doors opened, Harmony heard a piercing scream. When she got closer to their room, she realized the screams were Aria's. She opened the door, quietly crept in the room, and walked over to the bedroom where Aria's cries and whimpers were coming from. Yae was standing over Aria administering deadly blows to her naked body. Harmony gabbed the pistol from under the mattress and struck Yae over the head. "Nigga, what the fuck are you doing?"

*WHOP!*

Harmony yelled insults as she pistol whipped Yae non-stop. Aria willed her body out of the corner, grabbed her robe, and covered her naked body. Blood was everywhere, on the bed, the wall, and all over Harmony. Aria jumped into action. She had to stop this.

"Harmony!" Aria called out. "Stop before you kill her!" Harmony looked at Aria with a murderous stare. "If you kill her in here, they'll come looking for us. I don't care if you kill her, just not in here, baby. Just—" Harmony put her hand up, stopping Aria's words. She looked down at Yae who lay motionless.

"Get dressed and pack up this room. I'll be downstairs," she said coldly. Harmony had a million questions. *Why is this bitch even here?* She felt like taking her rage out on Aria. She couldn't even look at her, or she knew she would. Harmony went to the bathroom and punched the mirror. *This girl must think I am a joke.*

Once Aria and Harmony packed the car with the bags Aria brought out, they entered the car but didn't speak. Harmony maneuvered through the streets of Los Angeles as Aria sat quietly. Finally, Harmony looked over at her.

"Harmony, listen. I love you and—" Harmony's beeping phone pissed Aria off.

"Damn it! Can you put the streets on hold for just one second?" Aria asked. Harmony dropped her phone in her lap and gripped the steering wheel tightly. She tried to suppress the anger that was building up, but she couldn't. She was at her boiling point. There was nothing left to do but snap.

"Bitch, you don't have the least bit of room to say a damn thing about *anything* I do, and the way I am feeling at this moment I would advise you to be the fuck quiet," Harmony said, calmly. Aria's mouth fell open, but she took heed and shut it.

Eventually, Harmony pulled into the driveway of a two-story tan stucco building. "Come on!" she barked, grabbing Aria's things out of the trunk. Aria followed. Harmony unlocked the door to the empty two-story townhouse, went to the bathroom and locked herself in. Tears pooled in her eyes. She leaned over the counter and dropped her head. The pain she felt was overwhelming; she didn't understanding why Yae was even in their hotel room. Again. So many scenarios were running through her head.

Aria rushed to the bathroom. "Harmony, we need to talk. Please, baby. Open the door." Harmony snatched the door open, glaring at her.

"How about we start with why that nigga keeps finding her way into your presence?"

"How about we start with what the hell you've—" Aria's pride was back. Before Harmony knew it, her hands were around Aria's neck, and she was squeezing the life from her body. Aria dug her nails into Harmony, pleading with grunts and moans for her life.

"You are lucky I love you!" Harmony said, shoving Aria into the wall and storming past her. Aria grabbed her throat and sucked air into her starved lungs. Hot tears poured out of her eyes as she slid to the floor and cried. Harmony stormed out, leaving Aria waiting in deep thought and silence.

She hopped in her ride and smashed on the gas, willing her Chevy to get as far away from Aria as possible. She had lost her cool, and for a second she regretted laying hands on Aria. The pain that wracked Harmony's heart hurt physically. She took her shirt off and tossed it into the backseat. Then pulled into the Desert Eagle Inn. When she spotted Betta's truck, she hopped out and dashed up the steps. Then she opened the door, and the set of eyes that stared back at her made her heart fall into her stomach.

"Nice to finally put a face with a name," a beautiful woman said, her tone dripping with seduction. Harmony tried to regain her composure, but she knew that the woman had caught her eyes traveling from her model legs up to her contagious smile.

"Hey, uh, where is Betta?"

"I'm Reese, Money. It's a pleasure." She pointed to the bathroom. Betta came out of the bathroom and looked from Harmony to Reese.

"I see you two have met. Harmony, this is my right hand, Reese. She finally flew in from New York," Betta said. Harmony nodded.

"Uhh, Betta, I need to holla at you real quick." She stepped outside and Betta followed.

"What's good?" He looked at Harmony. "What's wrong? Reese is good people. She's my cousin, so don't—"

"Nah, it's not that. When I went to pick up Aria, Yae was there."

"So she really still fucking with her?"

"No—I don't know. When I walked in, she—man, I just pistol whipped that nigga."

"You did what? Did you kill her?"

"Umm, I don't know. I think she was still breathing."

"Well, you need to . . . Money, Yae ain't nobody to be playing with."

"Say no more." Harmony flew down the steps and went back to the hotel. The clerk couldn't even look her in the face. She knew something. Harmony willed the elevator to the third floor. When she went inside the room with her gun drawn, Yae was gone. Harmony sat down on the bed. She felt in her gut that she had just started something she was unsure she could finish. Her phone beeped again. She looked at the voicemail alert and listened as Yae's cold voice taunted and berated Aria. She had the truth on her voicemail. Even though every part of her wanted to be done with Aria, she was partially innocent—in this case. Harmony knew that when she saw Yae that she was going to have to bring it. This was her neck of the woods, and she was just hiding out in it.

\* \* \* \* \* \*

Aria climbed in the shower behind Harmony, who had not said much of anything since she came home. It was a bold move, but she needed to be close to her. Her bruises burned from the warm water, but she didn't care. She laid her head on Harmony's back and wrapped her arms around her waist. Harmony didn't shun her; she had heard everything that happened. Silently she forgave her for her fucked up choice to get attention by giving another woman some. Aria cried until her quiet cries turned into loud sobs.

"Everything is going to be fine, baby. We are going to get past this. Okay?" Harmony said softly.

"You promise? I-I'm sorry. I—"

"Shh, shh," Harmony said, silencing her with her fingers. "I said it is going to be okay, and I mean it. Let's just move forward." She kissed all over Aria's exhausted body.

A wild pulse beat between Harmony's legs as Aria kissed and sucked on her breasts and neck. She could hear her heart beating loudly in her ears. Aria gave Harmony the best sex she had ever had that night, sending her aching body into a frenzy. Aria ruled Harmony's body, and they both knew it.

Harmony lay in bed, her thoughts wreaking havoc. She was at a loss of what to do. Not only was her life potentially in danger; she needed to come up with a believable enough reason why she could not produce another key of pure cocaine and not draw suspicion. Reese's beautiful smile and mysterious eyes flashed across her mind. She looked down at Aria lying across her chest, then shut her eyes tight. But when she opened them, Reese still remained. *Damn!*

# CHAPTER 8

Harmony stuffed the swisher with kush, wracking her brain for a believable enough story to tell Betta about the connect she never had. *Fuck it. I'ma just tell him he got cased up.* She lit the blunt and blew out her frustration, displeased with her dishonesty. Betta and Harmony had become really good friends. He called her his little sister, something she took pride in. But she had no choice; she couldn't tell him the truth. There was no connect.

Reese came strolling in behind Betta. Her smile gave her away. Harmony could tell that Reese was feeling her and her eyes defied her every time and lingered on Reese's tight frame.

"What's good, Money?" Betta said, breaking the spell Reese always seemed to cast on her.

"Man, I got some bad news. My folks got knocked on the way to see me yesterday, and everybody is shook. So everything is on pause right now."

"Damn," Betta said, taking the blunt from her and sitting on the bed.

"I know, right. I called his wife, and she said that they are holding him without a bond." Harmony caught Reese's eyes lingering on her. "What's good, Reese?" Harmony said, suggestively.

"Life."

Betta smiled.

"Why don't you put her on with Notorious?" Reese suggested. Betta gave her the side-eye.

"I hate when you do that. Notorious has enough runners, and the percentage he wants is fucking ridiculous."

"Uhh, who is Notorious?" Harmony asked.

Reese walked across the room and opened the door. The smoker came in and she served him his vice, then he left. Harmony watched, intrigued by her skills.

"Money, we have a good thing going, and I'll see what I can shake as far as—" The sound of the door being kicked in made Harmony jump. Two armed men came in, pistols first.

"I'm only going to ask you one time. Where's the money?" the tall gunman asked calmly. The other gunman grabbed Reese by her hair.

"I'm not giving up shit until you let her go!" Betta said, matter of factly. The tall gunman walked over to Betta and smashed him over the head with his pistol.

"No!" Reese screamed. "Please stop it."

"Look, it's in the trunk," Harmony thought quickly. "Let her go. You can follow me out to the car," she said. Betta gave her an uncertain look. The gunman was uneasy, but he agreed.

"You, get over here!" the tall gunman said to Reese. "Hurry up," he said to his partner who nodded and followed Harmony closely into the dark parking lot. She knew that everybody's life depended on her next move. She needed a distraction.

"Which car is it?" he asked.

"The Chevy over there," Harmony said, grabbing for her keys and intentionally pressing the car alarm to stall.

"Turn it off!" he barked.

"I'm tryin'," she said, fumbling with the keys and dropping them to the ground. "Damn it." Harmony bent down to get the keys. The gunman's eyes followed.

"Hurry the fuck up!" he said, looking around.

Harmony popped the trunk, and in one swift movement gabbed the duffle bag and the silenced glock that lay under it, then sent a shot through his neck. She caught him, then stuffed his body into the trunk and placed the duffle bag full of clothes in the backseat. She tucked her pistol in her back and returned to the room and knocked on the door.

Reese answered. The gunman had his gun shoved in her back. Harmony put her hands in the air. "He took off with the money," she said. Her eyes met with the gunman's.

"He what?" He looked over at Betta, then dug in his pocket and pulled out his phone. In that split second, Harmony had her pistol in his face.

*Pfft.*

One shot to his forehead sent him stumbling back, then he dropped to the ground.

"Betta, pack up this shit. Reese, wipe this room down and hurry up!" Harmony ordered, searching the man's pockets, taking his money and valuables.

Betta looked over at Harmony, then at Reese, who was wiping everything down. "What are we going to do with him?" Reese asked.

"Don't worry about that. I'm going to handle it. Where's his buddy?" Betta asked.

"In my trunk," Harmony said.

"Reese, go home. Harmony, take my car. I will call you in a few." Reese hugged Harmony tight before she climbed into her Benz and sped off. They would forever be tied together after tonight.

\* \* \* \* \* \*

Aria stood in the bathroom and stared at her flawless reflection in the mirror. Harmony had chosen an all-white backless Dolce Gabbana dress with a pair of black Christian Louboutin's for her to stand tall in. She bumped her curls and smiled. Aria was now eighteen, but it felt more like twenty-five. She had endured so much and relished in the freedom to finally do as she pleased. The single karat diamond she wore around her neck matched her earrings. She rolled the karat between her fingers, thinking about how easier things had quickly gotten between her and Harmony. She finally came to terms with the lifestyle they lived, the early mornings and late nights, the coming and going. Because whenever the streets called, Harmony went running. But tonight was her night, and she welcomed the attention and quality time that came with the celebration of her eighteenth birthday. Harmony came into the bathroom dressed in a pair of white Dolce & Gabbana linen shorts and button up dress shirt with white red-bottomed loafers to match. She and Aria looked elegant and would definitely be the center of attention tonight. Betta had pulled a few strings, so they would be partying with the Los Angeles' elite.

"Babe, you look beautiful," Harmony said, taking all of Aria in.

"As do you," she said, smiling. "This dress, these shoes, they're beautiful," Aria exclaimed.

"Anything for you." Harmony tucked her pistol into her back and locked up their townhouse. She had a nice night planned. "Close your eyes, baby," Harmony said, leading her to the driveway.

"Okay, they're closed," Aria replied. Harmony led her to the driveway by her hand.

"Okay, you can open them now."

"Aaahhhh! Harmony! How did you—where . . . omigosh, baby! Thank you! It's beautiful." Harmony smiled at Aria's reaction to the 5 series BMW coupe she had sitting in the driveway on 20-inch rims with a huge pink bow tied to it. The BMW was a soft metallic pink with peanut butter interior. Excitement filled Aria as the engine purred beneath the hood. Harmony typed in their destination, and they pulled off into traffic.

\* \* \* \* \* \*

68

Betta checked his Rolex as he waited by the door to make sure everything went as planned. "Come on, Money," he said under his breath. Finally he spotted the pink bow weaving through traffic. The valet took the keys and helped Aria out of the car. Betta could not help but stare at her. She was beautiful. He had not seen her in months and to him she looked like a goddess.

Harmony shook his hand. Aria smiled and pulled him in for a hug. Caught off guard, Betta smelled her angelic scent. *Damn.* She was mesmerizing, and out of all the chicks Betta had been around, none had him fighting temptation the way Aria did. Money was his boy, and for that reason she was off limits.

The bouncer at the door let them in without asking for identification and led them to VIP. Iggy's new song was banging through the speakers, and the entire club was draped in white. Everyone danced in sync as Harmony introduced Aria to a few of Betta's friends that helped make this night possible, then she ordered their booth a few bottles. Aria was overwhelmed and caught the tears before she ruined her makeup.

"I love you, Aria," Harmony said, kissing her hand.

"I love you too, baby. Thank you for today. Thank you for everything."

"You're my queen. You deserve all of this and more."

Aria danced and drank for hours, enjoying every moment of this new lifestyle with the love of her life, two-stepping behind her.

"Excuse me, birthday girl. Let me borrow her for a minute," Betta said, pulling her out onto the balcony, where another dude stood holding a drink in his hand.

"Money, this is Notorious." Harmony stuck out her hand.

"Nice to meet you," she said. Notorious nodded.

"Same here. Betta told me that you were interested in doing business with me."

"I am."

"Honestly, I feel as though you're much more valuable than sprinkling a little snow here and there."

"No disrespect, Notorious, but I am not really into riddles," she said, seriously.

"Come on, baby. This is my song," Aria said, interrupting their conversation.

"Meet me next Friday at Roscoe's off Main Street, twelve noon and bring your wifey," Notorious said, smiling at Aria.

"Excuse me, boys, but tonight is my night," Aria said, dragging Harmony back to the dance floor.

* * * * * *

Reese's eyes locked with Harmony's as soon as she entered VIP. Her Versace dress looked as if it was painted across her thick, curvy frame, and her stilettos made her almost six feet tall. Harmony forced her eyes away, but not before Aria saw them trail up her legs and into her eyes. Reese strutted toward their booth.

Woo caught up, blocking Reese's view. "Cousin, what's good?" he said, hugging her.

"This party," she answered.

"Where's Betta?"

"Bathroom," Reese said, pointing at the restrooms. Reese reached Harmony and smiled seductively. "Money."

"Reese."

"How have you been?" she asked.

"Oh, I've been good livin'. This is my birthday girl, Aria. Aria, this is Reese, Betta's cousin."

*Birthday girl?* Aria thought.

"Oh, happy birthday. I've heard so much about you," Reese said, stretching out her hand.

"Funny, 'cause I have not heard a thing about you," Aria said coldly, staring and ignoring her stretched out hand. Her smile disappeared.

Harmony cleared her throat. The tension in the air was rising, and the atmosphere was becoming unbearable.

Aria stared Reese down, letting her know that she saw the attraction, felt the chemistry, and still didn't feel threatened.

"Reese!" Betta said, awkwardly.

Aria rolled her eyes at him. He immediately felt the tension. "I see you've met Aria. Money's girlfriend." They both stood toe to toe, neither one cowering, like most did when either of them walked in the room. Both women were filled with confidence and were flawlessly beautiful, and nobody could tell them they weren't the baddest.

Harmony cleared her throat. "Let's toast," she said.

Betta summoned a shot girl and grabbed a round. Harmony raised her glass. "To Aria, my friend, my queen, and the love of my life."

"To Aria!" Betta and Woo said. Reese threw back her shot, licked her lips seductively, and then looked at Harmony, who instantly looked away.

"Well, I am about to hit the dance floor," Reese said.

"Me too," Betta and Woo agreed simultaneously, leaving Harmony and Aria standing alone.

Aria turned to her. "This is your only chance to tell me the truth. Are you fucking her?"

"No, I'm not fucking her."

"You're not, or you haven't yet?"

"I'm not, I haven't, and I won't. You're all I need."

"I believe you, but don't give me a reason not to. I'm begging you." Aria leaned in and kissed her.

\* \* \* \* \* \*

Reese watched Aria with envy in her eyes. Harmony, had not once looked at her, but she wasn't fooled. She knew Harmony was into her, and Reese was going to make it her business to get rid of Aria. She had to give her a round of applause, at least she wasn't intimidated by her like most women.

"Are you enjoying yourself?" Betta asked, blocking Reese's view.

"I was. Who does this bitch think she is?" Reese asked, sipping her fifth drink.

"She's her girlfriend, and she's no fool either. Ray Charles can see that you have a thing for Harmony."

"It's not one-sided, Betta. Can you see that!"

Betta sighed.

"Don't get involved with her," he said. "And it's not a request."

"Why not?" she snapped.

"Because, blood is thicker than water, and I don't want to have to choose when things go wrong between you two. Money is my potna, and you of—"

"Oh, puh-lease, Betta. Who are you kidding? It's all about a coin when it comes to her, and she has made you plenty!"

"Reese, I'm not playin'—"

"You might have her fooled, but I'm not at all fooled. I know who you are," Reese snapped and walked off.

\* \* \* \* \* \*

Sex with Harmony was so intense, so sensual, Aria couldn't get enough of her. She lay next to Harmony watching her chest rise and fall. *I almost lost her to my ego. I can't let my pride trick me into thinking she isn't all I need, because without her I can't breathe. I love her till death do us part.* Her love for Harmony was genuine, and nobody would come between what they had. That was something Aria vowed to

God and herself. They'd die first before they accomplished anything close to it.

She slid out of bed and ran the shower for them. Harmony had asked her to accompany her to a meeting she couldn't be late to. Aria opened the closet and chose a creamy yellow Ferragamo pants suit with a white collar shirt and white Bally flats to match. Harmony had upgraded her in more than just one way. It was only up from here, and being a hustler's wife had perks Aria could get used to. They both washed up, refraining from having their way with each other again.

"Who are you going to meet with?" Aria asked, pulling her long hair into a high bun.

"His name's Notorious. He offered me a job. He thinks that I am too valuable to sell drugs in a trap somewhere."

"And how does he know your worth?"

"I assume Betta told him about me."

Aria screwed up her face. It was something about Betta she suddenly didn't like. Maybe the flaunting cousin was just too much for her. "So what is he getting out of it all, and where do I come in at?" Harmony shrugged.

"Notorious asked me to bring you," she said, disregarding what Aria was insinuating. Harmony kissed her forehead. "Come on, babe. Let's go before we're late."

Thirty minutes later, Harmony was guiding Aria's coupe into the parking lot of Roscoe's Famous Chicken and Waffles. Aria was surprised and a little irked to see Betta standing outside in front in his Sunday's best.

"What is this nigga doing here?" Harmony shook her head. Aria knew that he was Reese's link to Harmony, which meant he was also a threat and that was something she didn't take lightly.

"What's good, bruh?" Betta said, embracing her. "Aria," he said, nodding. She nodded back for Harmony's sake, who she knew was watching her every move and gesture.

Betta caught the drift and her stiff demeanor. "Listen, Money, Notorious is the man around this city. He damn near running this shit like the mayor, and anybody who is somebody wants to get down with him," Betta boasted.

"And?" Harmony said.

"And he doesn't like to be told no."

"Well, there's a first time for everything."

Aria smiled. Harmony had grown so much. The shell she had found her in seemed to no longer exist; she was no longer hesitating or unsure of what she wanted. She placed her hand on the small of Aria's back and escorted her inside. Betta stepped in behind them.

Nobody was inside, except a tall man with a light complexion, who sat way in the back in the corner. Off to the left, Notorious sat with two bodyguards, who were also dressed in black suits.

Betta shifted his weight from one foot to the other.

"Nervous?" Harmony asked.

"Hell yeah!" Aria said and rolled her eyes.

"For what? This nigga ain't God." Harmony smirked. She watched Aria strut beside her, and loved the fearlessness that lie within the layers of Aria's heart.

Notorious stood and shook their hands, then pulled a chair out for Aria. "Thank you for coming."

"You're welcome."

"I am glad that you guys could make it," Notorious said, taking his seat.

"You knew I would make it, so let's just skip all the pleasantries and get to the real reason I am here," Harmony said, not at all liking the way that Notorious' eyes continuously scanned up and down Aria.

Notorious unbuttoned his coat; he wasn't indifferent about

Harmony's smart mouth. He could tell right off that she was about business, and her time was precious.

"First, let me say that I've heard about the way you move in these streets—my streets . . . so—"

"And how did you hear that?" Aria asked, cutting Notorious off and shifting her eyes to Betta.

"Trust that I know everything that goes on in this city." Although Notorious was clearly unattractive, he had the confidence of the singer Tyrese. His smooth skin was coal black and his lanky frame fit his long legs perfectly. "Before I continue, I have a question. What do you think about at night once you have taken a person's life?" Aria crossed her legs impatiently.

"That it gets easier every time you do it," she cut in, getting tired of his riddles. She didn't like his beady, dark eyes.

"I agree." Harmony looked at her and smiled.

"Well, in that case, would you both like a job?"

"Depends on what you have in mind."

"I would like to let my enemies know that they can be touched."

Harmony sat in silence, unsure of how to place her thoughts and feelings.

"How much?" Aria asked, disrupting the silence.

"Depends on the hit and your success to deliver."

"Oh, we will deliver, but it must be worth our while," Aria pressed.

Notorious smiled; he liked her wit and the way she did business. "I am under the impression that nobody has time to waste. The first job I have for you is fifty grand." Harmony looked Notorious in his dark eyes. "Yes, fifty grand a piece," he said, as if he read her mind.

*Fifty grand?* Harmony thought. It had taken her months to make that kind of money. She couldn't help but wonder whose life was worth so much money.

"Can we have some details?" Harmony asked.

Notorious summoned one of his bodyguards, who handed him a USB flash drive and phone. "Everything you need to know is on this, and this phone is the only way we will communicate. I'll send you a text when I hear the job is done and I'll tell you where you can pick up the money." He reached in his breast pocket and slid an identical phone across the table to Aria. "Contact me when the job is done. You two have a nice day," Notorious said, dismissing them.

* * * * * *

Harmony sat in the car staring at the flash drive. "Fifty grand!" Harmony said, smiling.

"No. One hundred grand!" Aria corrected. She had taken control over the meeting, leaving Notorious intrigued with more than just her ability to deliver, but in Aria and what could come from this new alliance.

# CHAPTER 9

"Damn, is he gone yet?" Harmony asked, impatiently.

Aria set her binoculars down, faced Harmony, and grabbed her cheeks. "Baby, look at me! In my eyes."

"What?" Harmony asked.

"Get rid of that nervous energy, it will only make it harder, and I need you on this. We're a team, and I need to know without a doubt that we are on the same page before we go in here."

Harmony smacked her lips. "We are on the same page. I'm just ready to get this over with," she said and grabbed the binoculars, embarrassed by Aria's reprimand. Harmony looked down the street. Their target, Mr. Kelly was coming out of the house.

Finally Mr. Kelly pulled out of his driveway. He was running late, which was out of character for him. It made Harmony uneasy, but Aria knew that as hard as Mr. Kelly tried to stick to his schedule there was always room for error.

Aria climbed out of the rental car and then asked, "Are you sure?"

"Don't ask me again." Harmony mugged her, before taking a deep breath. She ran her hand over her face slowly, her body full of nervous energy. She had never killed anyone whom she didn't feel deserved it, or whom she felt threatened by. Mrs. Kelly's husband was an adulterer and a heavy risk taker. He needed to cash in on their $530,000 life insurance policy and retirement funds because he owed over half of that amount to Notorious. His gambling habit was serious and out of control. Being that his wife had caused him enough stress and embarrassment, he decided her death was easier than a divorce. Two birds. One stone.

Harmony went around the house to the backyard where she opened the back door with the key Mr. Kelly provided. She crept through the two-story house. The ding from the microwave gave away Mrs. Kelly's location. Harmony pointed the gun at the back of her head.

"If you make a peep, I swear I will put a bullet in the back of your head," she said harshly. Mrs. Kelly's hand shot to her mouth. Harmony checked her watch. The doorbell rang on cue. "Let's go." She led Mrs. Kelly through the house at gun point. "Open the door and invite her in."

"Avon Lady!" Aria chimed. Mrs. Kelly stepped back and let her in. "Have a seat," Aria said sweetly, pulling out a chair for her at the dining table. Mrs. Kelly trembled.

"W-what is going—" Aria pulled her glock out and pointed it in her face.

"Talk, and I'ma blow your fucking face off." Aria cocked her head to the side. "Got it?" Tears and confusion were all over Mrs. Kelly's face. She nodded. Aria set her Avon bag on the table. "Now, we can do this the easy way, or we can do this the hard way, which do you prefer?" Mrs. Kelly said nothing. "Speak!" Aria barked.

"E-easy w-way, th-the easy way," she stuttered, looking over at Harmony, who held the gun inches from her head.

"Good. Then this will only take a second," Aria said, smiling. She pulled out a syringe, a tourniquet with a few baggies of heroin and a spoon.

Mrs. Kelly cried silently as she saw the drug that almost took her life and ruined her marriage a year ago.

Aria cooked a few doses and shot them into her vein one by one. As Mrs. Kelly began to feel the effects of the drug, she became less tense. Her body swayed left to right.

"How does that feel?" Aria asked.

"G-goood," she replied in a whisper.

Harmony was amazed at how Aria handled herself. She avoided eye contact with her as she injected the final dose. Mrs. Kelly's body jerked violently, seizing as the lethal dose of heroin traveled through her body, shutting each organ down one by one. Harmony bent down and checked her pulse. "She is dead. Let's go." Aria leaned over and kissed Harmony.

"I'll meet you at the house in thirty minutes. I love you."

"I love you too."

\* \* \* \* \* \*

Later that night, Harmony sat on the balcony overlooking the neighborhood. The air was chilly, but the silence serene. She had just made an easy fifty grand. She replayed the entire ordeal through her head as she held another flash drive in her hand containing information on another mark. Only the stakes were higher this time; she had to do it all by herself, and it was worth sixty-five grand. She took a swig of her Corona, trying to place her thoughts and feeling on this new situation she had found herself in. The money was definitely good. Too good to pass up, but would God forgive her for stepping into his shoes and taking something so precious? Aria's soft lips touched the back of Harmony's neck, sending chills shooting through her.

"Don't think too much, or you'll get lost in there," Aria said, concern lurking in her eyes. She dug inside her pocket and pulled out an orange flash drive. "He sent for me and gave me a new client."

"A client?" Harmony asked.

"Yes, baby, a client, for seventy grand," Aria said and sat next to her.

"I got one too. Sixty-five grand." Harmony held up a black flash drive.

"That's 135 grand!" Aria stood up.

"I know, but the way he wants me to—"

"I know, baby, but we need this money." Harmony nodded in agreement.

"True, but it's just—"

"What, what's wrong? Tell me," Aria said, sitting back down.

"Nothing. I'm . . . it . . . never mind. I don't want you thinking that I am crazy."

"Don't say that." Aria looked at her seriously. "You're not crazy." Aria hated the word crazy.

"I just feel like once I start—listen, I just know that I'm angry, and I don't want to unleash this monster and not be able to control it."

Tears filled Aria's eyes. For years people had called her crazy and made her out to be this monster, when really it was all the hurt and anger living within her. "Baby, listen to me. You can control it."

"I don't know if I can."

"Trust me. If I can control it, I am sure you can. You're in control of it, remember that."

"I am?"

"Yes, and let it out so that we can get this money." Aria kissed Harmony roughly, tearing away her clothes. With every rip, Harmony grew moist between her legs. Suddenly Aria slapped her across the face. Then kissed her, driving Harmony insane. She grabbed a fist full of Aria's hair, pulling her into her lap, never breaking their kiss.

"I love you, Aria," she said, kissing down her cocoa skin, biting hard and licking wildly. Aria gasped in pleasure at the way Harmony was manhandling her. It was as if the monsters that lay within them both were having sex with each other. They were biting and passing licks, sexing each other into euphoria.

Silently Aria prayed that Harmony wouldn't disregard her, disrespect her, or dismantle their love life. Her late girlfriend Emily carelessly did exactly that. Aria was still damaged from the pain Emily caused and refused to make any excuses for anyone who thought it was okay to play games with her. She was all in and there was no turning back. She and Harmony struggled with the same issues; it only made their bond stronger and their love for each other deeper. Aria's uncle had raped her many nights until she took his life and revealed his secret. This destroyed her family and turned everybody against one another. Mr. Pratt had stolen a piece of Harmony's innocence every night until there was none left. Taking away her desire and trust for men. In their eyes, the monsters inside them would protect them from the world, from the people that had hurt, betrayed, and abused them for too long.

* * * * * *

It was as if Harmony had changed overnight. Her once warm spirit was shut off, and her laughs and smiles were strictly for the ones she loved. It was time to get this money, and that's where her mind was. She watched Andre Finks foolishly stumble out of his 745 BMW, dropping his keys on his porch. In seconds, she was pressing the .38 into the back of his neck.

"Move and you will never know why you didn't make it to see tomorrow," Harmony said, harshly.

"All right," he said, pushing the door open.

Harmony slammed the chrome caliber into the back of his head. Andre went crashing to the floor in the foyer of his elegant home. Harmony slammed the door behind them.

"Aarrgghh shit!" he groaned angrily, grabbing his head. Her steel toe boots pierced his side. "You fuckin' bitch!" he spat with an evil glare.

"That I am," she said, kicking him again. "And just so you know, Notorious sends his regards." Andre shook his head.

Using zip ties to bind his ankles and wrists, Harmony then removed his belt. Andre began laughing. "Some head would be nice," he spat sarcastically. Harmony reached in her pocket and pulled out a box cutter. His eyes grew big as she snatched his pants down his legs and cut his boxers off his body.

"I had intended on making this as less painful as possible, but since you insist," she said, stuffing the boxers in his mouth and gripping his manhood. In one swift movement, she sliced his pride clean off. He screamed so loud it gave Harmony the chills. She looked at him, kissed his dick, and then looped the belt around his neck, cutting off his air supply, turning his cries into pleas and grunts for air into mercy. Harmony left his squirming body inside and tossed his manhood over the fence for the neighbor's barking dogs.

*Aria was right. It does get easier every time.*

\* \* \* \* \* \*

*This should catch his eye*, Aria thought, standing in Neiman Marcus smiling at the Versace pants suit. She added the ensemble to her new mini shopping spree. Notorious had given her an unlimited spending budget for this "client" she had to take care of. He said she needed to dress the part and to get a little something for herself. She knew when somebody was hitting on her, but as much as she refused his every effort, he remained persistent, which irritated her. She added a few things for Harmony. Smiling at the saleswoman, Aria said, "I'll take all of this."

The woman rang it all up with no problem, asking only one question: "Cash or credit?"

"Cash," Aria responded as she glanced at her watch. She had to meet with Harmony for lunch before she flew out to San Francisco.

After making her purchase, she made a mad dash out of the store and climbed into her Coupe. Within a thirty minute window, she made it to her destination. She smiled as she approached the door to the restaurant. *I hope Harmony likes her gift.*

Harmony greeted Aria with a kiss. "Damn, babe. I'm going to miss you," Aria admitted. They had not been apart since the bullshit stunt she pulled.

"Don't worry, just handle ya business. I'ma hold down this fort." Aria smiled.

"I love you." Harmony winked.

They ordered their lunch and watched the groupies and paparazzi go crazy as they snapped pictures of Jamie Foxx and some model chick in Beverly Hills enjoying a meal.

"Well, I grabbed you a few things, courtesy of the boss man," Aria said. Harmony's smile disappeared.

"That nigga ain't your boss . . . mine either, and don't address him as such," Harmony stated. Aria nodded.

"I won't."

After they ate, Harmony drove Aria to the airport, kissing her softly. "Be safe, love."

"Bye, I'll see you in a few days."

"It's never bye. I'll see you soon."

"I'll see you soon, love." Aria couldn't help but smile.

Harmony knew that Notorious had a thing for Aria. She saw the way his eyes lingered on her, the way he watched her whenever they were in his presence, but she hoped Aria would remain loyal. She wasn't sure what or how she would react if she had to endure anymore heartache due to Aria's disloyalty. She had walls up, walls that neither she nor Aria knew existed.

\* \* \* \* \* \*

Reese smiled at the sight of Harmony pulling up to Betta's new spot. She had not really seen much of her lately, and even though she had stolen her number out of Betta's phone, she fought with herself every night, forcing away the urge to call. Betta had gotten the hook-up on some work from Notorious, his finder's fee for the two hit-chicks that delivered on time, every time. Reese made it her business to capitalize off of it, extorting Betta for a few grand. She had not gotten her hands dirty since she'd been back in town, but one thing she knew about Betta, there was always going to be a way to touch some money fucking with him. He had taught Reese the game, and she did it all in six-inch stilettoes. She had her eyes set on Harmony, and Betta was the link. She figured she might as well get paid while she secured a position in Harmony's life. *Kill two birds with one stone*, she thought.

"What's good, sexy?" Reese said, stepping on the balcony catching Betta and Harmony off guard.

"What's not good?" Harmony flirted back. She couldn't help but return Reese's smile. Betta looked at them both and shook his head.

Reese could not contain herself; she saw Harmony's swag dripping in her khaki Louis Vuitton shorts and brown shirt. Her Louis Vans set it all off, forcing Reese to stare.

Harmony was weak for her; the self-control she had could not withstand Reese's presence. Her eyes drifted from her manicured toes up to her eyes. Her chocolate skin beamed against her white dress that hugged her waist and fluffed out, leaving every eye to wonder what lie underneath. *Damn!* Harmony cursed.

Betta cleared his throat. "Ay, let me holla at Money real quick," he said, turning toward Reese. She stepped back out of eyesight.

"I see you've been doing ya thing. I knew you had it in you. I know a killa when I see one," Betta said, holding up his hand for a high five. Harmony shook her head.

"I'm not a killa," she said seriously. "But thanks for the connect though."

"Oh, no problem," Betta said, but Harmony knew there was more.

"What is it that's bothering you?" she asked.

Betta leaned on the balcony rail. "Look, I know you're grown, but my cousin plays for keeps."

"For keeps?" Harmony smiled. "I'm already kept." Betta smirked, knowing Harmony was intrigued.

"Then don't entertain her. She has entitlement issues."

"I'm not going to lie; she is beautiful, but Aria is where my heart's at."

"When is Aria due in town?" he asked.

"Sunday at the latest. Why? What's up?"

"Man, let's hit up the club. Have some fun."

"Fun?"

"Yeah, have you forgotten what that was? Too much of anything is bad for you." She looked over at Betta. "Yes, money falls in that category."

"Shit, I could never have too much of that, nigga, but we can go out," she said. Betta laughed.

"I'll meet you around nine." Betta said, following Harmony into the hotel room. She and Reese locked eyes.

"Leaving so soon?" Reese asked.

"Yeah, I have a few errands I gotta run," Harmony said, picking up a few baggies of kush. "I'll see you around." Harmony returned her smile, then embraced Betta. She left in a hurry and sped off as if the acceleration would erase her attraction to another woman.

Instantly, Reese popped into her head. *Damn it, Reese,* she thought, as *what if's* danced around in her imagination.

* * * * * *

85

Harmony looked at herself in the mirror, checking her swag. She had come a long way. The threads that Aria had piled in her closet exuded wealth, and her safe was so full she needed to get a bigger one. Her champagne Dolce & Gabbana short set and matching loafers lay against her skin well.

Betta sat on the sofa in Harmony's living room. He smiled as she descended into the foyer. "The place looks really nice and you look like a pretty ass little boy," he joked.

"Fuck you!" Harmony said, laughing. "I let Aria go crazy in the store. She did her thing though. Brought some life to the place. Betta looked around the living room.

"Turned the house into a home," he said. Harmony rolled her eyes.

"Shut up."

The club was live, and VIP was everything it could be. Harmony nursed her glass of Remy and watched Betta mack on the groupies. Woo two-stepped on the dance floor surrounded by some freaks. The women were choosing from the dance floor, making Harmony take refuge in VIP. The 'hos that sat in VIP were looking for a nigga to trick off, or give them a sip of the bottle he was sipping from, and she was doing neither.

"So, I see you stepped out." The sound of Reese's sexy, raspy voice sent a shockwave of energy through Harmony's body. Reese was so close that she could smell the berry lip gloss she had applied moments before stepping into VIP.

"I did," Harmony responded. "Are you enjoying yourself?"

"I am now," Reese answered. Harmony smirked. "Where's ya wifey?"

"Why? You don't really care," Harmony said, turning to face her.

"You're right. She's never far, I'm sure."

"Never." Curious, she wondered where this conversation was going.

"Money, you know what I want."

"I don't. Elaborate," she countered, never breaking her stare.

Reese stepped closer, closing the space between them and smiling. She could see Harmony fighting herself. In Reese's mind, this was going to be like taking candy from a baby. She whispered, "How about I show you?" Slithering her tongue across Harmony's ear. Her body tensed as she fought the urge to kiss her and check her about her distance. Not knowing which to choose from, she chose neither.

Clearing her throat, she leaned into Reese's ear and whispered, "I stand firm on the whole 'actions speak louder than words' theory, but I would love to hear it. I want you to tell me exactly what it is you want." Reese stared into her eyes as she pulled back and bit her lip. "And that thing you just did with your tongue could mean many things. So, if you don't mind, elaborate."

"Reese? What are you doing here?" Betta asked. He had headed their way after seeing the flirting Harmony and Reese were engaged in.

"I'm having fun. Isn't that what you called it?" She raised her glass sarcastically, rolling her eyes. "Umm, we will definitely have to finish this conversation," she said, raising her glass at them and strutting off.

# CHAPTER 10

Aria was growing impatient with the cat and mouse game she was playing with Donald, but forced herself to remain calm and focused. Giving it another try, she hoped to catch him today on his lunch break. There was no room for mistakes, too much money was riding on this one. Everything had to be perfect. Besides, this was right up her alley.

Donald came out of the courthouse and headed down Broadway Avenue. That was her cue. Aria climbed out of her car and walked behind him. The wind ripped through her fresh blow-out as she followed his every move. He stopped at a mom and pop cafe on the corner in downtown San Francisco. His eyes lit up when they met with hers as he held the door open. His fetish for beautiful black women was sickening. His blue eyes flickered as he watched her move throughout the cafe. He was intrigued by her beautiful presence; she had him. *Donald is very handsome*, she thought. His sandy brown ken doll cut was neat, and his slim build was draped in tailored Armani.

Notorious owed somebody a favor, and they had called it in. Aria learned that Donald hated black men and made it his goal to lock many of them away like the animals he thought them to be. His smile seemed so genuine, and so did hers. Aria shied away.

"Umm—I'm sorry. You're beautiful, and I just have to ask you: would you have lunch with me?" Aria smiled, showing her beautiful teeth.

"I'm flattered, but I am in such a hurry. I only have a few—"

"Well, how about dinner then?" He was making this too easy.

"Well . . ."

"I'm a great cook," he pressured.

"Okay, but I'll be in the office until seven."

"How about you come over at nine, wear something nice, and I'll cook something good to eat. Maybe grab a movie or something."

"Monica," Aria said, smiling seductively and extending her hand.

"Donald," he said, kissing her hand.

They parted ways and Aria returned to her hotel room. There, she sat on the bed and removed her pumps. She dialed Harmony's number. She missed her so much and was ready to hop on the early morning flight back to Los Angeles. In three weeks Harmony would be eighteen. Aria wanted to show out, do something grand for her. She had already started making arrangements for the party.

"Hey, baby girl," Harmony said.

"Hey, love. What you up to?"

"Nothing. I am at Betta's. Chillin'." Betta's equaled Reese, and Aria knew her motives. Reese wanted what she had.

"Aria, you there?"

"Yeah. I just wanted to check in with you, let you know that I am safe," she said, forcing the attitude out of her voice.

"When are you coming home to me?"

"Hopefully soon," she lied, knowing the job would be done tonight. The sound of a woman giggling in the background set her off.

"Babe, I have to go. I'll call you later," Harmony said, ending their call.

Tears welled up in Aria's eyes, jealous, angry tears. *How dare she be in the presence of that 'ho while I am away.* She started to call back and curse her out, but thought better of it. She had work to do and refused to misstep, or make a mistake because of her emotions.

She gathered her composure, dressed to kill, made up her face and decorated her neck and wrist. Aria didn't even need a mirror to tell her that her "bad bitch" status was beyond a ten. She arrived over to his place fully focused on the mission at hand. He answered quickly after she rang his door bell and took her on a tour of the lovely condominium.

Donald's condo was decked out. Only the finest art, rugs, and decor filled his bachelor's pad. He hugged her softly, sliding his hands across her ass. She didn't flinch; it only fueled her murderous thoughts. Aria wore a small black halter top dress that looked like it had been stitched onto her body. He took her coat, admiring her physique.

"You look absolutely gorgeous."

"So do you," she said seductively. Aria grabbed his hand and let him lead her to the candlelight dinner he had set up for them. Grilled salmon, mashed potatoes, and spinach. He was a great cook. *If he had to pick a last meal what would he have chosen?* Aria wondered. As she enjoyed her meal, she thought about Harmony. No matter how hard she tried to put her out of her mind, she couldn't. She was obsessed with her and didn't even know it. Her feelings had grown past the point of love. Normally she had several distractions to keep her mind and heart leveled; after Emily she vowed to never get too deeply involved. She promised herself she'd keep more than one woman in her life distracting her. But in this case, all she had was Harmony, and she couldn't live without her. She wanted to hurry and take care of Donald and catch the red-eye flight that left in a few hours. Aria hoped to catch it, but she was unsure of what the night would bring.

\* \* \* \* \* \*

Harmony watched Reese hustle as she gave orders and served fiends in her Jimmy Choo pumps. She could not help but be turned on. The attraction to Reese had caught even her off guard. She found herself wanting to be in her presence. Last night she lay in bed thinking about her, what it would be like and how good it would probably feel. She couldn't hide it anymore. Betta advised her, using three words: "Don't do it." Harmony wondered if this is what Aria felt toward Yae. Reese grabbed her hand.

"Come on. Let me holla at you," she said, seduction dripping off her tongue. And like a sheep going to slaughter, she followed her out onto the balcony.

Reese pressed Harmony against the wall with her body and kissed her. Harmony kissed her back. It felt so good and so wrong at the same time. Visions of Aria flashed in Harmony's mind, making her pull away.

"Reese, I can't."

"You can. Stop playing with me, Money."

"I'm not." *I just don't want to have to choose*, she thought.

"I'ma play my position. For now anyway, but you can't have your cake and eat it too," she said, leaving Harmony pulsing between her legs and with mixed emotions.

* * * * * *

"Now, I have a surprise for you!" Aria said, walking to her bag and pulling out a pair of furry pink handcuffs. Donald bit his lip, instantly growing hard.

"What else do you have in that bag?" he asked, excitedly.

"A whole lot of fun."

Donald scooped up Aria, tossing her over his shoulder. She snatched up the bag, and they headed for his master bedroom. Aria stripped him naked, allowing him to kiss and fondle her goodies. Then she secured his arms and legs to his bedpost. Donald's manhood stood at attention. He could only imagine what Aria had in store for him as he envisioned their sexual escapade. She unzipped her dress slowly, seductively making Donald more anxious by the minute. Aria bent over, pulled out a whip with metal and shards of glass on the tip, and a small ball with straps attached to it. Donald smiled.

"I have a request before you put that in my mouth."

"And what is that?"

"Fuck me hard and fast," he said. Aria smiled.

"I'll do my best," she said, putting the ball in his mouth and securing the straps behind his head. Aria turned to leave the room, her bag in tow. After a few minutes he grew agitated.

*I hope this coon isn't trying to rob me,* Donald thought. "Mmmmhhh!" he screamed, but his screams would only be heard in his head.

Aria slipped on a pair of black lace gloves and put on a velour jumpsuit, then poured herself a glass of Cristal that was left over from dinner. She wiped down the kitchen and dining room, leaving no trace of her presence. Then she put on a pot of water to boil. As she made her way up the steps, she could hear Donald trying to scream at her. She chuckled and set the pot on the dresser, then walked over to him. The whip that she held hung at her side.

*WHAP!*

The sound of Aria striking him, pierced through the silence. "Mmmhh!" he screamed.

*WHAP! WHAP! WHAP!*

"Now, Donald, is that any way to act?" Donald had pure fear in his eyes. "If you comply, we can talk and I'll untie you."

"Mm mmmh!" he cried.

"So?" Aria loosened the strap a notch, then popped the ball out of his mouth.

"Wait! Please, listen. I have a hundred grand in cash hidden in

93

the back of my closet. I-it's in a silver briefcase. The code is 1420. It's yours if you let me go." Aria placed the ball back in his mouth and tightened the strap. She held up one finger, then went to search out the hefty stash. *Guess I won't be catching that red-eye*, she thought. Aria went back over to Donald, who lay there bleeding and helpless. She removed the ball and loosened the strap.

"Thanks, but that's not nearly enough. I'm being paid much more," she lied. Tears fell down the sides of Donald's face. Aria reached to put the ball back in his mouth.

"P-please, we can negotiate any price. I-I will wire you any amount. I have a jewelry collection. It's in the top drawer of the chest in my closet. Please. I—it's worth hundreds of thousands. I'll give you anything, just please don't do this!" Donald begged. Aria sought out the collection.

"Again thanks, but it still won't save you. Do you know a Maurice Reid?" Aria sighed.

"Reid . . . Reid . . ." Recognition slowly crept over his face. Donald was pushing for him to be sent to prison for the rest of his life with no chance of parole. "His trial starts this Wednesday." Aria popped the ball back in his mouth. Donald jerked on his restraints that held him firmly in place. Aria grabbed the pot off the dresser and scalded Donald's face and chest. He wiggled and jerked as she emptied the pot. Aria picked up the whip and beat him repeatedly until she grew tired, taking every inch of her frustration out on him. His body was blistering and bleeding from the whip that cut him open every time she struck him. Donald lay there, his chest barely rising. She reached inside her bag and removed the glock. She put the pillow over his head and let off a silenced shot. Aria cleaned herself up, gathered his jewels and the money from the briefcase, and then drove toward the interstate. If she left now, she would reach Los Angeles by mid-afternoon.

\* \* \* \* \* \*

Harmony was surprised that Aria had delivered early and made an extra 100 grand, not to mention the crazy jewel collection she came up on. Notorious was so pleased, that he invited them to a party out in Malibu where they could network and possibly meet a couple of people who were interested in their services. Aria had gone on a huge shopping spree, creating a whole new image for them. No more sneakers or baggy jeans and everything tailored.

She watched Aria slip on a pair of nude red bottoms and smooth down her teal dress. She looked absolutely stunning, and she was all hers. The diamonds that graced her neck shined like her beauty and elegance. Aria grabbed her clutch, then caught Harmony's eyes on her. She smiled. "I'm ready."

"You look beautiful," Harmony said.

"Thank you. You sure clean up nice yourself," Aria replied. Harmony smiled.

"I love you," Aria said, searching her eyes for a reason not to.

"I love you too," Harmony genuinely replied. Guilt shot through her. She touched Aria's lips, remembering the sensual kiss Reese left on her lips.

\* \* \* \* \* \*

The ride to Malibu was filled with laughs and plans for their future. The two of them had made it, and life was looking up. Notorious was going to put more food on their plate, and they were ready to eat. Harmony laced her fingers in Aria's and gave the valet the keys. The mansion where the party was being hosted, was crazy. Three large stories of luxury, a huge pool, and the decor had to cost a couple hundred grand. Aria smiled as people followed Harmony with their eyes. She knew that her teal and nude lace dress would spark envy amongst the women and Harmony's matching Gucci knee-length shorts and V-neck T-shirt would set a trend. Their outfits were doing numbers; she expected all eyes to be on them. And they were.

"Hello, ladies. Glad to see that you could make it." Notorious greeted Harmony and Aria with a smile. Harmony didn't like him; there was something sly about him. He introduced them to a few major Los Angeles players and a guy from Miami who made it his business to give her his card and a date to meet. Harmony gave everyone that was interested in her service the green light to send her a few clients.

There were people everywhere, some drunk, some snorting cocaine off the mirrored table, and some popping pills and bottles. Harmony smoked and watched everyone watch her and Aria as she two-stepped behind her. *Damn, this is the life,* she thought as she inhaled the kush into her system.

"How'd this bitch get access to this party, especially without Betta?" Aria asked, watching Reese stare her down, only her look was different this time, making her antenna stand up. Harmony shrugged, attempting to appear nonchalant. She tried hard not to meet Reese's gaze, but it was difficult. Her heart beat sped up as Reese and Aria engaged in a stare off. Reese smirked as Aria rolled her curves into Harmony seductively, making it clear who Harmony belonged to. Reese met Harmony's eyes, then turned and disappeared into the crowd.

*Shit!* Harmony thought, juggling thoughts of them both as well as the consequences of her attraction to Reese should she ever act on it.

After a few hours passed, the night was finally winding down, and Harmony was ready to finish what they had started on the dance floor.

"Baby, I'm going to the bathroom, then we out. I'm trying to beat traffic," Harmony said.

"You're not driving, are you?" Aria joked.

"No, I am way too high." Harmony giggled.

"Okay. I am going to grab the car. I'll be out front."

Harmony squirted some hand soap into her palm and washed her hands. The door opened and shut quickly. Reese stood there in all black, looking damn good. A few seconds passed; they both stood there staring at each other. Then Reese pounced on Harmony, who gave in to her kisses and soft skin. Chanel No 5 invaded her senses and snapped her back to reality.

"Reese, are you crazy?"

"Crazy? Tell me that you have not thought about me since the last time you touched me, and I promise I will leave you alone. Tell me," Reese said. Harmony sighed and refused to respond, which Reese took as an open invitation. She attacked Harmony again, sucking and biting on her neck. It felt so good to Harmony that she got lost for a few seconds.

"Reese!"

"What?" Reese said seductively, lifting her dress over her head.

"N-no n-not here. Not like this."

"If not here, then where?"

"Hey, man, hurry up. I have to use the bathroom," someone called from the other side of the door.

Reese took Harmony's hand and slid it up her thighs between her legs and into her panties, soaking her fingers in her moisture. Reese gasped and threw her head back.

"Reese—I can't. Y-you know I can't."

"You can, and I know you want to."

Harmony lifted Reese onto the counter and slid her fingers deeper into her. Reese rotated her hips, almost coming instantly from the intensity and lust for her. Harmony touched every wall and kissed Reese with so much want. Reese rocked back and forth on

Harmony's fingers, moaning out in pleasure as she came. Harmony laid her head against Reese's forehead, knowing she was dead ass wrong. Reese slipped her dress back over her head and kissed her once more. "I am going to text you and you better answer," she said, walking out of the bathroom. Harmony washed her hands; she couldn't even look at herself.

"Why am I so weak for that girl?" she asked.

When Harmony climbed in the car, the floral scent of another woman wafted into the vehicle. Aria tilted her head upward and sniffed the air then Harmony, who didn't even look her in her eyes. "Chanel No. 5 mixed with dried saliva, huh?" Aria said. The sudden shift in Harmony's demeanor confirmed her suspicion. She reached back and slapped Harmony so hard it left her ears ringing.

*WHAP!*

"What was that for? Aria, you—" Harmony ducked to avoid another blow.

"I am not a fucking fool! So don't try to play me like I'm one!"

"Girl, you trippin' for real."

"Nah, I ain't tripped yet, but keep on playing with me and I will." Aria didn't say another word for the rest of the drive. She had already made up her mind; she knew what she had to do.

\* \* \* \* \* \*

The following two weeks seemed to drag by as Aria calculated her next move. She had to do something before she lost everything. Harmony's phone buzzed in Aria's lap. She had been checking Harmony's phone ever since the Malibu incident, and it was apparent that Reese was going to stop at nothing to get what she wanted. Harmony.

8:17 a.m.

**Reese:** *Meet me at Starbucks on La Brea.*

Aria grabbed the phone, climbed in Harmony's tinted-out Chevy and drove toward West Hollywood. She pulled into the parking lot. Reese pulled behind her and honked.

8:30 a.m.
**Harmony:** *With my wife. I'll get at you later.*

8:32 a.m.
**Reese:** *I hoped you would change your mind.*

Aria smiled at the text, thankful that Harmony had not betrayed her trust with this 'ho. Reese followed Aria to a secluded area filled with warehouses, one she had chosen a few days earlier. Reese hopped out of her car and opened the passenger door, her brow rising from shock.

"Reese!" Aria called out, stopping her from shutting the door. "I just want to talk." Reese bent down and looked at her.

"Bitch, you're a psycho. There is nothing for us to talk about," she said.

"You're right. There isn't," Aria said.

*Pfft! Pfft!*

Aria sent two silenced bullets across the passenger seat and into Reese's chest and neck. Her body went crashing to the ground. Aria climbed out of the car, snatched Reese's purse with her gloved hand and dialed on her phone. "Her car is parked beside the warehouse on Chamber Avenue." She hung up the phone after rattling off the address. Aria left no loose ends untied.

\* \* \* \* \* \*

Harmony woke up groggy. Aria had been acting distant ever since they left Malibu, and she had every reason to be. They had not shared the same bed, or spoken to one another in almost a week.

Today, all the silent treatment shit was going to cease. Harmony had texted Reese and told her they had needed to end their flirtation. That she loved Aria, and she deserved better and that creeping around was out of her character anyway. She searched for her phone, anxious to hear back from Reese, but couldn't find her phone anywhere. Harmony climbed in the shower, rinsing away her frustration and hoping to get things with Aria situated. Her silhouette appeared in the bathroom doorway. Harmony pulled the glass door back.

"Baby, we—" Aria had her silenced caliber at her side, tears streaming down her face. "What's the matter, baby?" she asked, never taking her eyes off Aria.

"I can't do this anymore." Harmony cut off the water and grabbed a towel. "Do you know why I was in a detention center for two years, huh?" Harmony wrapped the towel around her and stepped out onto the rug.

"No. Tell me, baby."

"Because I was in love with a bitch who thought she could play with my heart like it was a damn grand piano." Aria stepped into the bathroom.

Harmony's heart beat wildly against her chest. *Please don't let this bitch kill me*, she thought.

"Aria, I'm not playing with you." *Just tell her the truth. She isn't dumb.* "Reese and I never had anything serious. It was a—a crush, but I told her—I told her that I couldn't do it anymore—that I loved you." Aria pointed the glock at Harmony, then shot the glass door behind her. "Aria!" Harmony yelled, ducking from the shattered glass.

"Listen, I'm in love with you, Harmony, and I can't live without you. Promise me you won't see her anymore. Please promise me, promise me you won't break my heart. I'm full. I can't take any more heartache. I need you," Aria said, breaking down. Harmony closed the space between them, wrapping her arms around Aria, who began to sob and dropped the gun to the floor.

"I promise, baby. I won't hurt you. I love you. I'm sorry, Aria. Forgive me." Harmony held Aria's face up to hers.

"I love you too, and only will death do us apart," Aria said, her tone serious.

\* \* \* \* \* \*

The church was packed to capacity and Betta could not help the tears that fell onto his shirt. He listened to people as they took turns speaking about Reese and how they had such love for her. His heart ached. He had lost a piece of himself. Reese was his favorite cousin, aside from Woo, who had left the service because he couldn't take it. Betta was forced to be strong for Reese's mother. "She was a true diva," a friend of the family said. Betta wracked his brain searching for somebody that would want to do her harm, but kept getting the same answer: Aria. Betta smiled sadly and shook Harmony's hand as she approached with Aria at her side.

"I'm sorry for your loss, man. Have you heard anything?" Betta shook his head.

"The police have no leads. They're investigating several murders right now and because they're under the impression that it was drug-related—a drug deal gone wrong, Reese's murder isn't a priority.

"Drug-related?" Harmony asked.

"Yeah, but it's something fishy going on, and I'ma find out what stinks," Betta replied, looking at Aria.

"Betta," Aria spoke.

"Aria," he said dryly. Their eyes lingered on each other for a moment. Harmony sighed.

"Well, I'm here if you need me," she finally said.

"I know. Thank you for stopping by." The two friends embraced, then Harmony found her seat.

Harmony knew how much Reese meant to him. When she received the call, she could hear the pain in his voice. She knew that in spite of how Aria felt about them creeping, she still came to show Betta and his family love.

\* \* \* \* \* \*

Aria stood next to Harmony, who needed to support Betta in his time of need, but Aria wasn't at all moved. As they lowered the casket into the ground, Aria could not help but smirk. Reese had played a dangerous game and lost. When she looked up, Betta was staring dead at her, as if he knew her thoughts, or that she had something to do with his loss. She cut her eyes at him as he walked toward her. Aria cleared her throat.

"Betta, is there a reason you keep staring at me?" she asked.

"There is, but I want to be sure before I speak," he replied.

"Be sure of what?"

"If you had something to do with Reese being killed."

Harmony's mouth fell open. Aria chuckled. "Really? You think I'd kill Reese then attend her funeral?"

"I don't know what you would do." Betta shrugged.

"Whoa, Betta. Come on. Why would Aria kill Reese?" Harmony asked. Again Betta shrugged.

"I can only see you being the reason."

"You're delusional!" Aria said. "Harmony, I'll be in the car." Aria spun on her pumps, preparing to leave." Harmony stopped her.

"Money, I'm—" Betta started to say. Harmony held up her hand.

"I'm insulted, B," she said.

"Something is up. I can feel it in my gut," Betta said. "I gotta find out what happened to Reese. Who took her from me, so I can return the selfish favor?" His eyes met with Aria's just as she turned back to face him.

"Like I said, I'll be in the car. You coming?" Aria asked, gazing into Harmony's eyes.

Harmony turned and walked away, questioning the possibilities.

# CHAPTER 11

As the plane landed, Aria looked down at the buildings and lights of a city sprawled across a coastal plain. Los Angeles was so beautiful positioned next to the Pacific Ocean. The sky was clear, not a cloud in sight. She was so glad to be back in Los Angeles. She had been summoned to Texas by a close friend of Notorious, who'd paid all of her expenses and provided her with a fake ID and passport. She needed the break. It had been almost two months since Reese's funeral and she was growing tired of Betta and his middling.

Things between her and Harmony were so much better. Aria wasn't sure if it was because she'd cut Reese out of the picture, or because she genuinely wanted their relationship to work, or because she was afraid she'd kill her if she didn't tighten up. One thing Aria was sure of was that a person's true colors were bound to shine through, and if Harmony wasn't all in, she would soon find out. As she made her way to the exit, she spotted Harmony standing at the end of the ramp waiting for her. They smiled when their eyes locked.

"Hey, baby."

"Hey, how was your trip?"

"Successful," Aria said proudly. Notorious had put them on with some cat out of Texas, and he needed her to take care of something immediately and was willing to pay extra for any inconvenience. Harmony grabbed Aria's Gucci bag off the belt and laced her fingers in hers.

"I've missed you," Harmony admitted.

"Me too. What do you have planned for the day?"

"Nothing. I just have to meet with Betta. Woo said he isn't doing well." Aria rolled her eyes.

"I have to go meet with Notorious and pick up this money." Harmony was growing more and more suspicious of Notorious, who was always finding ways to conveniently meet with Aria, alone.

"I don't understand why he can't just drop it in the box like he does mine?"

"I have to meet with one of his colleagues," Aria said, climbing into the car.

"I don't like it."

"Aww baby, don't be like that. It's strictly business."

"Yeah, on your end. I don't mind seeking new business opportunities, just be careful and be on your shit."

\* \* \* \* \* \*

Notorious sat across from Aria looking dapper in his Armani suit. Le France was a nice restaurant, but too romantic for a business meeting. His beady eyes scanned over Aria hungrily. Her beauty was rare, distinctive, and he could not control himself. He had to have her. He seemed to never get enough time with her, so he set up a business meeting. He knew she wouldn't refuse the chance to make a dollar.

"Would you like wine, or—"

"No. I'll have a glass of cranberry juice please." Notorious ordered himself a glass of wine.

"Aria, I have to say that I am impressed, and I appreciate you taking care of business so swiftly and professionally. My business associates and I are very pleased." Aria smiled at his praise.

"Thank you. Harmony and I make sure we get the job done." She was being short with him. It had been almost twenty minutes, and his business associate was nowhere to be found, and more than likely wasn't coming.

"Have you ever been to the Hamptons?"

*What the fuck does the Hamptons have to do with anything?* "No."

"You should let me take you out that way. You know, expand your horizon." *Horizon? Oh, this nigga is definitely feeling himself.* "There's a few parties going on this weekend that I know you'd enjoy."

"Let me ask Money. I'm sure she'd love to go." Aria had no intention on being anywhere partying with Notorious, or any other man for that matter. Notorious smiled to hide his frustration with her turning down his every advance.

"No disrespect, sweetheart, but how'd you end up with—" Aria could see that Notorious was arrogant, but she threw him off his square with her nonchalant attitude. *Let me check him now so he will know where I stand.*

"Listen, I love everything about a woman. Especially *my* woman. She has the capability to make me feel wanted, appreciated, and respected. Something most men couldn't do if you gave them exact instructions." Notorious laughed, showing his crooked teeth.

"You just have not met the right man."

"Says who?" The waitress came with their drinks.

"Can I get you guys anything?" Notorious' phone rang. He said a few words, then hung up.

"You might as well order. My associate said he won't be able to make it today, and that he is sorry for the inconvenience." *How convenient!* she thought.

"No, I think I should go. I just flew in, and I have a few things to take care of." Aria didn't wait for his response. She stood and grabbed her jacket.

Notorious sat there fuming in silence. Nobody told him no, or rejected him. He watched Aria, realizing that he had a problem, and no problem was too hard for him to solve.

"You know how to reach me if you need to," Aria said, walking out of the restaurant.

\* \* \* \* \* \*

Betta dug deep into his hustle, serving fiend after fiend and filling his lungs with kush and his stomach with cognac. Something was nagging at him, telling him that Aria had something to do with Reese's murder. The smirk that she wore whenever he was around didn't help. Woo said he was being paranoid, but he could not shake the feeling, and because the detectives had nothing to go on, the case went cold, which only bothered him even more.

He heard a knock on the door, expecting Harmony. He was unsure of how to tell her what he was feeling, or if he should tell her at all. He remembered Reese being excited about seeing her. Did she? Had something happened, and was she helping Aria cover it up? So many things were going through his head.

"What's up, fam'?" Harmony said, coming in. She covered her nose. It smelled like shit and looked like a train wreck in there. Dirty clothes, empty liquor bottles of Paul Mason, and pizza boxes littered the floor. "Damn, bruh. You all right?"

"No, I'm not. The police have no leads! None. The streets act like they don't know shit, and I'm trying–"

"Listen, I know it's fucked up, but you can't let this shit take over you. When's the last time you slept or showered?" Harmony asked, cutting him off. Tears fell from Betta's eyes; he couldn't help it; he missed his cousin Reese. He cleared his throat.

"I'm just trying to figure this shit out. Weren't you and Reese supposed to meet up?"

"What?" Harmony asked, defensively. "I know you don't think . . ."

"Money, *please*! Just answer the question!" Betta barked.

"Yes, I was, but Aria trashed my phone. She knew me and Reese had something going on. How, I don't know, but she did and . . . You don't think she . . ."

"I don't know. Would she?"

"No!" Harmony answered, unsure of her own answer. "You trippin', Betta! For real," Harmony grew frustrated by his accusation and headed toward the door. How could Betta even ask her that?

"Wait, Money. It—"

"I came to invite you to my birthday bash. You're welcome to come through if you want, but I'll understand if you don't, and I am not going to take any offense to what you just suggested. I know you're grieving." Harmony tossed a flyer on the table and walked out.

\* \* \* \* \* \*

Harmony sat behind her limo tint in deep thought. She began to question Aria's innocence. *Would she kill Reese in cold blood then attend her funeral?*

She climbed the steps and entered their master suite. Aria was on the phone making some last minute arrangements for her party. In forty-eight hours she would be eighteen. No more running or living in fear of being carted back to the Pratts'. She waited until Aria ended her call before speaking. They had committed some serious crimes together, so what would make this a secret?

"What is it baby?" Aria asked.

"I just left Betta's."

"Oh, how's he doing?"

"He's real fucked up about Reese. He is taking it hard."

"Damn, why didn't you stay with him for a little while?" Aria asked, without flinching.

"Because he thinks you had something to do with her murder." Aria sat up looking Harmony deep in her eyes. "Did you—"

"Are you fucking serious right now? Harmony, if I was going to kill anybody it would be your ass. These 'hos can't fuck themselves.

I know it takes two. So, to answer your question—no. I didn't. I can't believe you would even ask me that," Aria snapped, storming out of the room and down the steps. Harmony came down the steps.

"Baby, I never thought you did. I just—" Harmony started but was interrupted. Aria pulled a bottle of Ciroc out of the freezer and some fruit from the fridge.

"What? Needed to be sure?" Aria snapped, pouring her ingredients into the blender. Harmony sighed. She didn't want to argue about another nigga's accusations. She had just gotten back in Aria's good graces and didn't want to fight with her.

"Can you make me one?" Harmony asked. Aria shot daggers at her, but put some extra fruit in the blender. "Baby, listen, I don't want to fight, okay?" Harmony said. Aria handed her a drink.

"Cheers to peace?"

"Don't ever try me like that again. If I make a move, I'll always tell you first. You know that." Harmony closed the space between them and lifted her drink in the air.

"Cheers," Aria said. She kissed her soft, pouting lips.

"You're right, and I am sorry."

Aria kissed Harmony back roughly, passionately. "I love you," she said, setting her drink down and picking Aria up onto the island. She kissed down Aria's neck and slid her panties to the side. Harmony's fingers entered her wetness, chills ran down her spine at the sound of Aria's moans. Aria lay back and let Harmony go to work. Spreading her legs eagle style while she devoured her, sucking her juices down her throat. She looked down at Harmony while she made love to her, squeezing her muscles around her fingers, inviting the sensation that rocked her body. Aria's hips involuntarily rolled on Harmony's tongue. Ecstasy filling her body and exploding in between her thighs.

\* \* \* \* \* \*

Harmony was draped in beige slacks with a navy blue dress shirt and loafers, compliments of Roberto Cavalli. She no longer wore the street garb or kept a thuggish appearance. Even her jewels were elegant. Cartier graced her neck and wrist. She was on top and it felt good.

The party was live and the attendance was filled with some of the most esteemed people in Los Angeles. She had to give Aria her props; she had definitely did her thing, sparing no cost. The Chanel dress that snuggled up to Aria's curves left her mouth watering. They had danced and drank champagne all night. The owner wouldn't let them smoke in VIP, so they were standing on the balcony in the chilly breeze, smoking some of the best kush California had to offer.

"Happy birthday, baby," Aria said for the hundredth time.

"Thank you, babe. I've never had anyone do anything so special for me."

"Nobody?" Harmony thought about her brother Peezy, whom she hadn't seen in almost five years. She thought about him often, but refused to feel any emotion for somebody that didn't care enough to come looking for her.

"Nope, no one." Harmony filled her lungs with kush, suppressing the pain that only continued to fuel her rage.

"I have to use the bathroom. I'ma meet you in VIP." Aria kissed Harmony's cheek and headed downstairs. She had to get ready for the grand finale. She stopped in the restroom to check her makeup. Aria dialed the valet's number. "Pierre, pull the car out front. We will be leaving in the next hour or so." Aria was satisfied with the outcome; she enjoyed watching Harmony have a good time. Aria smoothed her dress over and fluffed her curls. Her smile faded when Betta entered the restroom, charging at her. She didn't budge.

"You might have Money fooled, but I know you had something to do with my cousin's murder." Aria smiled at him, then chuckled.

111

"Prove it!" His jaw tightened.

"Oh, I am, and I hope Harmony sees you for what you are. A psychotic bitch!" Aria's smile disappeared.

"Well, be careful doing it," she said, standing on her toes, kissing his lips, and strutting out the restroom.

\* \* \* \* \* \*

Harmony kissed Aria on the forehead. She went all out for her party, sparing no expense. She smiled as the crowd gathered around outside the expensive hall she rented in downtown Los Angeles.

"I love it and it's so my style!" Harmony said, walking around the cocaine white Cadillac CTS that sat beautifully on 22's. The interior was filled with cherrywood grain and the seats, a mocha brown. Aria had their names engraved on the seats, and though Harmony wasn't the flashy type, she knew she had stepped up her game.

"You're riding like a big boy now," Betta said, coming through the crowd reeking of vodka. Harmony looked over at him. "That's what's up. I'm glad somebody can be happy." Harmony hugged him.

Aria stared Betta in the eyes.

"All right. Holla at me if you need anything." Aria smirked. She knew exactly how to erase Betta from the equation and kill any chance of him digging or snooping around . . .

\* \* \* \* \* \*

Aria had been watching Betta for the past week. He was foolishly set up in a motel where nothing but illegal activity was going on, which made access to his room a piece of cake. Harmony wouldn't be home until Friday, and it gave Aria just enough room to go and come as she pleased, but tonight was the perfect night. It was two o'clock in the morning when she made the call to the police about the drug activity and fighting she heard coming from inside Betta's motel room. She watched as the two officers approached his room. They beat on the door, but Betta took one second too long to answer, forcing them to draw their guns and kick the door in.

\* \* \* \* \* \*

Betta sat on the bed handcuffed next to a stripper he had met in the club a few weeks back while the police ransacked his room. He knew it was only a matter of time before they found his stash.

"Whoa, what's this?" the tall, lanky officer asked, holding up a chrome pistol. Betta dropped his head. Sick to his stomach. Somebody had set him up. *That bitch!* he thought. The officer escorted him to his patrol car through the crowd of onlookers. His eyes locked with Aria's, who stood there smirking.

"Betta, I told you to be careful," she said, sarcastically, turning and climbing into Harmony's CTS and speeding off. There was no fighting the inevitable. Betta was on parole, and no lawyer in the state of California would be able to get him out of this trouble. He dropped his head and climbed in the backseat of the squad car.

\* \* \* \* \* \*

Harmony sat across from Betta trying to grasp all of what he was saying. "She grimy, my nigga!" *How could Aria have anything to do with him getting caught slippin'?* Harmony didn't understand.

"Nah, my girl ain't that type."

"Money, she was there when I got arrested!"

"You don't even know—"

"No, you don't know her, nigga!" Betta shouted, trying to get through to her. "She was there when I got—"

"So, let me get this straight. You called me down here to tell me what? That Aria killed Reese and set you up because you were on to her?" Betta nodded yes. "I don't believe you. You don't even have an ounce of proof. Holla at me when you do," Harmony said, slamming down the phone. She couldn't believe this. There'd never been a word that came out of Betta's mouth that she didn't believe, but this was too extreme. She loved Aria and refused to believe that she had something to do with him being caught up. Harmony was livid and hurt as she walked out of the visitation room. *I'll never go against the grain*, she thought, handing the cashier five crispy hundreds to place on Betta's commissary account.

\* \* \* \* \* \*

Aria rubbed lotion on Harmony's back and listened as she told her about their visit. She tried not to laugh at how absurd Betta sounded when he was telling Harmony what he thought she had done.

"He probably wanted to fuck me," Aria said, poisoning Harmony's mind. The fact that Harmony knew how she despised men made Harmony smile. Aria had proven her loyalty. Aria kissed down her back. Her body was so beautiful, and she hid it well beneath her baggy clothes. Aria bit at her curves, then wrapped her lips around her weakness. The moans that bounced off the walls brought Aria to her height as she massaged her clit with her fingers. At that moment, she swore to erase everyone that ever posed a threat to what she and Harmony shared. Dangerously in love was an understatement, compared to what she felt, and no one but God himself could come between them.

# CHAPTER 12

Harmony sat in the truck watching Snake closely. He, like most niggas that were hood rich and had all the love in the streets, was slippin'. Not knowing that somebody had paid fifty grand to make him a memory. The only thing that bothered her was: she knew Snake, knew how he moved, and something just didn't seem right. He was being too careless. Harmony pulled off and onto the interstate. She always went with her gut. *There is always tomorrow.* Aria was at home waiting on her, and for whatever reason, she was anxious to get to her. Her mind wandered on the ride home, but when she pulled up and saw that the lights were off, she became alert and pulled out her gun. She unlocked the door. As soon as she entered, a large shadow charged at her.

*Pfft! Pfft!*

Harmony let off two shots, sending the large shadow crashing to the floor. A shot rang off upstairs, and a loud thud sent fear shooting through Harmony's body. *Aria!* Harmony ran up the stairs two and three at a time.

"Baby!" she called out.

"I'm up here!" Aria said. She stood over a man dressed in all black, with her gun drawn.

"What the fuck's going on?" Harmony asked, hugging Aria.

"I don't know. The lights just went off when I heard footsteps, so I grabbed my gun, then hid in the closet and—" Another gunshot cut her off, then the lights flickered back on. Harmony looked at Aria.

"Stay right here."

"No, I'm coming too," she whispered defiantly. They descended the stairs slowly, Aria in back, their guns drawn. *What the fuck is going on?* Harmony thought, her mind racing. The tall, light-skinned man that was struggling to tie up the intruder, stood to his feet.

"Peezy?" Harmony yelled in disbelief. His eyes softened at the sight of his baby sister.

"Harmony!"

"What the fuck are you doing here!" she asked.

"I came to look for you when I heard you fled from the Pratt's."

"So, you knew where I was this entire time?" she asked, hurt.

"No. Not the entire time. Once I found you, the next day you were gone."

"I thought you forgot about me. How come you didn't come after mom—" Tears pooled in her eyes and fell down her face.

"I tried. They moved me around so much, and when I couldn't find you, I got discouraged. I looked for you for three years. They kept changing your case worker," Peezy said, tears in his eyes. He looked over at Aria. Her gun was still drawn. It was something familiar about him, but she couldn't place it. Peezy nodded to her.

"He's cool. This is my brother Peezy. This is my girl Aria." Aria lowered her gun.

"I was shocked when I saw you were, were—" Peezy started.

"Yeah, I'm a lesbian," Harmony said, laughing and wiping her eyes.

"Umm, the police are probably on the way, so maybe you two should go," Aria said.

"You're right. Sis, help me carry this nigga to my van," he said.

"We're going to find out who sent these niggas and why." Harmony's mind went into overdrive. Betta was the only person who knew where they lived. Had he sent some niggas to kill Aria because he was convinced she killed Reese? Fear rose inside of Harmony. Was Karma catching up with them? Was it their turn to fall? Harmony helped carry the man to Peezy's van and put him in the backseat.

"Don't worry. I'll deal with the police. Give me your gun," Aria said. Peezy looked at her. It was very rare that he would find a chick that would ride. She kissed Harmony and went back inside. "I will call you once they leave. I'll be at the Marriott."

\* \* \* \* \* \*

*WHAP!*

The sound of muffled screams, metal hitting flesh, and breaking bones sent chills up Harmony's spine. "Mmmh mmmmh," Antwon screamed.

Harmony snatched the towel from his mouth.

"I-I'll t-tell y-you. I'll tell you."

Peezy had tortured and beat him for hours, and even though Harmony's mind was distracted, she took note of Peezy's brutality. "Who sent you to kill my sister?" he asked. The guy's heavy breathing and foul smell reminded her of something out of a horror movie.

"N-Notorious sent me. H-he said he wanted u-us to—H-he wants th-that girl. Your . . . your girl. He said to kill y-you."

"He sent you to kill me so that he can have my girlfriend?" Harmony asked again for clarity. Notorious' goon nodded rapidly.

"Who's Notorious? You know him?" Peezy asked.

"Yes, very well." Harmony dug in her pocket and screwed on her silencer, then looked over at Peezy. "You done?" He nodded. Harmony put two holes in his head and left him slumped over and tied to the chair in a vacant warehouse. She couldn't believe that Notorious was trying to take her out only to steal the love of her life. "I knew it was something I didn't like about that nigga." She texted Notorious from Antwon's phone.

It's done.

\* \* \* \* \* \*

The two overweight detectives that reported to the scene were floored by Aria's beauty. Being the manipulator that she is, she used her beauty to her advantage after she had made the hysterical 911 call and roughed herself up. She told them that the wounded men lying in her foyer had tried to rob her. The detectives questioned her for hours, then she was released. They kept her gun and other evidence for their case, but she wasn't worried. Manipulation was her game.

She called Harmony and gave her the room number to her suite at the Marriott, then took a shower. Aria could not believe that somebody had come into their house and tried to kill her. Had Biggs found her? Was Los Angeles not far enough? Tears came to her eyes. If he had found her, she wasn't running this time. *It is war,* she thought, drifting off into a comfortable sleep.

* * * * * *

"So how are you going to get at this nigga?" Peezy asked as he sped down the interstate. Harmony sat silent in the passenger seat.

"I don't know yet. It's crazy 'cause I knew he liked her, bruh. Maybe even wanted to fuck her because true—she is one bad ass bitch."

*Damn sure is,* Peezy thought.

"But him trying to kill me, now that's deep. I honestly thought that her past had caught up with her. I never would've thought that this fat fuck nigga would cross me like that. I love her so much I would do anything for her, and nobody is going to take her from me. Nobody!" Peezy swallowed hard. Biggs had sent him to do just that. He cleared his throat.

"Harmony, I have to tell you something. I didn't just come out here to find you. I came because I was paid to track down Aria and bring her back to San Diego dead or alive, but when I found out that you were with her at the Pratt's and had fled, I really had to find her so that I could find you."

"What?"

"I love you. I never forgot about you, and if we are going to establish a relationship, I want to be truthful. I was sent to kill her, or bring her back with me."

"Well, you might as well cancel that because you will have to kill me first," Harmony said, reaching for Peezy's gun and placing it on her lap. "And trust that it won't be easy."

\* \* \* \* \* \*

Aria woke up out of her nightmare gasping for air. "Peezy is Biggs right hand! Oh my goodness! He found me!" she said, tears pooling in her eyes. The sound of her phone buzzing startled her. "Hello?"

"What's up, beautiful? It's me. Notorious." *Beautiful?* Aria looked at the phone, then down at her watch. It was almost three in the morning. Aria thought about how out of line Notorious was. "I'm sending you a car to come get you. We need to talk. Where are you?"

"I'm not at home. I-I'm going through it." The knock at the door startled her. "Um let me call you back."

"Don't keep me waiting."

Aria hung up and answered the door. Relief washed over her when she saw Harmony was alone. "Where's Peezy?"

"He's getting his own room. Listen though, we have a serious problem."

*Oh God! He is going to let him kill me! Blood will always be thicker than water.* Unarmed and trapped in a corner, Aria began to panic. *Think, Aria, think,* she coached, bracing herself for the worst. "Notorious sent his goons to kill me." Harmony chuckled.

"I guess he feels as though I'm the only thing standing in his way."

"He what! I know he—"

"Whatever you said or did to him has him thinking."

"I don't have him *thinking* a damn thing!" Aria barked, defensively.

"There you go again trying me." Harmony sighed.

"He just called my phone."

"Yeah, because he thinks I'm dead!"

The knock at the door made Aria jump. Fear rose from the depths of her stomach when her eyes locked with Peezy's. She looked at Harmony.

"He said that he would send me a car. He wants to meet," she said, trying to suppress her fear. She wasn't sure if she would tell Harmony, or wait to see what Peezy's next move was going to be. Aria couldn't show her hand; she had to play dumb. For now. If he tried anything, she'd kill him and expose his real reason for finding his long lost sister.

"Well then, let's go meet him," Peezy said.

\* \* \* \* \* \*

Aria sat in the back of the Lincoln Navigator Notorious sent. Peezy and Harmony tailed her. *How dare this nigga play me close and try to take the only person I got.* She would get rid of Notorious first, then Peezy. She thought hard, organizing her priorities. *Nobody will take her away, especially not my past, and anyone who even attempts to do so will pay with their life.* The truck pulled up to Notorious' condo, and the driver helped her out. Her stilettos clacked on the marble floor.

"You sent for me?" she asked.

Notorious turned around and smiled, drink in hand. "I did."

"You're so charming," she lied, forcing herself to smile.

"And you are the epitome of beautiful."

"What is it that you wanted? You got a client for me?"

"No. I actually wanted to treat you to a day on the town. That is, if your girl won't mind," he said, smiling devilishly. Aria frowned.

"Me and Money, we are—umm . . . I caught her with another woman and have not spoken to her since. I'm not with that foolish shit."

"I would say that I'm sorry, but then I'd be lying. Aria, I've wanted you ever since the first time I saw you at your birthday party." Aria blushed. He was flattering, but fat, black, and very ugly was nowhere near her type. Dingy, charcoal-hued skin and long crooked teeth. He towered over her even in her pumps. Notorious reminded her of the Boogey Man. Yeah, his money was long and he had his hands in every illegal chain there was, but nothing about him was appealing, the first, being that he was a man. Aria laced her arm in his and smiled.

"I'd be more than happy to be treated to a day on the town. Only if you promise to be good." Notorious' eyebrows rose. "Be good?"

"Yes," Aria said, looking up at him. "Be good. I'm sure you are used to getting whatever you want, but you are going to have to work for this good shit," Aria said, placing her hand on her hip. Notorious laughed.

"Girl, you are something else, but you have my word. I'll be on my best behavior." Notorious released a deep sigh. "I can't really explain why I can't get you off my mind." Aria smiled.

"Maybe because I gave you a hell of a chase." He grinned.

"I'm just glad you're giving me a chance. I was waiting for the lil nigga to fuck up."

*You mean kill her*, Aria thought as she met his beady eyes. "Yeah, she fucked up royally."

"Good! Now I can show you I'm not like the rest." He smiled

triumphantly. Who would've thought that she and Harmony would be on bad terms when he took the life from her body?

\* \* \* \* \* \*

Harmony and Peezy were parked across the street from the fancy five-star restaurant. She was becoming restless watching Notorious wine and dine Aria. She was seeing red, and if it wasn't for Peezy, she would have blown their cover on more than one occasion. Peezy patted Harmony's shoulder.

"Just chill. It's all an act, even though she is doing a damn good job of it. You and I know she wants him dead, maybe even worse than you do." She exhaled hard.

"You're right. It's just killing me."

"I'm sure it is. You love her, don't you?"

The dead hitman's cell phone buzzed. Harmony checked the text.

"He made the drop, and he only paid this nigga ten grand to kill me?" Harmony gave Peezy the directions to the drop, frustration filling her.

\* \* \* \* \* \*

Aria had become completely impatient with every passing moment, but she knew she had to play her position. For the past two weeks she let Notorious wine and dine her, spending ridiculous amounts of cash on the frivolous things she desired. She had practically moved in with him, but only to further mislead him and get the combination to the monstrous safe he kept pulling thousands out of in an attempt to impress her. Her sex appeal and charm had him slipping. *Fuckin' fool.* The Birkin bag that sat in the chair next to her was well over fifteen grand. Aria had decided that tonight she was going to end this little charade. She couldn't take it anymore.

They sat in Madera Heights dining at the five-star establishment, and she stared deep into his eyes as if she was smitten, but murderous thoughts raced through her mind.

"So, have I been a good boy?" he asked. Aria chuckled.

"Surprisingly, you have, and because you have been such a good boy, I have a surprise for you. Tonight." Notorious smiled. "And I'm into all kinds of kinky shit, so we will see if you can keep up."

"Oh, I am more than sure that I can, but I have a surprise for you," Notorious said, reaching into his breast pocket and pulling out a purple velvet box. He slid it across the table.

"Why do you spoil me the way you do?"

"Because I want you to know that if you were mine, there is not a thing in this world that you couldn't have." Aria opened the box and a princess cut diamond tennis bracelet sat inside. She gasped at the beautifully crafted jewelry.

"It's gorgeous, Notorious, but don't think that because you are giving me all of these expensive gifts that I'm going to give it all up. I'm feeling you and all that comes along with being yours, but like I said before, I'm not with no foolishness."

Notorious smiled hard, all his patience and persistence wasn't wasted after all. She would be his in just a matter of time.

\* \* \* \* \* \*

Harmony sat across from Peezy in the huge hotel suite. She lay back and put her hands behind her head, listening to Peezy catch her up on his life and the years they had missed. He was married and had a son. Harmony couldn't help the anxiety that flared up in her. She too was excited to live happily with Aria. So much had gone on in her life; some things she had not even digested.

"I have so much to tell you, but before I start, I have to know why you were sent to kill her. What did she do so bad that he wants her dead?" Peezy looked over at Harmony.

"She hasn't told you?" he asked, shocked. Harmony shook her head. "Well, I'd rather she did." Harmony smiled. Peezy had not changed much, and the love that she had for him had not gone anywhere; it had resurfaced from where she'd buried it the moment she saw his face. One that resembled hers so much, even more now that she rocked a low Caesar.

"I have so many questions, but I want to know why you left the Pratt's. What happened? Why did he poison his wife?"

"Poison who? Mr. Pratt?" Harmony scoffed. "He didn't have the—" Then it hit her hard in the chest. Aria had made good on her promise of killing two birds with one stone, then fleeing with her to Los Angeles. "He was abusive; I had to go," was all she could say.

"They gave him life in prison," Peezy stated. Harmony sighed.

"He deserves it."

"Damn, I'm sorry I didn't find Aria sooner. Biggs somehow came up with the resources to find you, even though I had begged him to call in some favors to help me look for you. But when he found out where Aria was, he sent his men to find her. He had been searching high and low for her when he got word that she was out of the detention facility, but once I found out that you were with her–"

"How did you know I was with her?"

"I saw a picture of you guys together, but a few days later you disappeared. Then somebody sent word that she was shacked up with some nigga out in LA. That nigga ended up being you." Harmony chuckled.

"One day I will tell you all about it. Here," she said, handing him five of the ten thousand dollars that was paid to take her life.

"What's this for?"

"I know the price on Aria's head was much more, but it's the least I can do."

"I'm not sure what I'm going to tell Biggs, but I know he isn't going to like it." The siblings smiled at each other. Peezy tucked the crisp hundreds in his pocket. "Matter of fact, I'm not going to tell him nothing. I'm going to show him."

"Show him what?"

"That friends make the best enemies."

# CHAPTER 13

The black corset that hugged Aria's body accentuated her frame nicely. Notorious lay on the California King-size bed stretched out, a glass of cognac in one hand and a spliff of kush in the other. His eyes followed Aria's curves as she lit candles and emptied her goody bag. She exhaled.

"You promise to be gentle?" Aria asked. Notorious set down his glass.

"I would never hurt you," he said, seriously. Aria looked at him with uncertainty.

"Oh, come on, baby. Don't freeze up on me."

"I'm not. It's just . . . this is a big step for me."

"Okay, look. I will let you control everything. I won't even touch you." *I didn't plan on letting you do that anyway, nigga!* Aria held up her green silk straps, and Notorious put his hands up in submission.

"Just don't tie them too tight." *I won't have to.* Aria nodded as she licked her lips.

"You ready?"

\* \* \* \* \* \*

Harmony aimed her silencer at Notorious' guard and let off a round. He fell to the floor before he could reach for his gun. Peezy had unarmed the guards and let Harmony know the coast was clear. She tucked her glock in her back. "Nobody will disturb you. Handle your business," he said, standing guard. Peezy welcomed the silence; he had so much on his mind. Biggs was nobody to play with, and if a decision wasn't made quickly, he would have a problem on his hands.

Rounding the corner, Harmony admired Aria's ability to seduce and secure her prey like a black widow. She swayed seductively to Rihanna's voice, as Notorious lay in a trance under her, drooling, oblivious to what awaited him. As the song ended, Harmony clapped her hands.

"Bravo, baby! Bravo!" she said. The look of fear that spread over Notorious' face was priceless.

"You bitch!" he said, jerking on his restraints.

"You snake!" Harmony countered.

Aria jumped off the bed, walked over to her and kissed her. "I've missed you."

"Me too." Notorious glared at them with hatred in his eyes, still struggling to free himself. He knew how ruthless they were. He had sent them to kill plenty of people, and they never returned empty-handed.

Harmony kissed her deeper as Aria began undressing her. She kissed down Harmony's neck and shoulder, breasts, then stomach. Notorious burned with envy as he was forced to look on. Aria dropped to her knees and spread Harmony's petals with her lips, beckoning her body into submission. Harmony moaned loudly, gripping Aria's hair as she rocked her hips into her rhythm. Notorious tried desperately to free himself. The silk straps were designed to tighten at the slightest resistance. "I'ma kill you dike bitches, if it's the last thing I do."

Tuning him out, Harmony let the murderous thoughts and Aria's expertise take her over the edge.

* * * * * *

Peezy's cell phone buzzed. It was Biggs. He had put this call off for as long as he could; he just couldn't go against the grain, against his flesh and blood. Ever since he realized Aria was the love of Harmony's life and that she was willing to go to war with anyone that posed a threat to their relationship, he knew he had to do something. What was he going to do was the question. Peezy cleared his throat.

"Speak."

"Nah, nigga, you speak. What's the hold up?" *Who the fuck is this nigga talkin' to?* Peezy thought. "You have been gone for almost three weeks?" Marcus barked into the phone. Peezy looked down at the phone. He and Marcus had been good friends for years, but ever since his father Biggs placed Peezy at his side, Marcus had gotten beside himself with envy.

"Who the fuck are you talkin' to, lil nigga? I'm handling my business, so pipe down. I don't take orders from you, or report to you. You are straight trippin'! I need more time; this shit ain't as sweet as our informant said it to be." Marcus was growing impatient with Peezy, whom he had envied since their childhood.

"My dad said you got a few days and that's it," Marcus barked, hanging up. *Both these niggas got me fucked up.* Peezy thought. He had been the enforcement behind a lot of the new business deals and territory Biggs had gained over the past few years. He knew Biggs' organization inside and out, his connects, his stash houses, and him.

"I'm the last nigga you want as an enemy," he said aloud as the wheels started to turn in his head.

* * * * * *

"I'm really disappointed in you, Notorious," Harmony said, buttoning up her shirt. "I have been nothing but loyal to you and your cause." Harmony grabbed her glock and pointed it at him.

"Wait, Money—hear me out." Aria began to cook up a deadly dose of heroin. "It was her idea," he lied, nodding toward her.

Harmony pointed the gun at Aria. "So you were going to have me killed?" Aria burst into laughter.

"Yeah, me and him were going to live happily ever after." Harmony chuckled.

Notorious jerked at her. "Ahh!" He winced, looking up at the restraints that were sinking into his flesh. Aria filled the syringe with heroin. Notorious' eyes grew big. "Wait. Listen. I can make you a deal," he begged.

"Tell me the combination." Notorious looked over at Aria.

"I'll die before I do that."

"So be it then." She held the gun to his head.

"Okay, 34-32-26."

"He's lying!" Aria said, walking over to him and wrapping the tourniquet around his arm. "Last chance. Tell me the combination and I'll let you live." He thought about it for a second, then smiled.

"Okay. It's f-u-c-k y-o-u!" he replied.

Harmony looked over at Aria and nodded. She walked over to the photo of Los Angeles and lifted it off the wall.

"It's 4-20-88," Aria said. Notorious turned pale as he screamed every curse word there was. Harmony smiled at the safe that sat behind it. She entered the code and the light turned green and the safe slid open like a drawer.

"There are some duffle bags in the closet," Aria said.

Harmony looked at her. "Kill him."

"But wait. I thought—"

"I lied," Harmony said, opening the door for Peezy.

"Damn, it took you forty-five minutes to kill the—" Peezy froze as he watched Notorious attempt to resist Aria as she administered the deadly dose into his veins. She was dressed in close to nothing, leaving Peezy aroused. *Damn, she is a bad bitch,* he thought, admiring her beauty and flawless body. Notorious' body began to jerk and convulse as the heroin made its way into his blood stream. Aria got up and started to wipe the entire room down.

"Come on, bruh. Help me load this money up." It had to be at the least, half a million in the safe.

Aria grabbed all the luxuries she had accumulated, then pulled the van around to the back. Her pumps clicked on the marble floor, but the sound of a bullet being loaded into a chamber made her freeze. Her eyes met with Yae's. The scars that graced Yae's face and neck from the vicious beating Harmony administered were visibly permanent. *Oh. My. Goodness!*

"Yeah, bitch. It's me. Now move!" She dragged Aria into the room by her hair, gun in her face. "Move and I'ma kill you."

"Fuck you!" Aria barked.

"Nah, fuck with me," Yae said, chuckling as she looked around the large room.

"Baby!" Aria cried. Yae held her at gunpoint, and the cold look in Yae's eyes let Harmony know that she had better do something quick. But if she missed, Aria's life would be in jeopardy.

"You might as well hand over your gun and the money."

"Bitch, please! I know revenge is what you want."

Yae laughed hysterically. "I want more than that," she said, looking over at Notorious. "I want the air you breathe to cease," she said, tightening her grip on Aria's hair.

"Well, hurry up and get it over with," she said.

Yae pointed her gun at Harmony's head and pulled the trigger.

"No!" Aria screamed, jerking on her arm as Harmony's body fell to the ground. "Harmony!" Aria cried, piercing Yae's ribs with her elbow. They fumbled over the gun. "I'ma kill you, bitch!" Aria screamed hysterically, then dug her manicured nails into Yae's eyes.

"Ahhh!" Yae punched Aria in the jaw, and she hit the floor hard. Yae scrambled toward the gun and pointed it at her. "Your turn," Yae said coldly. "I'll tell Satan you said hello." Yae screwed up her mouth, then jerked as the bullets entered her back. Blood trickled out of her mouth as she dared to take a breath. Peezy stood behind her as her body dropped to the floor. Aria lay there confused.

"Baby? Harmony, are you okay?" *Had he saved my life so that he can take pleasure in ending it? Does Biggs want me alive?* Aria thought, as she scooted over to Harmony.

"I'm okay. Let's just get this money into the car and get the fuck out of here," Harmony demanded, staggering to her feet.

"You good?" Peezy looked at her.

"Yeah, thanks for saving her."

"I gave you my word," he said, watching Aria's ass jiggle out of the room.

* * * * * *

Aria sat in the hospital room watching Harmony sleep. She was thankful the doctors had removed the bullet from her shoulder, and in a few days she would be able to go home. The knock at the door broke through Aria's reserve.

"Aria Fayette?"

"Yes," she said, standing at the sight of the two detectives.

"Hi. I am Detective Sanders, and this is my partner Gonzales. We are from the San Diego Police Department, and we have a few questions we'd like—"

"Concerning what?" she interrupted.

"I'd rather speak with you at the station."

"I'm not in any kind of trouble, am I?"

"No, ma'am."

"Give me a second. I will be right out," she said, bending to kiss Harmony's cheek and scribbled her a note. Aria knew what they were here for. They had been looking for her and Harmony for more than two years, and she was prepared for every question they could possibly ask.

\* \* \* \* \* \*

The room they sat her in was cold and stale. She wasn't moved. She had rehearsed this moment in her mind at least a thousand times. The first detective that came in was fat, pale, and short with an extremely thin, strawberry blonde comb over. She guessed he was the bad cop from the frown on his face.

"Can I have some coffee?" Aria asked, before he could take his seat. He sighed. *You made me wait, now it is your turn, fatty,* Aria thought, smiling on the inside.

"Thanks," she said, taking the hot Styrofoam cup from him. He nodded.

"Ms. Fayette, we have been looking for you and Miss–"

"Harmony. Her name's Harmony."

"Yes, it's been two years," the cop said. Aria nodded.

"We had to get away from there; Mr. Pratt was abusing us, and it was getting worse and—"

"He was abusing you and Ms. Reymos?"

"Yes," she answered. He jotted something on his notepad. "Are we in trouble for running away?"

"No, I just want to know what went on inside the Pratt's residence. Can you tell me a little about him and Mrs. Pratt's relationship?"

"Relationship? There was no relationship. He beat and abused her verbally, physically, and I'm sure emotionally. She told me that she was leaving him one night. I wonder if she found the courage to do it." The detective cleared his throat.

"Are you aware that Mrs. Pratt was murdered?" Aria gasped.

"What! By who? How!" she cried.

"We believe Mr. Pratt had something to do with her murder." Aria worked up a few more tears. "We found her poisoned body on the highway and—" Aria's sobs interrupted him.

"Sh-she was a great woman. I-I've missed her." He scribbled a few more things on his notepad and handed her a box of Kleenex. She wiped her tears and suppressed her smirk under the tissue.

"Excuse me for a minute." The detective left and returned with his partner and a statement form. She wrote about the abuse and mistreatment Mr. Pratt pressed upon them and why she and Harmony ran away.

"Here's my card, and Ms. Fayette, if you need me for anything, call me," he said, showing her out.

* * * * * *

Harmony opened her eyes. Peezy was standing by the window staring out at the traffic lights with a strained look. Harmony winced at the pain, but she sat up.

"What's the matter?" Harmony asked.

"Listen, you know I'ma have to answer to Biggs," Peezy replied.

"Well, tell him she got away." He sighed.

"I can't. He'll only look harder. It's personal, and when he comes I won't have any control over if she lives or not." Harmony dropped her head.

"We can take the money and run," she suggested.

"He'll find her," Peezy said. Harmony's jaw tightened.

"What are you getting at?"

"You guys can't run forever. I mean, do you really want to live your life like that? There is only one way to stop this manhunt."

"Spit it out, Peezy!" Harmony snapped impatiently.

"By killing him."

"How?" Harmony sighed. "Doesn't he have a thousand goons?"

"I know how to get at him. I can predict his every move. Remember, I am his right hand. Besides, I think it's time I took what's mine, what I helped build."

"And what's that?"

"The city of San Diego."

\* \* \* \* \* \*

After Harmony was discharged from the hospital, she was contacted to speak with the detectives who were working a murder case out of San Diego. Her heart fell into her chest; she was nervous as she sat in the interrogation room, sweating. The tall, lean white man came in with a serious look in his eyes. "Good afternoon, Ms. Reymos, I have a few questions about the Pratts, who you and Ms. Fayette stayed with before you two ran off." Harmony swallowed hard. "And why did you two run off?"

"Uh, um . . . we—we were being abused."

"By we, do you mean yourself and Ms. Fayette?"

"Yes. Both of us," Harmony said, remembering the note Aria left her. "He abused us both." The detective shook his head and scribbled on his pad.

"How would you describe the Pratt's relationship?" he asked. Harmony looked at the man.

"He was the master and she was his slave." The detective scribbled again. "Am I in trouble?"

"No. Mrs. Pratt was murdered, and we are under the impression that her husband had something to do with it." Harmony sat up, stunned. It all made sense to her. Aria poisoned Mrs. Pratt and framed Mr. Pratt for her murder, sending him to prison for the rest of his life.

That chapter of her life was now closed. She had unfinished business to tend to. Biggs had to go. She refused to run for the rest of her life, and thanks to her brother, she didn't have to run ever again.

# CHAPTER 14

Peezy knew that this takeover was possible. Biggs and Smoke had taken over Rambo's empire single-handedly. Once they infiltrated the few loyal soldiers he had, everything else around them fell. When Peezy was sent off to a group home, he wasted no time joining Biggs' crew. He carried out hits, took over territory, and spotted most snakes before they got close enough to bite. Biggs took him in, seeing him as an asset, almost instantly promoting him over everyone, even his son Marcus. Peezy wasn't oblivious to the envy Marcus carried in his heart for him. Mainly because Biggs took him in, treated him like a son, and often told Marcus he needed to take notes. Nobody would ever suspect Peezy. He would catch them with their pants down. Everything he'd heard about Biggs when he was a boy was true. Partially. Biggs gave the orders and lives were taken, but Biggs himself had not shot a gun in almost an entire decade. He was slipping. Peezy had his own idea of how things should be run, and the more he thought about it, the more power hungry he became.

\* \* \* \* \* \*

Aria sat across the hotel suite staring at Peezy. He had yet to make an attempt on her life. *Had he even told Harmony?* She could kill him right now and tell her the real reason he was here. To kill her. Aria stood, and in seconds was across the room. She held her .38 to his neck. "I know who you are, and I know why you're here, but I'm telling you now. I am not going down without a fight, and the only reason I haven't put you to sleep is because Harmony loves you."

"Whoa, Aria! Calm down. Harmony knows why I'm here," Peezy said, his hands in the air. Aria mashed the silencer into his neck.

"Liar!" she said through clenched teeth.

"You know Biggs. And he would not have sent me out here just to come back empty-handed. I wouldn't have let you live this long if I changed my mind about killing you," Peezy said calmly.

"Fuck you! You came here to do a job. Me and you both know what will happen if you fail to produce me or my death certificate."

"Listen," Peezy said impatiently. "Harmony and I have a plan. We—"

"Aria, what are you doing?" Harmony yelled, coming out of the bathroom.

"Remember the men that I was running from? Well, here is the head honcho of the manhunt. How much are you getting paid, huh? What's the price on my head!" Aria yelled.

"Baby, calm down and drop the gun. I know everything." Harmony walked toward Aria. Tears fell from her eyes as she gripped the gun tighter.

"They want me dead, but they don't even know why I did it. Emily hurt me to my core. She played with me like a puppet, killing me softly slowly every day. I told her. I tried to warn her to stop, that I was at my breaking point, but she wouldn't listen," Aria cried. "So yeah, I killed her, slowly, like she did me day in and out with the late nights and constant phone calls. And no, I'm not sorry I did it!" Harmony wrapped her arm around Aria and her hand over the gun. Aria let it go and fell into her arms. "I'm sorry I didn't tell you."

"I don't care about your past. You are the only one that can make me leave you. Nothing, or no one else has that power but you." Peezy eyed Aria, his jaw tight. Then he grabbed his coat and headed for the door.

"Peezy!" He held up his hand.

"Let me cool off for a minute!" he barked.

* * * * * *

Harmony followed Peezy's van with Aria tailing her. They were headed back to San Diego, a place she thought she'd never return to willingly. She was not sure what to expect, but knew that she wasn't leaving until she had Aria's freedom. She and Peezy were back together; it felt good to have the two people she loved the most next to her. She thought about Betta and Woo, whom she had grown close to, but with Betta being locked up and Woo hustling non-stop, they rarely had time for each other. Harmony sent Betta some more cash and a few cards, letting him know there were no hard feelings. But still, she wondered if things between them would ever be the same. *Damn, Betta,* she thought. Her mind shifted back to what she had set out to accomplish as they merged onto I-805: Hunt or be hunted.

* * * * * *

Peezy called Biggs and let him know he was in town. He was not at all surprised that Biggs knew nothing of the phone call Marcus placed with strict orders. *Figures,* Peezy thought as he sat across from Biggs.

"How is Samore and Junior doing?"

"They're doing well," Peezy said, anxious to skip the pleasantries and get to the business at hand. "I almost had her, but she was surrounded by security. It was hard to get her by herself, so I'm going to give it another shot. I have something in mind. You said to do it quietly, but when Marcus called, I thought you needed my presence immediately."

"No, and I apologize about that. I will be sure to remind Marcus of his place. To be quite honest, I am tired of wasting money, favors, and manpower on this thing, but Natalie won't let this thing rest, and I promised her I'd take care of it."

"I understand. You have my word that everything will be handled promptly."

"Good," Biggs said, standing to leave. "Let me know when you're going to head out." Peezy nodded, then signaled for the waiter. Everything was going as planned; so far so good.

\* \* \* \* \* \*

Harmony turned up the television and watched the team of DEA agents storm into each and every trap house that Biggs had around the city. Everyone, even Peezy, was brought out in handcuffs. It was all for show. Peezy had tipped the agents off, siccing them on Biggs and his team, only to turn everybody against one another. Peezy rounded the corner into the living room; he was deep in conversation.

"But, Biggs, I want answers. I feel like I was set up or something. There's a snitch lurking amongst us, and I refuse to put up with this. I wasn't gone but a few weeks, and all of this chaos is in the air. They raided every single spot we had! That's bullshit! Call a meeting or something, and everyone needs to be there. I want to get to the bottom of this and quickly. Yes, I understand . . . okay. See you then," Peezy said, hanging up the phone.

Harmony looked over at him. He smiled. "You were right. It worked! Biggs is calling a meeting. Everybody will be in attendance."

"That's what's up."

"Exactly! And I know the perfect chick to call. Come on. I have someone I want you to meet."

\* \* \* \* \* \*

Harmony watched intently as Byou wired the basement with explosives. She was taken aback by the elegance of the huge flat that sat in the middle of poverty on Ocean View Boulevard. The marble floors and red oak wood furniture all blended nicely. Harmony was still unsure of how easy it was going to be to back Biggs into a corner, but everything was going as planned so far.

"Hold this," Byou said as beads of sweat formed on the bridge of her button nose. Harmony looked at her like she was crazy, but complied. The way that her locks were twisted up on her head were neat, stylish, and beautiful. Her toffee-colored skin was smooth, and every word that rolled off her tongue made Harmony smile. She had a serious, sexy swag. The New Orleans native intrigued her. "All set," Byou said, tucking the wires back into the socket. "Don't be nervous. This detonator is the only thing that can activate this beast," she said, smiling. Byou was normally standoffish toward new faces, but because Peezy spoke so highly of her, she eased up and erased her initial attraction to the beautiful woman, especially when her girlfriend Aria pulled up.

"I'm Aria, Harmony's woman," Aria said, introducing herself. Byou shook her hand and led them both over to the van. "So now what?" Aria asked.

"We wait for the call, and then BOOM!"

\* \* \* \* \* \*

Peezy stood beside Marcus. Nothing but hatred filled the man's eyes. *Hate me, nigga. So killing you will be so much easier,* Peezy thought. Marcus turned to him.

"So, you went and ran your mouth to my father like the bitch-nigga you are, huh?" Peezy chuckled. His insults didn't faze him. They both knew who the bitch was, and it wasn't him. "What's so funny, nigga?"

"You're funny." Marcus' face flushed blood red. He pulled his glock and pointed it at Peezy, who grabbed his wrist, bent it back and in seconds, had him on the ground.

"Let's wait until the grand finale, fuck boy. I'm going to kill you, but it will be on my own terms," Peezy whispered in his ear. Marcus' eyes grew big.

"Marcus, that's enough!" Biggs' deep baritone echoed through the basement hall. He was getting old, and his patience was running thin with Marcus' attitude and entitlement issues. Peezy snatched Marcus off the ground and stood in his face.

"We are on the same team, nigga. I don't know where all this animosity is coming from, but we have much more pressing matters to tend to besides your bruised ego," Peezy said coldly, shoving his glock into his chest. Peezy straightened his Burberry blazer and brushed past him. Biggs' eyes were cold, and he shook his head at Marcus in disapproval, then fell in step beside Peezy.

* * * * * *

Biggs had already decided that Peezy would take the reins. The cancer was taking over his body at an alarming rate, and not even chemo would be able to fight it off. He had maybe another year at the most, and because Peezy handled every situation like a real boss should, he was left with no choice but to leave him the keys to the city. Yes, he had built this very lucrative organization, but Marcus was selfish, spoiled, and arrogant and had a sense of entitlement toward everything. Whereas Peezy had to hustle for every grain and morsel he had. Peezy would cherish the organization, maybe even take it to new heights. Marcus would more than likely ruin everything that he'd worked so hard to build. So when the time was right, he'd give Peezy all his connects and every key he needed to keep this organization going. He had earned them.

* * * * * *

Peezy's eyes searched every single persons' eyes that were present in the basement. Biggs called the meeting to order, and then gave Peezy the floor. He had everyone's undivided attention. The power that surged through him felt close to heaven. He cleared his throat before he gave his speech.

"We have a serious problem. Somebody inside this organization is giving information to the police," Peezy said slowly and carefully as he paced back and forth. Everyone sat quietly around the oak table. Some stood in the back of the room. Everyone's eyes were on him. "But before we start pointing fingers, I'd like to let you all talk amongst yourselves and see what you all come up with, or any other information you might have." Biggs nodded in agreement. Peezy walked over to him and whispered in his ear.

"Can I speak with you and Marcus outside?" Biggs nodded again and stood to his feet.

"Marcus, can I speak with you outside in private." Marcus' eyes shot to his father's. Impatience filled Biggs eyes. Marcus stood and buttoned his Armani coat and followed them out the door. Peezy smiled, closed the door, and then slid the cinder block in place. In less than a minute, accusations began to fly across the room.

"We shall have our rat in no time," Peezy said, with a sly grin on his face as he led them down the hall to safety.

"Peezy, that was genius!" Biggs complimented.

"Thanks, I instructed Boo to call me when they have reached a verdict." Marcus cut his eyes at him. "I would like to invite you two to lunch, on me, so that we as leaders can figure out how to situate this problem and find a common solution." Biggs smiled.

"Great, because I'm starved." He loved Peezy's take-charge attitude, and soon would have to break the news to Marcus about his plans for Peezy and the organization. He knew that it would be a hard pill for Marcus to swallow, but it wasn't about him, not this time. Biggs thought he had nurtured and raised Marcus for the time when he would have to take his place, but real bosses aren't made— they are born.

"How 'bout we just kill them?" Marcus said, sarcastically. Peezy sighed.

"First, we have to get the information they gave the police so that we can be and stay a step ahead of them. Killing whoever it is won't give us nothing," Peezy countered.

"You remind me of myself years ago," Biggs said to Peezy.

Marcus rolled his eyes. He longed to make his father proud, but with Peezy around, it would never happen. That was something they all knew.

* * * * * *

"Damn, what is taking them so long?" Aria questioned.

"Patience, grasshopper. Everything is all about timing," Byou said, puffing on her black and mild. Harmony smiled. She was so thugged out, but sexy with it; she liked her style. Byou was trained in explosives and survived by blowing shit up for a living.

"There they are," Harmony said.

Biggs, Peezy, and Marcus came out from the back of the house. Peezy held the door for Biggs as he climbed inside the tinted Escalade. Marcus climbed in the backseat, contempt written on his face.

"Here," Byou said, handing Harmony the detonator. "Want to do the honors?"

"Hell yeah!" Harmony said, excitedly. Peezy's name popped up on the screen. "Hello?"

"I'm headed out to lunch, Samore," Peezy said to Harmony. "I'm probably going to be late, so go ahead and put Jr. down for his nap."

"Okay. I love you," Harmony replied, pretending to be Samore.

"Okay. I love you too. Bye."

Byou started the van up and drove to the end of the block.

"Go ahead," she said, looking over at Harmony. Harmony pushed down on the walkie-talkie button, and the ground rumbled behind them as flames and smoke rose from the structure. Byou smiled.

"Music to my ears," she said.

# CHAPTER 15

Aria stared at Samore like she was crazy. This 'ho has two seconds to get her hands from around my bitch, or I'm going to straight lose it on her ass, Aria thought.

"Peezy's told me so much about you! You're so beautiful. You do look just like him. Peezy, you didn't tell me she was a lesbian."

"She is, but just comfortable in men's clothes and likes bad bitches," Peezy said, smiling at Aria. Every day she was becoming more and more appealing to him.

Harmony smiled, completely missing the real meaning of his statement. "This is my girlfriend Aria."

"Hey, nice to meet you," Samore said, dryly. Instantly Samore was intimidated by Aria's beauty, like most women, and Aria sensed it. She made a mental note to make her feel as inferior as possible. Insecure ass bitch. Aria smirked to herself. When she looked up, she caught Peezy staring at her with lust and want lurking in his eyes; her body got hot. He was a spitting image of Harmony, only his eyes were hazel brown, and he had a curly afro the color of dark roasted coffee beans. Aria blushed and turned away. She didn't identify with the strange feeling that shot through her. *Why are you blushing?* she thought.

"Umm, where's the bathroom?" she asked, anxious to escape. Peezy led her down the hall.

"It's right here," he said, pushing the door ajar, looking down on her. She refused to make eye contact. The smell of lavender and the golden shower curtains calmed her. Aria washed her hands, then splashed water on her face.

"What is wrong with you? You need to get a grip. We don't like men!" She scolded herself. After a few minutes, she shook off her unwanted attraction to Harmony's brother and returned to the living room in her old state of mind.

"Aria, meet my nephew Junior. Isn't he gorgeous?" Harmony asked, excitedly. Aria could not help but smile. "Say hi, Junior," Harmony said, smiling. Instantly, Aria fell in love with the toddler that sat on Harmony's lap rubbing his eyes. His head was full of black curls, and his eyes mirrored Harmony's, minus the pain.

"Hi," he said shyly. Aria stooped to her knees.

"Hello, handsome." He smiled again, showing his baby teeth.

Peezy spoke loudly into the phone while coming back into the living room. "Money, let's ride." Samore picked up Junior and kissed Peezy on the lips before he left out. A jolt of jealousy shot through Aria as Harmony kissed her good-bye. *What is my problem?* she questioned.

Samore cleared her throat. "Let me get you some fresh linen. I'm sure you're tired."

"Actually, I have some business to tend to. You can just put them in the room. I'll arrange it later. Thanks," Aria said sarcastically, grabbing her Birkin bag and heading for the door.

"Business?" Samore suppressed her attitude. "That's fine, I'll see you later." Aria didn't reply, which was only the beginning of her antics.

"Bitch!" Samore said to herself.

\* \* \* \* \* \*

Harmony found it easy to act as if she was oblivious to everything that was going on as Peezy introduced her to Biggs and Marcus. They would not stop staring at her. She kept one hand close to her pistol just in case. The tension was thick. Biggs didn't have the slightest clue as to who was trying to destroy him and tear apart his organization. He had made so many enemies throughout the years that he wasn't sure who wanted to see him fall, or if it was Karma that had slowly caught up with him. The DEA would not catch him with a dime of dirty money, a crumb of any kind of illegal substance, or any unregistered firearms. That is what he had soldiers for, so he was entrusting it all to his most loyal and trusted soldier and instructed him to take it to his vacation house in La Jolla where it would be safe. The police had raided every trap, and Harmony had blown up his safe house with his army in it. They had backed Biggs into a corner so that his every move could be predicted, like this one.

"What's up with that nigga Marcus?" Harmony asked as she eyed Peezy loading his trunk with the last of their weapons.

"Jealousy and pride is eating him alive," Peezy said, laughing. "He wants to be where I'm at so bad, but will never amount. Even his father knows that. I'll be right back." Peezy went to shake Biggs' hand. They parted ways, and then Peezy climbed into the van. They drove to La Jolla in silence. Their minds filled with plots against the enemy.

* * * * * *

Aria was skeptical of Peezy's plan, but something made her trust him. Whatever it was she couldn't definite it and didn't like it very much. She sat loosely tied in the trunk of the van. Harmony en route behind her.

"We are almost there, ma. Just remember what I told you." Peezy put his game face on. It was time to end this. In his arrogant mind he had already won. Biggs had introduced Peezy to all his connects and had secured a position for him at the table of wealth and prestige in and out of the country. Peezy was well on his way to being a real boss thanks to the lack of confidence Biggs had in his own son, and Marcus' inability to take the reins.

Peezy pulled up into the circular driveway of the mini mansion Biggs had been hiding out in. "Game time," Peezy said to himself, climbing out of the van and dragging Aria from the trunk and through the living room.

"Watch it, nigga," she murmured.

"I found her! Finally." Biggs clapped his hands, but Marcus' eyes grew dark with suspicion. Upon Peezy's arrival, nothing but havoc had been rearing its ugly head, and his father was blind to it all. There was no other explanation for it all.

"You see, Marcus. This is the reason Peezy is in the position he is in—because he's earned it," Biggs said forcefully.

"Whoa, boss man. What did I walk into?" Peezy said, holding his hands up.

"Marcus here, seems to think that he should take the reins. See, I'm getting too old for this shit. I probably have another year left in me at the most," Biggs said, thinking optimistically.

*Not even that*, Peezy thought.

"And if I thought that you could handle this on your own without getting yourself killed, then I would've been more than honored to hand the keys to this city and all I've built to you, but you and I both know you don't have what it takes to run this organization," Biggs said, mockingly.

"But you can't just—" Marcus started to say, but Biggs held up his finger and dialed on his phone.

"Natalie, baby. Daddy has a surprise for you."

Aria suppressed her smirk as she stood there with her hands behind her back. Biggs hung up the phone, then looked at Peezy. "Here is the funniest part. Marcus is trying to convince me that you're behind all of my sudden misfortune. That *you're* the one behind the scenes trying to take down my organization, the one you helped me build." Peezy and Biggs both began laughing hysterically.

Marcus stood there embarrassed; he couldn't ignore what his gut was telling him. It wasn't his ego or pride that most times consumed him. It was what his mother spoke of before she was set up and killed. Intuition. Aria stood looking on as Marcus held his composure while they humiliated him.

"What's so funny, Daddy?" Natalie asked, coming into the room.

"Nothing, honey." Aria rolled her eyes at Natalie. She still wanted some sort of position in her Daddy's organization, but sadly she didn't make the cut either. Natalie's looked over at Aria.

"You can run but you can't hide," Natalie said, contemptuously.

"See, that is where you're wrong. I can run, but I quickly grew tired of hiding." In one swift movement, Aria was out of her restraints sending a bullet flying through Natalie's brain.

"Nat!" Biggs cried, dropping almost instantly with Natalie's body. Marcus drew his gun. Peezy drew two, one on Marcus and the other on Biggs. Aria trained her gun on Biggs.

"Good shot, ma." Peezy smiled. Aria smirked and winked at Peezy. Biggs stood to his feet, a look of horror on his face.

"P–"

"Don't act shocked, old man. You knew this was coming. Even Marcus' dumb ass saw the shit coming," Peezy said coldly. Marcus let off a shot. Peezy chuckled. "You're an idiot just like your father said you were. A real killer knows the weight of a gun when it's loaded and not full of blanks." Peezy scoffed. "Now say good-bye to your beloved father." Peezy sent a bullet soaring across the room and into Biggs' head.

"Noooo!" Marcus screamed, charging at Peezy, knocking him to the floor. His guns flew in two separate directions, and they began wrestling. Aria held her gun on them as they beat each other mercilessly, both fueled by the need to own the keys to the city.

Marcus couldn't hold Peezy; he was too strong for him. Marcus kicked him back, crawling toward the gun. Peezy grabbed Marcus' leg, pulling him away from his only defense, then snapped his ankle.

"Ahhh!" Marcus screamed, holding his ankle, eyes full of despair. Peezy smiled, enjoying the torture he had caused.

"Sounds like you're the bitch to me."

"Fuck you!" Marcus cried.

"Nah, fuck you!" Peezy said, grabbing his other leg. Marcus kicked Peezy in the chest, sending him flying to the floor, then he scrambled for the gun and let off a round. Junior's face flashed in his mind followed by Harmony's and Samore's. *Oh shit! Get up!* Peezy screamed inside his head. He sat up and looked at Marcus attempting to take a breath as his lungs filled with his own blood. His eyes rolled up, then dropped with his body. Aria stood over Peezy and held out her hand.

"Now we're even," she said, winking flirtatiously.

\* \* \* \* \* \*

Aria chopped Biggs' hand off at the wrist, then bagged it up. She didn't hesitate when Peezy asked her to do it. Killing had become second nature to her. She did it without remorse or any thought, aside from what she would gain for doing such a deed. She helped Harmony dump the three bodies into the acid and watched them disappear. *I've got to get me some of this,* Aria thought as it ate away at Natalie's flesh.

"Come on," Peezy said. "And bring that hand with you." They followed Peezy through the house, and at that moment Harmony knew that she had not been living. Peezy stopped in the middle of the long hallway, placed Biggs' hand on a picture of a beautiful woman whose hair was down the back of her fur coat, with legs as long as a flamingo's sticking from under her mini skirt.

"Damn, who is that?" Harmony asked.

"His wife Emma. She was a bad bitch. One of the baddest I've ever seen in the game. She was a stone cold killer."

"What happen to her?" Aria asked.

"Karma," he said shortly. A green light shined on the right side of the frame, and a wall opened up, giving them passage to a small room stocked with guns, money, drugs and jewels. Harmony's mouth dropped open. Aria's eyes began to water, and Peezy smiled. They now had access to every penny Biggs had stashed away. He never believed in bank accounts, and because of it they were now millionaires. "Let's check the rest of the house, load up some of this money, and then get out of here."

"I'll take the second floor," Aria screamed, and took off running down the hall.

Peezy and Harmony laughed. "I'm glad I found you, sis. It's only up from here. I promise everything we lacked, we will have in abundance." Harmony hugged Peezy. Then watched as he reset the code authorizing Harmony's and his prints only.

\* \* \* \* \* \*

Aria watched Peezy double check the two-car garage and smirked at the muscle shirt that wrapped around his firm build, exposing every crease and bulge his sculpted body had. The sudden attraction puzzled her, but she couldn't deny it or hide from it. *Mmmph! Damn!*

"You did good, ma," Peezy said, after a few minutes without turning around.

Startled, she stumbled over her words. "Th-thank you. Y-you should've taken up acting because you could have won an Oscar for that act." Peezy turned around and smiled, closing the space between them. He was drawn to her just as she was to him. Her body instantly grew hot and butterflies swarmed through her. Peezy towered over her.

"I'm not going to act like there's nothing going on here, but I love my baby sister, and I've missed out on too much to ruin it over the urge I'm having to fold your fine ass up and give you what your eyes are begging me for." Aria gasped inwardly.

"And what exactly are my eyes begging for?" she responded, stepping closer. Peezy smirked, trying to hide the want that surged through him. Aria spun on her heels and headed down the hall.

"What am I doing?" she whispered the question to herself.

# CHAPTER 16

Harmony forced the thought out of any and everyone's head that she and Peezy's crew were soft, or that they were in any way giving up the keys to the city. Whether it be with a caliber or her bare hands, she wasn't playing, making it known in the streets of San Diego that she nor her money was to be toyed with. The only unsettling issue Harmony had was her feeling as if she should be standing next to Peezy and not under him, something he was not aware of. But they'd have to cross that road eventually.

Now seated comfortably in the lawn chair, Harmony watched Junior play in the pool that Peezy had built in the backyard of his beautiful home. She was thankful to be spending time with the ones she loved. She and Peezy had been so busy establishing things in the streets that they had very little time to do much else.

By the time she got in she was dog tired, only to have to get up in a few hours and hit the streets. Her phone chimed. She smiled at the email from JPay. Finally she had gotten Betta to write and keep an open line of communication. Harmony was hoping that Betta spoke to Woo about getting down with her so she could set him up in a few of their spots to get the money flowing. Woo's whip game was on point, and she decided she'd keep her hands as clean as possible as far as the drugs went, especially after seeing how easily Betta had gotten banged up. Hands down, Woo would be a good asset to the team, and he was trustworthy, even though Peezy felt indifferent about it. Harmony didn't care because he had her surrounded by one too many people she didn't care for or know well.

She began reading the email:

*Money,*

*What's good, sis? Man, I miss you, the streets, and my daughter the most. Thanks for sending that bread my way and to my baby mom's triflin' ass. It means so much more than you could ever know. A nigga wouldn't know what to do without you and Woo looking out. I told him what you had in mind so he should be calling you soon. I'm working on an appeal. Ten years flat just won't cut it. My daughter will be sixteen, man. Anyway, stay safe and remember most if not all people have a motive whether it be good or bad.*

*I love you sis. Get at me.*

*B*

Harmony slid her phone in her pocket and leaned back in the chair. The streets gave them all the respect in the world. Biggs' close friends and distant relatives searched for him and his family relentlessly. Peezy made sure to be supportive in every way, careful not to draw any suspicion. Harmony and Peezy had begun to bond slowly, becoming inseparable as she and Aria were drawing further apart, seeming to always be at odds. She watched her play with Junior, her laugh sounding angelic and bringing a smile to her face. She couldn't understand what had happened to them.

Samore brought out some ice tea and sandwiches. Harmony forced her eyes away from her butterscotch skin tone. She was beautiful and could see why Peezy married her. "Money, you thirsty?" Samore asked.

"Yeah thanks," Harmony said, taking the spiked tea from her. She followed Samore's eyes as they landed on Aria, who was in the pool with Junior and Peezy playing and splashing water everywhere. Aria and Samore had some unspoken animosity, and the fact that Peezy and Junior took to her didn't help the situation.

\* \* \* \* \* \*

Aria couldn't help her growing desire for Peezy. She could not remember the last time she was even attracted to a man, so this sudden attraction to him had her feeling crazy. She tried to calm her nerves, but to no avail. It was like she had a jones in her bones for him that wouldn't go away. Whenever they were in the same room with each other for too long, Aria found any excuse to escape his lustful stare. Harmony had done nothing but run the streets since they'd been back in San Diego, leaving her lonely, making her eyes wander and her desire shift toward Peezy, who still made time for his family.

Aria rubbed Oil of Olay all over her body, then dressed in a soft pink Emilio Pucci two-piece jumper with white sandals to match. She bumped her bangs and straightened her unruly hair. She had a few errands to run and some light shopping to do. She refused to sit around the house and wait for Harmony to return, only to have to run back out into the streets or fall asleep on her.

"Where are you headed, ma?" Peezy demanded in a low tone, coming into the guest room she shared with Harmony.

"I'm going to Horton Plaza. Why?"

"Because I want to know. I might want to pull up," he said seriously, then winked at her. "Have fun." Aria blushed through her chocolate skin.

*Mmm.* He had a way about himself that was beginning to drive her crazy. *Why do I want him so bad?* She grabbed her phone:

2:12 p.m.
**Aria:** *Headed out in a little while to run a few errands.*

2:17 p.m.
**Harmony:** *Okay. Love you*

"Yeah right, nigga. You love them streets," Aria said, throwing her phone in her Birkin bag and heading out.

* * * * * *

Samore rolled her eyes as Aria came down the hall. "Bye-bye, Junior," Aria said, bending to kiss his forehead.

"Bye-bye, Auntie," he chimed happily. Aria walked past Samore, not even acknowledging her.

"Didn't I tell you to stop kissing my baby on his face?" Samore said. Aria turned around.

"Peezy doesn't seem to mind, and neither does Junior," Aria snapped quickly, cutting through Samore's confidence, then slamming the door behind her.

Junior made Aria's day every time she laid eyes on him, making her long to have a child of her own. Something Harmony wanted no part of, at least not right now. Aria grimaced as she played their conversation over in her head.

"No, we are not ready for that yet. That is a major step."

"You mean you're not ready!" Aria argued.

"No, I'm not. I want to be settled and financially secure."

"Harmony, we are settled and financially secure. How much more money do you need?"

"It's not just about the money . . . it's—look, I said no. End of discussion," Harmony said, rolling over and going to bed.

Aria was beginning to resent Harmony. She had in so many words paved a way for her in these streets in this lifestyle, and now her and all of her needs, aside from buying her whatever she wanted, had taken the back burner to Harmony's street dreams. All she wanted to do was hustle, and all Aria wanted was to settle down and start a family, maybe open a business or two. She almost regretted taking her with her. She would probably be knocked up by now anyway if she would have left her with Mr. Pratt's pedophile ass. Aria wanted to say this, but thought better of it. Her aim was never to hurt Harmony, but she could see that she had lost total control over her. Aria's old tricks no longer pushed her buttons, not even her sex game could keep Harmony in line anymore. They argued and fought about petty issues, quality time, and her disregard for Aria's feelings. Their relationship was definitely on the rocks. Aria was clueless, and her stubbornness wouldn't allow her to submit to the monster she had unchained and crowned as her king.

\* \* \* \* \* \*

Peezy pulled a crisp white T-shirt over his curls and grabbed his keys off the dresser. He had to make a few runs, meet with a few people, and be sure that his clients got all that they ordered on time. Harmony was doing an exceptional job, but once Biggs came up missing, the streets had begun to stock up just in case an unexpected drought hit. Peezy was sitting on a million-dollar enterprise, and because his team was so small, everyone would eat and get full. He had taken note of his sister's take-charge attitude. He was excited about their future.

"P, where are you going?" Samore asked, irritated that he was leaving out in a rush.

"I have to go handle some business. Why? What's up?"

"I want you to talk to your sister's bitch about putting her lips on my baby!"

"You mean *our* baby. Samore, what is your beef with her anyway? The woman has done nothing to you."

"I don't have no beef with that bitch. I just don't want her dike ass putting her lips on our son."

"I'll holla at her." Peezy chuckled.

"Good. One more thing, P. This bitch goes shopping damn near every day. When are they planning on moving?"

"I told my sister that she and Aria are welcome here for as long as they want. This is my house, bitch. Please don't forget that," Peezy said sharply.

"Don't worry, Samore. We will be outta your hair like yesterday," Harmony said, coming into the den. Peezy cut his eyes at Samore who dropped her head. "I just came to drop off this bread. I picked it up while I was out. I'm gone though."

"All right, sis. Holla at me."

"Most definitely," Harmony said, slamming the door.

"Junior, go in your room and play, poppa," Peezy said.

Once Junior was out of sight, Peezy hauled back and slapped Samore into the couch. "I *told* you about that insecure shit. You know I just found my little sister, and I will be damned if your insecurities come between us," he barked, shaking his hand from the impact, then stormed out.

Peezy drove the speed limit, thinking of the business he had at hand. He was meeting Byou downtown at the pawnshop to collect a few grand she had picked up from a mutual friend of theirs. He wanted a few keys, and Peezy was willing to come off of them at a special price under one condition. That he spread the word out of town that he was now the go-to guy. Before he could leave, he felt the urge to buy Aria something nice. Thoughts of her led him a few blocks down the street to Horton plaza.

"What are you doing here, Peezy?" she asked, looking completely surprised. He scolded himself as he tried to rationalize his actions. He had spotted Aria's BMW and made sure he parked within walking distance. He figured she would more than likely be in BeBe or Nordstrom. He checked BeBe, then headed up the escalator to Nordstrom. His thoughts were racing, telling him to leave but he couldn't. He wandered through the aisle in search of her chocolate-coated skin.

"Peezy?" Aria said, stopping in the aisle.

"What's good, ma?" he said, smiling.

"Nothing." Aria had butterflies, as a soft pulsation began to beat throughout her entire body. She slowed her breathing, trying to control the effect his presence had on her. Peezy stuck his hand in his pocket.

"I got you something," he said, stepping close to her and handing her a red velvet box. She smiled.

"What's this?"

"I was out, and I thought about you." Aria opened it.

"It's beautiful, but I don't have a belly ring?"

"Not yet." Aria smiled at the three karat diamond and shook her head.

"Peezy, what are—"

"No questions—it makes it easier." Aria dropped her head.

"Do you always have to say the right words?" she muttered.

"Come on. I got you," he said, nodding to her handful of high-end fashions. The silence between them on the way out was filled with questions they refused to ask, and the chemistry was unbearable. Peezy loaded her bags in the trunk.

"Thank you for everything." He pulled her door open, leaving no space for her to squeeze through. Aria's heart beat wildly. She had never been so close to him before. Peezy pulled her toward him and slid his tongue in her mouth, raking his hands through her hair. Aria's knees became weak, heat filling her body from the top of her head to the soles of her feet. They kissed so passionately it melted their defense, and there was no turning back. The line had been crossed, erased, leaving them no choice but to feed their desire for each other.

* * * * * *

Harmony rented a room at the Ritz Carlton for a few nights against Peezy's request. "Never will I stay another night where me and my woman are clearly not wanted," she snapped at Peezy, who was desperately trying to change her mind. She loaded her and Aria's bags into her trunk.

"This is my house, Money. That bitch don't run a thing."

"Peezy, I'm out," Harmony said.

Aria pulled up and hopped out, avoiding Peezy's stare. She had stopped to get her navel pierced. "What is going on?" she asked.

"Just go grab the rest of your things, baby," Harmony stated.

Aria stormed up the steps and into the house. Samore was sitting on the couch watching television. Her eyes bucked at the cold look Aria shot her on the way in.

"Don't be muggin' me, 'ho. This ain't no shelter," Samore barked at Aria's back. She turned and doubled back and in seconds Aria was at Samore.

*WHOP!*

"Bitch, I don't know who you thought I was."

*WHOP!*

Samore jumped into action, her arm flailing like a windmill.

"But we don't need."

*WHOP! WHOP!*

"Your fuckin' charity!"

*WHOP!*

"But I do know."

*WHOP!*

"You have every reason—"

*WHOP!*

"To be the insecure bitch that you are!" Samore jumped up, dodging Aria's blows and retaliating with a hard punch to her face.

"Fuck you, bitch! You don't know shit about me." Aria grabbed Samore's hair and slung her into the entertainment center.

*WHOP!*

"I know enough, bitch!"

*WHOP! WHOP!*

Aria mounted Samore, sending deadly blows to her face. Samore pushed up, using all her strength and wrestled Aria to the ground.

*WHOP!*

Aria knocked Samore back down, hitting her in her eye, then wrapped her arms around Samore's neck. "I'm going to taint what you hold dear to you, bitch, starting with your man just because I can."

"I'd like to see you try, 'ho."

"I'll save you a seat." Samore bucked back, busting Aria's lip, then charged at her.

"Samore!" Peezy yelled loudly, coming into the house.

"Man, get your crazy ass bitch off of me!" Aria screamed, holding Samore's arms.

"Let her go!" Peezy said, pulling them apart.

"Try it again, bitch!" Aria said, sucker punching her. Samore charged at her. Aria sent two hard punches over Peezy's back.

*WHOP! WHOP!*

"Aria, let's go!" Harmony yelled. Peezy shoved Samore into the kitchen.

"P, she—" He raised his hand, silencing her. "Quiet and sit!" he ordered, pulling out a chair. "And don't you *dare* move!" Peezy snapped.

* * * * * *

Harmony grabbed a few more of their bags and piled them into their trunks. Peezy came outside with an ice pack. "You all right?" he asked, handing it to Aria.

"Yeah, I'm good," she said, putting the ice pack on her jaw.

"I want to see you again," he said seriously.

"Victoria's Secret is having a sale at Plaza Bonita Friday. I'll be there around one."

"I'll see you then."

Aria nodded and climbed into her coupe. Peezy walked over to Harmony and helped her put the last of their bags in the trunk. He felt a tinge of guilt, but he shrugged it off. Aria had his attention, and it became clear to him that he lacked self-control when it came to the beautiful woman. She was the love of Harmony's life, making her forbidden fruit. But just like Eve, he was drawn and wanted more than a bite.

# CHAPTER 17

It took Aria two weeks to find her dream house. She chose a three-story house in Fashion Valley. Harmony gave her free reign to do as she pleased inside and out. She filled each story with the hottest decor sparing no cost. She had customized an office for Harmony with a crazy view out of ceiling-to-floor widows, giving it a cozy vintage feel. A huge picture of them a year ago in Hollywood hung on the wall, and her library was filled with a floor-to-ceiling book shelves stacked neatly with her favorite authors and self-help books. Aria did a three sixty in the middle of the office, stopping and smiling at the picture. Guilt struck her hard; she thought about the time she had been spending with Peezy, the secret lunches, kisses of betrayal, and all the fun she had been having with him. She knew there was no rationalizing her betrayal, even though she tried to. This office and the other extra miles she had been going to make up for her deceit were only evident to her and Peezy.

Aria checked her Cartier watch that was filled with LeVian diamonds, another gift from Peezy. *Harmony will be here any minute*, she thought. Aria went to freshen up, her Roberto Cavalli ensemble fell loosely around her curves, bouncing at her sides as her pumps drummed against their arabescato marble floor. She fixed Harmony and herself a glass of Twenty Grand and sipped hers slowly. She could hear Harmony's music in the driveway. She braced herself as she heard Junior's little footsteps, followed by his shouts of joy.

"Auntie! Auntie!" She scooped him up in her arms and hugged him tight.

"Hey, little guy. I've missed you so much. How are you?"

"I'm fine," he said happily.

Samore hated for Junior to come over, but Peezy made it clear that he would be in Harmony's life, and with her came Aria, end of discussion. Aria set up a room for him for overnight visits, or when Harmony and Peezy were going out of town. The Ben 10 decor had everything a five year old could ask for.

Harmony appeared in the kitchen smiling with Peezy at her side. He glanced at the beautiful dress Aria wore and scrunched up his face. Jealousy surged through him at the sight of her looking good for his sister. Aria sat Junior down, then stood and smoothed out her dress.

"Hey, Peezy. I didn't know you were coming."

"My little man begged and begged. I couldn't tell him no," Peezy lied. They hadn't seen each other in a few days, and for whatever reason, he felt compelled to see her. Aria's heart fluttered as he stared at her. She had a hold on him, a hold that she couldn't explain, and one that she didn't want him to let go of.

"Auntie, can I go upstairs and play?"

"Yes, just as long as you come check in with me for dinner."

"Yes, ma'am," Junior said, spinning on his heels and running out the room.

"Babe, I have a surprise for you," Aria said.

"For me?" Harmony's eyebrows rose.

"Yes," Aria said, pouring Peezy a glass of cognac. They followed Aria to the third floor and down the hall. "Close your eyes," she said, playfully covering Harmony's eyes with her hands, pressing her body into hers. She avoided Peezy's jealous stare and opened the door.

"Okay, you can open them now." Harmony gasped.

"Baby, it is beautiful." Harmony wrapped her arms around her small waist, kissing her deep. Chills crept up Aria's back, reminding her that Harmony still owned her body, even though their love was failing.

Peezy cleared his throat. "Umm, I'm gon' let you two enjoy this moment."

Harmony took in the entire office and all of her hard work. She was thankful and sat behind the huge mahogany desk. A picture of her and Junior floated across the screen.

"Damn, ma. You went all out," Harmony said.

Aria froze. Peezy called her ma. It was his little name for her. Hearing Harmony say it made her feel guilty instantly.

"Baby, I know that I have been running the streets heavy since we left Los Angeles, but after I situate this last bit of business, I'm going to be spending a lot more time with you." Aria smiled

"You promise?" she asked, knowing it was probably another lie, or some unfortunate event was going to take place and take precedence over the quality time she said she would spend.

"I promise. Come here." Aria sat on Harmony's lap. *There is nothing wrong with having your cake and eating it too.* Harmony kissed her with so much passion. Passion she had not felt from her in a long time. It frightened her. "Baby, I'm sorry that I've been neglecting you. I swear I will do better," she said between breaths. Tears pooled in Aria's eyes as Harmony undressed her. She set Aria's body up on the desk and laid her back spreading her legs eagle style. "I love you, Aria. Forgive me for putting anything before you," Harmony said in a low whisper. Tears burned down the sides of her face, guilt eating away at her resolve.

"Yes, baby, I forgive you." Harmony stuck two fingers inside Aria's mouth, then inserted them into her wetness. Aria's body shuddered. Harmony sucked on her clit while she stroked her with her fingers. "Please . . ." Aria moaned. "D-don't stop." Harmony dug deeper, sucked harder, willing Aria to reach her height. She sucked her sweet juices off her fingers, and then slid them back inside. "Oh, baby, I am a-about to c-cum. I loove y-yooou," Aria moaned loudly, her body jerking from satisfaction. Aria lay there, tears pooling in her eyes, then spilling down the sides of her face.

"Baby, why are you crying?" Harmony asked, concerned. Aria sat up and wiped her tears.

"I . . . I just love you so much, and I feel like we have not connected like that in a long time."

"I love you too, baby, and I'm so sorry. I meant every word I said."

"You better had," Aria said, punching Harmony in the chest playfully.

The couple walked down the hall hand and hand. Aria's mind shifted to Peezy. She wasn't sure if she was happy. She found herself comparing her relationship to Peezy's marriage. She longed for the constant presence of her better half, something Harmony refused to give her. She looked over at her and sighed inwardly. "I'm going to check on Junior," Aria said. Harmony nodded, then headed down the stairs. Aria opened Junior's bedroom door. He wasn't there. Toys were scattered everywhere. Junior knew better. Aria smirked. *He left with Junior! Peezy's jealous!*

* * * * * *

"Get ahold of yourself, Peezy. You trippin'!" he said, coaching himself. "Come, poppa. We have to go. Mommy just called," he lied.

"Aww, but Daddy, you said—"

"Let's go. Now!" he snapped.

"Yes, sir," Junior pouted.

Peezy had to go. He couldn't look Aria in the eyes after she had just been worked over by his sister. It made his betrayal all too real. He grabbed Junior's coat, and they left quietly. He had business to handle anyway.

Within thirty-five minutes he arrived home with his little boy fast asleep in his car seat. Although Peezy was parked outside, he didn't feel like staying home. So he picked up his cellphone and called home. "Samore, come get Junior. I'm outside. I have to shoot to the hood real quick."

*Click.*

Samore came to the car and pulled Junior out of the backseat. She bent down in the passenger window and looked at him. "Peezy, I want you to know that I am not stupid, okay?"

"What are you talking about?"

"You know good and damn well what I am talking about. Keep playing with me, nigga," Samore snapped and stormed up the steps and into the house. Peezy put the car in park. The way he was feeling right now, she was liable to get her ass kicked. He sighed, ashamed that Aria had begun to consume him. He stormed in the house behind her, sent Junior to his room, and slammed the bedroom door behind him. Peezy pushed Samore down on the bed and climbed on top of her. She stared at him, unsure of what was next. They stared into each other's eyes for a brief moment, then he kissed her roughly. Samore was taken aback by his sudden want for her. Peezy lifted her nightgown and ripped her panties loose.

"Is this what you want?" he asked.

"Yesss. I need it, Peezy. I—" Peezy covered her mouth with his, then shimmied out of his jeans. Flashes of Aria entered his brain as he slid inside of Samore.

"Ahh, baby," she cried. "Peezy!" He buried his face in her neck and viciously pumped in and out of her wetness. Samore took every thrust, matching him. "I love you," she cried.

"I love you too," he said, but as he reached his peak, his mind shifted to Aria, and he imagined how wet and tight she was. "Damn!" Peezy said, rolling over onto the bed.

Samore cuddled up to him. After a few moments of silence, she asked in a serious tone. "Are you cheating on me?"

"What?" Peezy snapped? "Bitch, I just—"

"Answer the fucking question, nigga!"

"No. I have not stuck my dick where it doesn't belong, Samore," Peezy said, irritated, getting up and putting on his clothes. "You so damn insecure."

"Yeah, 'cause you made me this way!" she said, throwing a pillow at his back as he stormed out the room.

For the rest of the evening, Peezy busied himself in the streets trying to keep his mind off of Aria. Things had begun to pick up now that the Feds were no longer lurking, trying to investigate the bombing and their search for Biggs had come up completely empty. Now Peezy could claim San Diego as his own and let everyone know that he was the head nigga in charge. They only had two options: fall in line or die. Byou had recruited a few gunners from New Orleans who had settled out in Oakland, California. The dread head trio had a deadly reputation and a "shoot-first-ask-questions-later" kind of policy.

\* \* \* \* \* \*

The sky was a light gray and tiny drops of rain fell to the ground. Lightning flashed just outside of the hookah lounge, leaving a rumble of thunder in its wake. Despite the gloomy weather, this was a great day for Peezy and Harmony. This would be the first expansion to the empire they were building. They greeted the siblings, and they all ordered drinks.

Derek was the oldest out of the three New Orleanean crew. He stood a striking seven feet tall and weighed almost three hundred pounds. His fair skin and black eyes gave him a mysterious look. He had a no nonsense stare and smoked nothing but joints filled with kush. He towered over Peezy and Harmony and smiled, his teeth white as snow.

"It's a pleasure to meet you both. Byou told us so much about you and the love you have shown her," Derek said.

Peezy nodded.

"This is my baby sister Deon and my brother Devin." The twins were beautiful with their pecan-colored skin and long dreads.

Deon had a serious body on her, one that most women paid thousands for. Her cold, honey-brown gaze was filled with pain, and her silence spoke volumes. She was said to be the most dangerous out of the bunch. Deon nodded, acknowledging them.

"Call me D. I'm not into that first name basis shit," Devin said angrily. Peezy labeled him as the hot head.

"Well, it is an honor to be able to be a part of this team. All we ask you for is your loyalty and respect because with that, everything else will follow," Derek said.

"I totally agree. We ask for the same in return." Harmony raised her glass.

"Now that the introductions are out of the way, let me say that we are going to run this city together with an iron fist, and anybody that refuses to fall in line are like gangrene. I want them cut off immediately, quietly, and professionally. We don't need any more heat. This place just cooled down. I have a few traps set up around the city to keep the money flowing, but I am looking to do bigger and better things. I'm looking at things on a much larger scale, and now that we have a solid team to do so, everything will go as planned. Any questions?" Silence filled the room. "Good," he said, looking over at Harmony.

"Here are your phones. They are secured lines, and the only way we will be contacting each other. So, keep them charged and keep them on," Harmony said, handing each of them an iPhone. "We will meet every Monday morning for breakfast and every Thursday night for dinner. I will send a text with the times and location."

"Derek, here's the keys to your new place. I need eyes all over the city, so you each are stationed throughout it with a contact person to keep you all updated on what's going on in the streets," Harmony explained, handing Byou, Deon, and Devin a set of keys attached to an addressed note.

Deon smirked. "I'm glad you got your shit together." Peezy smirked at her boldness.

"So with all that being said, rest up, get settled, and we will see everybody Thursday."

\* \* \* \* \* \*

Aria had begun to search Harmony's phone regularly for something, anything to justify her betrayal, but as always, it revealed nothing. Until she stumbled upon a JPay app. Instantly, she became irritated as she read through Harmony and Betta's messages. It bothered her to know that she was taking care of his daughter and paying his bills at home. Aria thought she had crushed Betta completely and warned him to stay away from them both. She checked the clock. It was 6:23 in the morning. Could she make it to visitation on time? She eased out of bed, slid on a pair of jeans and a gray cardigan, then headed out. Aria sped up the interstate, anger surging through her. *I should've just killed his ass,"* she thought. After the long drive, she pulled into the maximum state prison, slid her feet into her Chanel pumps, and grabbed her bag.

The female guard at the front desk smiled at her. "Can I help you, ma'am?"

"That's what I want to know. Look, I'm going to be honest with you. Me and my husband got into it, and he removed me from the visitation list. Do you think you could—"

"I can't."

"Will this sway you?" Aria said, sliding a hundred dollar bill toward her. The overweight woman didn't budge. "How about this?" Aria asked, counting four more crisp hundreds.

"What's his name?" the guard asked.

"Gamble. Jamal Gamble." Aria smiled.

"Yes, I see your name right here. Please fill out this form and go through the double doors to your left."

"Thank you," Aria said.

"No, thank *you*," she said, tucking the cash in her bra.

* * * * * *

Aria stood by the vending machine in the visitation room staring at the entrance where the inmates were coming in at. Finally, Betta came in and the officer told him what table he was at. Aria walked briskly to the table once he was seated. She set the chips, candy, and soda down and took a seat across from Betta and crossed her legs. Malice and hate filled his eyes at the sight of her.

"Bitch, what the fuck are you doing here?"

"Now, Jamal, is that any way to greet an old friend?" Aria asked, wearing the same smirk she wore the night he was arrested.

"I swear on everything I've ever loved, when I get out of here I'm going to kill you, bitch." Aria laughed hysterically at his threat.

"Understand something, I have the means and the power to make sure that never happens, so you better watch it."

"Aria, what do you want? Because I'm not going to stop writing Money, if that is why you're here."

"Oh, you know me too well, don't you?" Aria said, putting her hand on her chest dramatically.

"Bitch, you're a psycho," he said. Aria chuckled.

"Just make sure you keep your mouth shut about whatever it is you *think* you know, or I will shut your mouth for you, for good this time," Aria said, standing to leave. "Oh, and if you so much as speak of this visit, I will kill you myself, and that's a promise, not an idle threat. So don't take it lightly. Toodles," she said, blowing Betta a kiss and sashaying out of the visitation room.

# CHAPTER 18

"I appreciate you coming out, my nigga. I need your hands and your passionate hustle," Harmony said, pulling into her driveway.

"No problem, Money. You know you my lil nigga. I got you, and I know Betta would've definitely rode with you," Woo said. "When he called, I came running. Shit got real crazy when you left. The police found Notorious tied up, overdosed on heroin. Whoever would have thought that nigga was getting high on his own shit?" Harmony laughed.

"Well, this here is the land of milk and honey," she said, changing the subject. "And I promise you there is nothing but money to be made."

"That's what I'm talkin' 'bout." Woo slapped five with her.

Harmony led Woo into her plush home and smiled proudly as he took in the luxury. "Damn, Money. Aria did her thing in here. I see you coming up in this world."

"Thanks," Harmony said, walking over to the bar. "You want something to drink?"

"Yeah, what you got?"

"Everything," she said arrogantly.

"In that case, I'll take Jack D on the rocks."

"You still a clown I see." Harmony laughed.

"That will never change."

Aria stopped in her tracks when she saw Woo standing in her kitchen. She forced a smile on her face.

"Hey, baby," Harmony said, smiling. "Look who I found."

"Woo," Aria said, nodding her head.

"Hey, beautiful one."

"What's good?"

"This crib. I was just telling Money what a great job you've done."

"Thanks. Should I set another place for dinner?"

"No, baby. That won't be necessary. I have to go and meet with Peezy later on around seven, so don't wait up for us."

Aria looked at Harmony sadly. "Another lonely night in the palace, huh?" Harmony frowned.

"I do what I do so you can live in this palace."

"Whatever!" Aria snapped, walking up the stairs.

Woo looked at Harmony who started up the stairs, then turned back. She shook her head at him. "Come on, bruh. Let's go."

* * * * * *

Harmony pulled up to the hookah lounge in Lemon Grove. She had to introduce Woo to the team so everybody could get acquainted and get on one accord. Although she and Betta were close, Woo always kept it real with her, no matter if it caused her pain or drama, and for that and many more reasons, had she grown to love and respect him. Betta, on the other hand, tried to shield and protect Harmony from the harshness of the streets. They were like her family.

Her red bottom loafers tapped against the floor as the neon light outlined the stitching throughout her expensive threads. The team greeted Harmony with love.

Introductions were made and the meeting began. Deon's eyes lingered on Woo a moment too long, something only Harmony took note of. She excused herself and disappeared in the crowd. Harmony smiled at the thought of Deon being shy. "I'm going to order another round of drinks and grab me some wings, any special requests?" Harmony took their orders, then headed into the crowd.

"Oh, excuse me," a woman said, bumping into Harmony.

"No, excuse me," she replied, looking into the woman's soft, golden brown eyes.

"I'm Ginger," the petite woman said, holding out her hand.

"Money," Harmony said, taking in her beauty.

Ginger was five feet with flawless cashew-colored skin. Her big baby doll eyes were the color of brown sugar and her lips were pouty and pink. She was sexy. Harmony quickly shook the twinge of guilt off as butterflies filled her stomach, making it hard for her to speak.

"Uh, can I have my hand back?" Ginger asked.

"Umm yeah. I'm sorry. It's just . . . you're so . . . beautiful," she said nervously.

"Thank you. You're beautiful too." Harmony released the woman's hand, then walked off when she turned around. Again their eyes locked one last time before she disappeared into the crowd. Harmony ordered a round of drinks and a few baskets of appetizers, then headed back to their table. Her eyes involuntarily searched the crowd for the stunning beauty.

\* \* \* \* \* \*

Harmony and Peezy listened intently as everyone reported what they had gathered from their end of the streets. Who was who; who was trying to enforce or take over uncharted territory. Deon spoke softly.

"Lincoln Park is affiliated with Brims and they have a few troops pushing kush and pills. Their coke connect is dry right now because I pulled the plug on his order."

"Quick thinking," Peezy said.

"Them neighborhood niggas don't have nothing going on but a whole lot of gang activity. No money is being made around that way. They are dry," Derek commented next.

Devin cleared his throat dramatically. "Mason thinks he is running shit. He is cutting the dope a million times, and that is why the money has slowed down. Nobody has really been fuckin' with us because our product isn't worth smoking, let alone buying."

"You know fiends will walk a green mile for good dope," Deon said.

"Oh, don't worry about that, sweetheart. I'm going to take care of that," Woo replied. Deon looked at him.

"My heart is anything but sweet," she said coldly. The entire table grew silent.

"I didn't mean anything by it," Woo apologized.

"Good. Anybody want another drink?" she asked, not once looking at Woo.

Peezy and Devin raised their hand.

"Damn, she is cold," Woo said, watching her hips sway.

"Yeah, and she's my baby sister too," Derek said, protectively.

Slowly everybody filed out one by one.

Woo stayed seated, allowing the meeting to sink in. He decided he'd enjoy some hookah and mingle with the crowd while Harmony sat at the bar nursing her drink, plotting for their next mission. Mason had to go. He was already showing signs of being power hungry, and because that is what motivated Peezy to take down Biggs, they were left no other choice.

* * * * * *

"Drowning out your sorrows?" a familiar voice asked. Harmony smiled and spun on the stool.

"Not hardly, are you partying yours away?" Harmony responded.

"With the stress of work and other issues, I wish it could be that easy." Ginger pulled herself up onto the barstool next to her.

"What kind of work do you do?"

"I'm a district attorney," Ginger answered.

Harmony raised her eyebrow.

"What?"

"Nothing. I just didn't think that this was the kind of place where DAs hung out."

"Just because I'm successful doesn't mean I have to forget my roots." Harmony nodded and threw back a shot. "I was born and raised in this area. I made a choice to be successful."

"Good choice," Harmony commented. Ginger laughed.

"Don't let this outfit fool you." They laughed.

"It did, and you look gorgeous in it, by the way." Ginger blushed, then released a yawn.

"Thank you. Oh, excuse me. I guess that's my cue," she said, looking down at her diamond infested watch.

"You're welcome." *Get her number!* Harmony thought as Ginger slid off the stool, adjusted her purse strap, and stuck out her hand. "It was a pleasure meeting you, Money. It really was," she said, hesitantly. Ginger turned to walk away. *Don't let her leave.*

"Hey, uh, Ginger."

"Yes," she said, spinning around, her dark brown curls bouncing at her sides.

"Can I take you out some time?"

"Take me out? Oh, I'm not—I." Harmony nodded, then smiled.

"You have a good night, Ginger, and drive safe." Ginger nodded back and walked briskly away.

"Damn! Who is that!" Woo asked. Harmony shrugged. "Yeah, you better not know. Aria gone lose it on your ass." Harmony looked down at her watch, then cursed.

"Come on, man. It's late."

\* \* \* \* \* \*

Aria woke up wrapped in her silk sheets alone. She checked the clock. It was 10:00 a.m.

"Dammit"!" she yelled, hopping out of bed. Peezy would be expecting her in an hour, and it would take her that long to get ready. She washed away the make-up sex that she and Harmony had last night and climbed into a Ralph Lauren design. The sundress flowed freely around her thighs, and the peach color complimented her chocolatey complexion. She applied a thick layer of Dior to her lips, grabbed her clutch, and then dialed Peezy's phone.

"Ma, what's good?"

"Babe, I'm on my way. I'm running a little late," Aria said as she slid into her car.

"I'll be waiting impatiently," he said, hanging up. Aria looked down at the phone, then threw it in the passenger seat.

She pulled into Mission Valley mall a few minutes late, hopped out, then searched for Peezy's truck.

"Boo!" he said, scaring her.

"Peezy!" she screeched. He grabbed her hand.

"Come on. Let's go." Aria followed him around the mall buying a few things here and there. She was in a trance as they walked and talked about everything. He had some depth to him, which allowed their conversation to flow.

Aria modeled a few dresses for him from H&M. "Here, try this one on," he said, handing her a dress over the dressing room door.

"Come in," Aria said, opening the door. Peezy bit his lip as he saw her naked frame.

"Damn!" he whispered, nodding from left to right. She pounced on him, shoving her tongue down his throat, moaning from the overwhelming feeling of want. Peezy lifted her body on his, slamming her against the wall. The feeling that rushed through him confirmed what he had been trying to deny. *I'm fallin' for her,'* he thought, as Aria attacked him, biting and sucking on his neck. He slid two fingers into her wetness.

"Ooo, Peezy!" Aria moaned breathlessly. She began to rock on his fingers. He dug deeper inside her. "Omigoodness," she moaned, as her juices began to run down his hand and onto her thighs. Aria freed her breasts, pulling Peezy toward them. He kissed and softly kneaded her nipples with his teeth and tongue, sending her body into a frenzy. His manhood stood at attention as her body shuddered against his. Peezy had never felt or fallen so fast for too many women, but something about Aria made him cross all boundaries. He wanted her bad.

Once Aria gained control over her body, she refused the guilt that attempted to seep in. Peezy had become a part of her, and letting him go would be close to impossible. *It's her brother, Aria. Damn!* Aria closed her eyes. She had lost the fight.

"Peezy, we can't do this," she admitted, breathing heavily. He laughed.

"You and I both know that is no longer an option." Aria dropped her head. He was right.

* * * * * *

Byou slipped her clip in place as she and Harmony pulled up to Mason's spot.

"You ready?" she asked Harmony.

"Yes, I'm ready." Harmony crept behind her. In the distance, Mason was running his mouth about somebody's business.

"I always find it funny how people are so oblivious to the last few minutes of their lives. Here Mason is, clowning and talking shit, not knowing that we about to bring it to his ass," Byou said, then chuckled.

Harmony thought Byou, Derek, and the twins were a little

creepy. They were all beautiful, but they were crazy as hell. Whatever happened during Hurricane Katrina changed them. They didn't speak on it often, and Harmony didn't pry. Byou tapped on the door with the butt of her glock.

"I'm closed for the night!" Mason yelled. "So get yo' crack head ass away from my damn door!" Harmony twisted up her face, and Byou banged harder this time.

"We 'pose to be open twenty-four hours. This nigga is trippin'!" Mason snatched the door open.

"Didn't I tell yo'—." His evil glare was replaced with fear when he saw Harmony standing there.

"Nigga, open the fucking door!" she barked, pushing past him. Byou, in step behind her, gun drawn.

"My, my bad, M-Money. I thought—"

"You thought what, nigga? What could you have possibly thought? That Peezy wasn't going to hear that you been playin' with his money?"

"Mason, baby, what's—" A red-boned model chick with beautiful long legs came from the back room in nothing but a thong and stilettos. She gasped, then turned to run.

"You might as well have a seat," Byou said, pointing her gun at her. Tears pooled in the sexy woman's eyes.

"Please don't—"

"Bitch, shut the fuck up!" Byou demanded.

"Now, Mason. What did Peezy say about having 'hos in the trap?" Harmony asked.

"He said no 'hos in the spot." Harmony pulled her pistol from her back and slapped him across the face.

"Silly ass nigga. Now you have cost her, her life."

"No, please. I swear I—"

*Pfft Pfft.*

Byou let off two rounds into her chest.

*Pfft.*

Harmony shot a round into Mason's head. "Check the back, clean out the safe, and let's go!" Harmony said, searching Mason and bagging up the dope. Byou cleaned out his safe and grabbed the surveillance tape, then followed Harmony.

\* \* \* \* \* \*

Harmony sat across from Peezy at TGI Fridays taking in the haste of downtown. Everybody gave their weekly report. Biggs had taught Peezy how to run an organization, and he was in turn, teaching her. Everything had fallen in line. It was just a few others that needed to be reminded that he was the HNIC.

"Now it is time to let the streets know who got that work and what it is going for. I have a few out-of-town buyers, but I want to supply those within the city limits as well," Peezy said. The waitress brought a round of shots to their table. "Let's toast to us, our success, and to all this damn money we about to make." Everybody raised their shot glasses and turned them up. Harmony smiled at Peezy. She was proud and happy for him. He saw a vision, and they were all carrying it out. She never thought that she would ever be sitting next to him toasting to their success. Her mind drifted to Aria and the distance she continuously placed between them, not sexually, because she was always down to fuck, but mentally and emotionally she was dead, leaving her a small list of options. It seemed as if there was nothing Harmony could do to comfort her and let her know that she was hers. Their relationship was falling apart rapidly.

"Are you here or here?" Woo asked, pointing to his head. Harmony smirked. Woo knew her too well. He could tell that something was eating away at her. "Come on. Let's take a walk," he whispered. Deon caught his eye and smirked. Pretending that she wasn't interested was becoming harder and harder to do. Woo smiled at her openly and excused himself and Harmony.

"Where y'all off to?" Peezy asked, clearly agitated by their side bar conversation.

"We're about to go to the store real quick. Anybody want anything?"

"Yeah, some Newport shorts in the box," Devin said.

Harmony noticed Peezy's jaw clenching. Is *he jealous of my bond with Woo?*

She and Woo made their exit, and Harmony strolled beside him.

"What is it, lil sis?" he asked straight out. She sighed.

"It's Aria," she admitted.

"Aria?"

"Yes, she's been straight trippin'. Hard. Every day I come home, she's accusing me of sleeping around with random 'hos. She always has an attitude . . . just bullshit, man . . . for real. I feel like she's trying to push me away, and whether she knows it or not, it's working." Woo looked at her. He could see the stress on her face. He knew that Aria wasn't even the insecure type. Harmony didn't give her a reason to be.

"More times than not, when a chick is doing all that, she is the one who is—"

"Hey!" Ginger said, walking toward them.

Harmony could not refuse the smile that formed at the sight of Ginger in her cream pants suit and natural brown curls.

"What's up, Ms. Lady?" Harmony said.

"Ms. Lady?" Ginger asked. Harmony shrugged.

"What have you been up to?"

"Work, work, and more work." Ginger smiled.

"So when do you get a little free time?"

"Rarely." Ginger fell in step with them.

"Nice to meet you, Ginger. I'm Woo," he said sarcastically, looking at Harmony. Woo turned into the store, leaving them outside.

Harmony rubbed her hands together nervously. *Play it cool.*

"Where are you headed?" Harmony asked.

"To my car."

"Let me walk you."

"Oh, it's just a block or two away," Ginger said, running her fingers through her hair, something she did when she was nervous. The green man appeared on the traffic signal, indicating it was safe to walk. Harmony looked at Ginger and smiled, then crossed the street with her. Ginger looked over at her. "You're persistent, aren't you?"

"Are you afraid that you might like my persistence?" Again, she ran her fingers through her hair and smiled. "I promise I don't bite." *Ask her again. She can't say no twice.*

"Money, you don't understand," Ginger said, stopping in the parking lot facing her. "My life is so complicated." Harmony stepped closer.

"Then help me understand. Let me un-complicate things." Ginger brushed past her and defused her car alarm to her black ATS coupe. Harmony smiled. "Come on. Let me take you out," she said, opening her door. Ginger sat in the car. "We can go wherever you want to go." The curly haired beauty put her hands on the steering wheel, willing herself to fight temptation.

"Okay, Money. You win," Ginger said, smiling. "But I won't be available until—" She looked into her bag and pulled out her iPad. "Until next Friday night."

"How does eight sound?"

"Good, eight is good." She handed Harmony her business card and started the car.

"Ginger Demasci-Grand!" Harmony said aloud, taking note of the three letters printed in front of her name. *She's married?* Before Harmony could glance down at her ring finger, she was pulling off.

* * * * * *

In the two-bedroom flat, Woo stood in the kitchen near the table and stole a glance at Deon while he whipped another pot of the purest fish scale he had ever seen. The word had spread, and sales were up in a matter of a week. Harmony had made the decision to place Woo over the trap houses. He was experienced in that area. Even though Peezy didn't like it, he had to agree that he wasn't a killer like the rest of them. Maybe if he was pushed to do so, but one can never be sure. That wasn't the life the rest of them knew; they killed day in and out with no remorse or questions asked.

Deon sat with her long legs crossed, serving the fiends in silence. Strangely, it turned him on. The women in New Orleans were bred completely different from the ones he had run across. She was mysterious. Deon had eased her toffee-colored frame into Woo's mind numerous times since the first day he saw her. The neat blonde micro dreads she kept twisted up hung down to the middle of her long torso. They smelled like sweet cherry blossom, enticing him in a way that left him wanting to be close enough to bury his nose in them. *This woman done put roots on me. I swear*, he thought, as she kept creeping into his mind. He had even dreamed of her.

Derek was not at all happy when Peezy said that he needed Deon to stand guard while Woo cooked up a few keys and got them ready for the traps to distribute, but there was nothing he could do. Peezy had spoken. His presence was needed. For Woo, luck could not have come at a better time. He knew that Deon was feeling him, but could he break through her resolve? It seemed to be as hard as a brick.

The knock at the door broke through his courage to spark up a conversation with her. "Ay, let me get a slab," a man known as Arab asked. He always spent no less than a hundred every time he came by. The man rushed past Deon.

"Man, stop playin', lil mama and let me—" Deon cocked her calico and pointed it in his face.

"Listen, you lil fucker. Your mama is at home, and the smallest thing on me is my feet, which I don't mind shoving up your ass." Arab swallowed hard. Deon held out her hand, and he handed her a hundred dollar bill. "*Here!*" she barked, handing him his vice. "Now, beat it!" she yelled, slamming the door in his face.

Woo smirked at her and shook his head.

"What?"

"Deon, you have to be nice to the customers," Woo replied. Deon chuckled.

"No, I don't. Who made up that rule? You?" Woo flipped over the Pyrex dish, and a perfect cookie fell into his palm. She eyed him.

"Yeah, I did actually."

"Well, I only follow *my* rules," she said, tucking her gun in her back. Woo sighed and went to the sink to wash his hands.

*Do it now, or you can forget it.* He dried his hands, then strode across the room toward her. She didn't budge.

"Listen, Deon," he said, choosing his words carefully. "I can't keep walking around here pretending like I don't think about you when I lay down at night and rise in the morning, or when I am out handling business throughout the day, and for real, this shit is torture." He stopped in front of her. Deon wrapped her arms around his neck and looked him in his eyes.

"Then don't," she said, sliding her tongue into his mouth. She too had been holding her composure for months. She felt like she was going to burst if she didn't taste his soft lips. "My brothers are going to kill you," Deon said, coming up for air.

"You wouldn't let them do that, would you?"

"Yeah, if you hurt me, you're a dead man."

\* \* \* \* \* \*

Peezy pulled up in Harbor Manor apartments, known for its notorious gang activity. Lil Man ran the Crips on this side of town and had sent word to Peezy that he, or nobody else in his hood would be playing by his rules or paying taxes to flip bricks in their own hood. Peezy rallied up his team and a few recruits who were ready to prove their loyalty at all costs, and fill any and everybody with hot lead on command. Peezy climbed out of his Denali and leaned against the hood. He made eye contact with a young mother who gathered all the children off the playground. A mob of thirty or so men came toward him. Peezy didn't budge as he chewed on a toothpick. He could see the underestimation in the young men's eyes.

"What are you doing in my hood, nigga?" one man asked.

"I'm looking for Lil Man." The crowd parted and a short, lanky, brown-skinned man emerged from the crowd wearing a blue rag tied around his mouth.

"I'll take it you got my message," he said, lowering the rag around his neck.

"Yeah, it's unfortunate that you refused my offer."

"Offer? You might run these other niggas around here, but me and my hood don't answer to nobody. That shit died when that nigga Biggs skipped town." Peezy smirked. A red dot appeared on Lil Man's chest.

"See, you must have it misunderstood. I'm only asking for what is rightfully mine by offering you and your hood protection from SDPD and anybody else who feels the need to try to take what's yours. I don't want to run your hood. I simply just want my cut for making sure you niggas don't starve to death, 'cause you all look like you could use a meal or two," he said, calmly. A red light appeared on everyone who was standing in the crowd. They all looked down, then at each other. "Everyone in favor, say I," Peezy said.

"Nigga, you ain't Don fuckin' Corleone!" Lil Man snapped, looking around at his crew, who had begun to snicker. "Fuck this nigga! It's neighborhood Crip, on m—" Lil Man's body dropped to the ground, and his blood squirted on everyone standing beside him.

"Man!" a woman yelled, running to his side crying and cradling his body.

"Anyone else feel the need to protest?" A few men pulled their guns. Red lights landed on everyone's face simultaneously. "Go ahead, I dare you. If you think you can get a shot off before your body is lying next to his," Peezy said, crossing his arms over his chest. The men lowered their weapons. "So I take it we have an agreement?"

"Yeah, we do," a tall, flaxen-colored man answered from the crowd.

"Good, and your name is?"

"Squally."

"Squally. I'll be in touch," Peezy said, climbing into his truck and pulling off, his music beating loudly, setting off car alarms on the way out.

# CHAPTER 19

Harmony banged on Woo's door impatiently. Normally, she would've called and let him know first, but he wasn't answering his phone, and since Peezy had left town to meet up with a few potential clients, she needed him.

Woo snatched the door open wearing nothing but a pair of basketball shorts. His buff, chiseled chest was shining like he had just taken an oil bath.

"Eww! Go put some clothes on," she said, brushing past him. He and Deon were having the best sex he had ever experienced in his life, but Harmony was like his little sister, and she would not have come over if it wasn't important.

"Last time I checked, this was my house." Harmony went over to the bar and poured her a glass of Jack Daniels. Woo sighed.

"What's the matter?"

"Aria is gone. She left."

"She did what?"

"I woke up to a note saying she needs some time to figure things out," Harmony said, balling the note up and throwing it across the room.

"Time to figure what out?" he asked. Harmony shrugged, drank the whiskey and poured herself another glass.

"Don't tell me she found out about Ginger?"

"No! No . . . or you and Peezy would be planning my funeral."

*Or hers.* Woo thought.

"Speaking of Ginger, I'm supposed to take her out tonight, but I'm just not feeling it. Maybe I should go and try to find Aria."

"I don't. I think you should take Ginger out, show her a good time, and enjoy yourself. If Aria wanted to be found, she would be at home. Always keep you a bitch lined up, sis, and for real, something doesn't sit right with—"

"Keep you a bitch lined up?" Deon said, storming into the living room in a trench coat. "So, who is in line, Woo? Me, or the other bitch?" she yelled, throwing her sandal at Woo. Harmony stood there in awe.

"No. Baby, wait!" he pleaded, ducking.

*Baby?* Harmony thought, pouring herself another drink.

"I didn't mean it like that. I'm talking about her line, baby, not mine. I don't even have a line."

"No, fuck you, Woo! I'm out!" Deon said, scooping up her shoe and storming out, slamming the door behind her. Woo turned and looked at Harmony.

"So when were you going to tell me you was smashin' Deon?" Woo ran his hand over his face.

"I'm not smashin' Deon. I'm falling in love with her." Harmony shook her head.

"Well, your secret is safe with me. You do know that when Derek and D find out, they are going to kill you though, right?" Woo sighed.

"Man, pour me one." Harmony poured him a drink and sat on the stool.

"It's crazy, because when I envisioned Aria leaving, I saw myself all twisted and sick over it. I mean, don't get me wrong. I'm fucked up, but I'm feeling more confused and disrespected than anything, but it is nothing at all like I thought it would be."

"That's because you felt it. You knew that it was just a matter of time before it happened. Now, I'm not trying to plant no seed in your head, but it sounds to me like ya' girl got something else going on."

"I will not lie and say that I have not entertained the thought,"

Harmony said, knowing it was definitely a possibility. Their relationship was crumbling right before their eyes, and every effort she made to try to mend it, went unnoticed or unappreciated. They had been through so much together, and as much as Harmony didn't want to admit it, something just wasn't right.

* * * * * *

Aria stood in front of the airport clutching her MIU MIU carry on, waiting for Peezy. She could not actually believe that she had left. Even though it was only for a few days, she had led Harmony to believe that she needed space and was torn over their rocky relationship that she was the cause of. Aria played with Harmony's feelings, pulling and pushing her as she chose. Only this time she didn't get the reaction she thought she would. The things Harmony was doing to try to save their relationship made Aria feel guilty, but it didn't change the fact that Peezy had become her new drug, and she was strung out. She could only imagine what was going through Harmony's head. *Well, maybe if she would step her game up,* Aria thought, attempting to justify her actions. When the truth was, she had fallen for Peezy, and the time she spent away from him was pure torture.

When he texted her, Aria was ecstatic. He told her to pack a small bag and catch the red-eye flight out to New York to meet him. She couldn't tell him no. Ever. He knew that. Harmony had to take the reins for the weekend while he was away, so Aria would be the last thing on her mind. Or so they thought.

Peezy pulled up in a stretch Hummer, taking in the sight of her. Her hair was blowing down her back in the wind as she stood there like a stallion. Her yellow BCBG dress hugged every curve, lying snug against her hour-glass shape. *Mmmph! I swear if I wasn't with Samore, and she wasn't my sister's bitch, I'd wife her fine ass,* he thought momentarily. Peezy stepped out the back and helped her into the truck.

"Hey, P!" she screeched, smiling excitedly. He was looking dapper in his black Armani slacks and gray button up. She wrapped her arms around him and breathed in his scent. "Love this nigga," she murmured, then slid her tongue into his mouth. "I missed you," she said between breaths as they kissed each other like long lost lovers.

"Missed you too, that's why I sent for you. I hoped you would come," he said, half running game.

"Hoped? Nigga, you *knew* I was coming. Stop frontin'." Peezy smiled. "I love Harmony, but . . . it's complicated."

"I understand." Peezy was dealing with his own betrayal toward his sister and didn't want to discuss it with her. It made it too real. "Come on. Let's make the most of these forty-eight hours." Aria nodded and let him lead her to the limo. She grabbed the Dom Perignon that sat in a bucket of ice and poured them a glass.

"To us," she said. Peezy raised his glass and swallowed it down. She set her empty glass down as he placed soft kisses down her neck and onto her breasts, filling her with heat. *Dammit!* Aria's body shuddered at his touch. Peezy worked her body over, then slid her moist panties to the side, sliding his fingers in and out of her wetness, moving in circles, touching every wall she owned. Her mouth formed the shape of an 'O' as he did what her body needed him to do. "Baby!" she cried out. His manhood wanted to feel the deepest parts of her, feel her walls contract against him. He put his fingers into his mouth and sucked on them. Aria smiled. She tasted so good to him. He craved her late nights after Samore had done all but satisfy him.

"What are you doing to me?" he asked, burying his head between her chocolate thighs and sucking her sweetness into his mouth. Peezy kissed and sucked on her clit as she rolled her hips to her own rhythm. He could feel her building up, feel her muscles tightening.

"Oh!" she screamed. "Peezy, I'm coming. I'm—" she moaned loudly. He sucked softly, and guided two fingers deep inside her. "Mmmmph!" she said, breathlessly. *I love you,* she screamed inside her head.

\* \* \* \* \* \*

*One week later . . .*

Ginger had changed clothes more than ten times before she found something to wear. The beautifully crafted red Ferragamo long-sleeve cotton dress stopped right above her knees, showing off her soft, flawless model legs and lay against her skin like a thin layer of paint. Sexy, but not too sexy, Ginger thought, eyeing herself in the mirror. She was nervous and finally got up the courage to return Harmony's persistence with a yes. She had not been able to keep Harmony, who she initially thought was a man, off her mind.

The week seemed to drag by, but only because she was looking forward to her weekends out on the town that had become more frequent than her husband would ever admit. His constant infidelity had driven her so far away from him that the only thing they did together was fake it through the holidays with her parents. A divorce would be much too messy and embarrassing on her end, and the fact that her father would make sure that Trenton didn't have two red cents to rub together was the only reason they were even still married now.

"You look beautiful," he said, watching her apply a thick coat of Mac gloss to her pouty lips.

"Thank you, Trenton," she said dryly, grabbing her black trench coat, covering herself. "Don't wait up," she remarked coldly as she walked past him. That was a line he often spoke when he was having his affair. Something she constantly reminded him of and couldn't let go.

Twenty minutes later, Ginger pulled next to Harmony in the downtown parking structure and smiled, noticing they had yet another thing in common. Cadillacs. Harmony grinned at Ginger as she admired her car, making her stomach fill to the rim with butterflies. *This woman is seriously sexy.* Ginger could not believe her thoughts. *What are you doing? You're not even into women. Start up the car and go home!* her responsible self yelled. A part of her wanted to stay; the other part wanted to run like a frightened animal.

Harmony climbed out of her cocaine white CTS in a dark brown linen Marc Jacobs short set with a pair of Tom Ford loafers and no socks. She looked good enough to eat, and she had just left the barbershop, so her line up was as sharp as the straight razor that cut it. She opened the door and helped Ginger out. The black trench coat she wore revealed nothing, making Harmony's mind wonder exactly what Ginger intended it to do. Harmony placed her hand on the small of her back, sending electricity up her back and down to the soles of her Ferragamo pumps. *Wheeew!* she gasped inwardly.

"Where are we headed?" she asked, recovering from her touch.

"Well, since you told me to surprise you, I was thinking we could go to a movie, grab a bite to eat. Then maybe if you're up to it, we can go and hit up Club Bloom." Ginger smiled, something she caught herself doing a lot at the mere thought of her.

"That sounds like fun."

"Good."

On the walk to the theater, Harmony noticed how she had not once spoken about her marriage. *How serious was it?* she thought. *For her not to mention it.* Ginger seemed so young and free-spirited, a thing Harmony never remembered being. Her ruthless, no nonsense attitude and money, made her not care about needing, nor was she fearful of much. Only now, something seemed to be missing and she felt it.

"Ginger, how old are you?" Harmony asked after a few minutes of silence. She gasped.

"You're not supposed to ask a woman that!"

"Yeah, if you're a man. Something I am clearly not or want to be," she said, grinning.

"I'm twenty-three."

"How did you become a district attorney so quickly?" Ginger smiled.

"I graduated from high school at the age of sixteen with honors, and when I told my father what I wanted to do, he pulled some strings, and from there I was studying law. This is actually my first year in the courtroom. My father runs this city, so whatever I want I get. They hate me at my office, by the way," she said, laughing, leaning into Harmony. Harmony was turned on by her ambition and confidence. Most chicks from around her way lacked the most important qualities. She seemed to possess just about all of them.

They reached the theater after a few blocks, and Harmony purchased their tickets. Surprisingly, Ginger wanted to watch an action movie instead of the sappy romance film she had originally prepared herself to sit through. Ginger bypassed the snacks. She couldn't eat when her nerves were all bundled in the pit of her stomach. She didn't expect to speak so freely. Ginger was a great listener and not much of a talker, but with Harmony, they vibed instantly. The theater was chilly, so Ginger kept her coat on and snuggled up to Harmony, whose stomach was so full of butterflies and lady bugs, she thought it was going to burst. Her sexy, seductive perfume was enticing her in a way that was new to her. They watched the action-packed film in mostly silence. When the movie was over, all Harmony could think about was how to get close to her again.

"That was a good movie," Ginger commented.

"I enjoyed it too," Harmony said, strolling beside her on 5th Avenue.

"There is a great bistro a few blocks ahead; their food is wonderful."

"You have not had wonderful food until you have had my Mema's cooking," Ginger flirted.

"Oh, we will see," Harmony countered, taking her up on her indirect offer. They shared another smile. Ginger seemed to like her more and more with every passing second.

Because the wait could be crazy, Harmony made reservations ahead of time. They were quickly seated. Ginger unbuttoned her trench coat and laid it on the back of the chair that Harmony pulled out for her. Harmony's eyes took in her thick curves and small waist. *Damn, this chick is the truth!* She watched her intently. Finally she cleared her throat. "You look—umm . . . that dress is—"

"Hello, my name is Tina, and I'm going to be serving you tonight," the skinny brunette said with a little too much enthusiasm, interrupting Harmony and their flirtatious stare. "What can I get you guys to drink?" Ginger ordered a margarita. Harmony ordered a few shots of Patron.

"Your dress is beautiful. Did you wear it for me?" Ginger's face flushed.

"No!" Harmony laughed. "Okay, maybe," she said, laughing.

They chatted over their meal with ease, charming one another with smiles. Harmony gave her a little background, leaving out the grimy details. Just talking to Ginger made her want more out of life besides the keys to the city. Ginger made her question her dreams and aspirations to run the streets and what her motives were when it came to them. In that moment, Ginger had unknowingly broadened her thinking and captured her in a way that no other woman had, giving her a different perspective of life. A better one. She wasn't sure if it was her or the liquor that warmed her.

Harmony paid the hefty tab and left Tina a nice tip, who blatantly stared every time she came to the table. She was used to it by now. It didn't bother her anymore. Harmony held Ginger's coat as she slid her arms in. The smell of her traveled all the way down to Harmony's stomach as she whipped her hair over her collar. *Damn she smells so good.*

"You still up for Bloom?"

"I'm down for whatever." *As long as I can spend more time with you.* Harmony smiled at her thoughts.

Ginger was impressed with the night club. Its three dance floors, three bars, and the lavish VIP section she had set aside for them was elegant.

"This is nice," Ginger said over Nicki and Beyoncé. Harmony grabbed ahold of her hand as they were led through the club by the bouncer. Ginger couldn't help but notice the envious stares and smirks throughout the crowd. They were seated next to a dance floor, and Harmony ordered a bottle of Patron with salt and limes. She looked over at Ginger, who was watching her. *Mmmmph! Those lips,* Ginger thought, as Harmony intentionally licked them. Ginger just couldn't understand the attraction. Harmony was sexy and confident, her open mind and optimism turned Ginger on. Most women were close minded and prude. One of the reasons she didn't deal with too many women.

After a few shots, Ginger was on her feet and swaying seductively to the music. Harmony wasn't much of a dancer, so she sat and watched. A Nicki Minaj song banged through the speakers. Ginger was feeling every piano key and drum as the beat took over her body. She grabbed Harmony's hands, pulling her to her feet.

"Dance with me!" she said, seduction dripping from her lips.

"I don't know how to dance," Harmony admitted.

"It's easy. Let the beat move you," Ginger said, lacing her hands in hers. She swirled and swayed against Harmony, sending an electric shock through their bodies. Harmony's hands trailed down her arms, then curves.

"Oh my goodness!" Ginger said aloud, thankful the music covered her outburst. She laid her head back against Harmony's shoulder, losing herself in her touch. Harmony tried not to explore her body too much, but the way she was grinding her ass into her lap was turning her on. If she had a dick, it would've been rock hard. She smelled Ginger's neck and hair while two stepping behind her. Ginger held her breath from the sensation that followed. "Omigosh!" Ginger screamed. *She has no clue what she is doing to me. Or does she?*

\* \* \* \* \* \*

Peezy squirted Oil of Olay onto the loofa and washed Aria's body. They had just shared a nice meal, drank some champagne, and were lit. Aria was falling for him, and he could tell. It was something about the way a woman looked at you that let you know she was falling for you. As much as she tried to hide it, he could still see it. Women never did a good job at hiding their emotions, not from him anyway. His mind shifted to Harmony and how hurt she sounded when he spoke with her. She told him that Aria had left. He knew how she would feel if she knew that Aria was in New York with him. Their betrayal made him sick, but he couldn't help it. All he could think about was how long they would be able to hide it. Samore knew he was cheating. She always knew, but never had proof. She had told him before he left on his *business trip*.

"What are you talking about?" Peezy had asked.

"Your touch is not the same. I'm your wife. I know you, Peezy. We've been together almost eleven years."

"Girl, whatever! You trippin'!" he said, kissing Junior and leaving for his early flight. He shook his head and started his car. She did know him. Peezy would sleep around until he got bored, or things became too complicated, then come home. He was a dog, but Samore loved him and he loved her. He never allowed his affairs to affect his home life, but he wanted Aria, and there was no denying it, only to the world.

\* \* \* \* \* \*

Aria wrapped the plush robe around her naked body. Tonight would be the night she gave Peezy all of her. Peezy handed her another glass of champagne. Before she took a sip, she kissed him softly. Then downed her glass of courage. He unwrapped her moist body and kissed every inch of her soft skin. Spreading her legs slowly, he kissed her most private part. His warm lips against her wetness sent her into a frenzy. Her heart beat wildly against her chest. Her knees felt weak as he sucked hungrily on her pleasure. Aria spread her legs wider, giving him more.

"Peezy," she moaned, looking down at him. "I love the way you do that." *I love you.* He pushed her back on the bed and crawled up her frame, kissing her roughly. She rolled on top of him, snatching at his robe to untie it. Aria had never been aggressive with him. She never took control, but tonight, everything would be different. Tonight, she would make him love her too. She was a master at seduction, and once they landed in her web it was over. Aria bit at his hips and nibbled at his thighs then kissed his long, thick, pulsing wood. Peezy gasped. She had not given head since her uncle forced her to learn the art of it. As Aria French kissed his manhood, his muscles clenched.

"Mmm, so you been holding out on me?" Aria giggled, then swallowed every inch of him at once.

"Oh shit!" Peezy yelped. "Damn, ma. I-I ain't know . . . Mmmph! You . . . damn, Ariaa—Ohhh," he moaned. Aria sucked and swallowed Peezy's ten inches like a pro, leaving him speechless as she sucked hard then soft, slow then fast, sending his body into a state of want. Peezy grabbed her face. "Aria!" he moaned. She smiled.

"Peezy, I want you to fuck me," she moaned, rolling over on her back and playing in her wetness. His eyes grew wide. "Are you—"

"Shhh—no talking. It makes everything easier," she said softly. Peezy climbed on top of her and guided his girth slowly inside of her. She bit her bottom lip as his manhood stretched her virgin-like pussy. Aria clawed at his back from the mixture of pleasure and pain. Once his length reached the depth of her, they both let out a loud moan. Peezy buried his head into her curls. Her wetness gripped him so tight he almost came instantly. Her muscles drummed against his flesh involuntarily. "Peezy!"

"Yes."

"Don't stop—please," she begged as she saturated him. He stroked her strategically, but with ease and care. Her moans and pleas for more sent him over the edge into another world. He rocked and worked her body into a frenzy. "Tell me—tell me you love this pussy," she demanded, meeting his every stroke.

"Oh sh—I-I . . . l-love this pussy," he moaned.

"Now, tell me I'm all you want," she ordered, rolling over on top of him and dipping his inches inside of her.

"Ahh! You—you're all I want, baby," he moaned. Aria rode him into oblivion.

"Say it. Say I'm all you need," she said, smiling down at him. Peezy rolled her over and began to pound her slowly.

"You're. All. I. Need. I swear!" he said, barely pulling out in time to release on her stomach. "I swear you are," he admitted.

\* \* \* \* \* \*

"Are you sure you're not too drunk to drive?" Harmony asked. *No,* Ginger thought.

"Yes, I'm fine," she assured her.

"Okay. Text me when you make it to your doorstep," Harmony said, opening Ginger's car door. She placed a kiss on her cheek. Ginger turned her head, then slid her tongue into her mouth, surprising herself and Harmony, who kissed her back. Running her fingers through her hair and pressing her body into hers. *Mmmph! Her lips are as soft as they look,* Harmony thought, devouring her. Suddenly Ginger pulled away.

"Oh, I'm-I'm sorry," she said, climbing into her car. Harmony touched her lips. *Shit.*

"Hey, everybody! There is a road block before almost every freeway entrance. Be careful!" a guy yelled to everyone in the parking lot. Harmony looked at Ginger and reached inside her car, then removed the keys from the ignition.

"Come on. Neither of us need to go to jail tonight." Ginger laid her head on the steering wheel. *Go home, Ginger.* She ignored her thoughts and followed Harmony to a hotel. She stood in the lobby as Harmony rented them a room for the night. They boarded the elevator in silence once the doors closed. Harmony grabbed Ginger's hand. She smiled at the gesture.

"Here. You're in room 402. I'll be right across the hall. I'll see you in the morning," she said, handing her the room key and guiding her to her door. Ginger didn't revel in the thought of being alone for another night, but the fact that Harmony didn't take advantage of the road blocks made her even more irresistible. Harmony kissed her forehead.

"Good night. I had a wonderful time," Ginger said again. Harmony looked at the want in her eyes, then forced herself to say good night.

# CHAPTER 20

Harmony took in the scent of the salty ocean as she and Woo sat on the Santa Monica Pier. Woo looked over at her.

"What is weighing so heavily on you?"

"Ginger. We had a real good time the other night, but she has not hit me up or returned any of my calls?" Harmony said sadly. "Have you and Deon made up?"

"Yeah, it took a whole lot of convincing and a few long strokes," Woo said, laughing. "She can't resist the kid."

"Be careful. She seems dangerous."

"Seems? More like *is*, but I like her a lot."

"That's all that matters."

"So what's up with Aria?"

"She called." Harmony sighed. "Told me she is in New York, she loves me, and that we need to talk. So she'll be home later this afternoon." Woo scoffed. Though he had nothing against Aria, he even knew bullshit when he heard it. "Man, she's trippin'! What woman tells her mate, the one she loves so much, that she is on the other side of the country and will be home, *after* she left a note saying pretty much nothing and has been gone for almost a week?" Harmony shrugged. She was far from dumb and knew that whatever Aria had going on was consuming her just like their relationship had when it was fresh and exciting.

"If you know like I know, that whole situation sounds like some straight bullshit," Woo stated. Harmony nodded in agreement. Everything about Aria had changed, from her patterns of jealousy, to the things she did or said, something Harmony was sure she had not grown out of.

"What did your brother say?" Harmony shrugged.

"He said to give her some time, to not give up on her." Woo's eyebrows rose.

"I guess. I wouldn't give her ass a damn thing but a deuce," he said, holding up two fingers in the air. Harmony laughed.

"I am thoroughly pissed, but most of all disappointed. For real, I am not sure what I'm going to do. Besides, Ginger has my full attention."

"Ginger? What's so special about her that she deserves that?"

"She is smart, sexy as hell, and works for the DA's office."

"Bruh, she's a DA? That's always a good card to have in your hand."

"I know, but it's really not about that, and what makes it so much better is, she isn't into women."

"Well then, how—why are you even bothering to—"

"Because the fact that I'm going to be the first to own that pussy excites me in a way I cannot explain." Woo burst into laughter.

"You sound like a nigga, bruh."

\* \* \* \* \* \*

Aria climbed out of the cab, her hands filled with Saks Fifth and Neiman Marcus bags. Compliments of Peezy. He had let her tear the Avenue up after she had put her sex game down on him for two days straight. Her body still ached from the wild sex they had. Aria's heart dropped into her stomach forming a ball of guilt when she glanced up at Harmony's office window and caught her staring. She had a look in her eyes that she had never seen before.

Woo's Infiniti truck sat in the driveway along with a few other cars she had never seen before. She smacked her lips. "I told her I'd be home around this time, and I wasn't expecting company," she mumbled.

"Aria," Woo said dryly, nodding his head. A beautiful, tall, fair-skinned woman sat at his side. Her ice-blonde sister locks were hanging down her back in spiral curls, the tips honey brown. Aria could tell by her attire that she had money. "Deon, this is Aria. Money's—"

"*Girlfriend*," she said matter-of-factly, cutting him off.

"Aria," Deon said without a smile.

"Deon," Aria said, matching her tone and rolling her eyes at them both.

Aria carried her bags to her room, her heart began to beat uncontrollably fast as she walked down the hall to Harmony's office. She had no clue what Harmony was going to say to her, or how she was going to explain herself. The guilt she felt was now clouding her mind. How could she do this to her? Harmony had been nothing but good to her from the beginning. Tears threatened to pool in her eyes, but she quickly dried them up. She opened the door to Harmony's office. Then everyone grew silent as her beauty enveloped the room. Her eyes met with Peezy's, who quickly shifted his gaze.

"Oh, excuse me," she said, turning to leave.

"Sit," Harmony said, coldly. "I want you to meet two of my friends and colleagues. D and Derek. They're here to support me and my cause, along with a few others that I may introduce you to." *May?* Aria thought, getting an attitude.

"It's nice to meet you guys. Welcome to the family."

"Likewise," D said.

"What's good with you, Aria?" Peezy asked. He could feel the tension in the room. Aria shrugged.

"I'm okay. Just flew in from New York. I needed a little break."

"I feel you. Well, I'ma catch you all later. D, you ready to roll?" Peezy said, being short and standing to leave. Derek followed everyone, giving Harmony their love as they filed out the door.

Aria sat frozen in her seat. The silence punishing her with every minute that passed by. "Baby, we need to talk," she said, taking the initiative.

"Talk?" Harmony scoffed. "The time to talk was four days ago, or four months ago, or whenever things had gotten so bad that you felt like you needed some time and space to figure things out!" she said coldly. "So now *I* need some time. *I* need some space—a lot of it. There's a few things *I* need to sort out." Harmony chuckled. "Aria, I tried to accommodate you. Nothing was good enough though, was it?"

"Harmony, please just hear—" Harmony held up her hand, silencing her.

"I'm out here in these streets taking chances so that you don't have to, so that we can live the way we want and do whatever we please. Your disregard and inability to be understanding of my position has pushed me far away." Harmony cut her eyes at her. "I put a little money in your account, and I've paid up the bills. I'll holla at you when I feel the need," she said, sliding her fitted cap over her head. Aria stood to her feet.

"This conversation is not over." Harmony laughed and stepped past her.

"What, you want to tell me that you're sorry? That while you were on the other side of the map doing God knows what, you realized that what? You still loved me? Missed me? Bitch, please!"

*WHAP!*

Aria slapped Harmony across the face. She smirked.

"Be mad all you like, but I've made up my mind, Aria," she said, walking to the door. "But just know that you did this to us." She shut the door behind her.

Aria sat down and let her tears fall freely; she was hurt and confused. Had Harmony just left her for good? "Fuck her!" she said aloud, a feeble attempt at salvaging her ego, but deep down she knew that Harmony was the only person that ever loved her genuinely, for no other reason, no motives, no incentives, just love.

\* \* \* \* \* \*

Ginger had not returned any of Harmony's calls, or responded to the notes and fresh set of roses she had sent every few days. It bothered Harmony more than she let on, and even when her body craved some attention, she refused Aria's texts and endless phone calls. Harmony stood in the lobby of the District Attorney's Office and scanned the directory for Ginger's name. She held a single rose in her hand as she boarded the elevator and rode it to the eleventh floor. Harmony smiled at Ginger's secretary, who stood and greeted her with an unreadable expression. She scanned her gray Dolce and Gabbana slacks and powder blue dress shirt.

"Is Mrs. Grand in?" Harmony asked.

"Yes, um—she is. Let me—uh . . . who should I say is—"

"Harmony Reymos is here to see her," she said, ignoring the woman's judgmental stare. Surprisingly, the petite blonde didn't keep her waiting long.

"Right this way, Ms. Reymos." Harmony took in the woodsy smell and bold decor that had caught her off guard. Ginger seemed so sweet and gentle. "Mrs. Grand, Ms. Reymos is here."

"Great, have a seat," Ginger said, not looking up from her paperwork.

"Ms. Reymos, can I get you something to drink? Mrs. Grand, would you like me to brew you some fresh coffee?" Ginger looked up to see who was keeping her nosey secretary in her office for so long, and her eyes locked with Harmony.

"Um no. That's—we're fine. Thank you."

"No thank you," Harmony said, smiling. The woman looked

209

from Harmony to Ginger. *Is our chemistry that obvious?* Harmony thought. The secretary closed the door behind her. Harmony stood abruptly and walked up to Ginger, holding out the rose.

"Thank you, but what are you doing here?" Ginger asked, taking it from her and smelling it. Harmony smiled.

"Damn, Miss Lady. Is it like that?" Ginger had made the decision to stay as far away from her as possible.

"Money, I shouldn't have—"

"Shouldn't have what? Spent time with me and had the most fun you've had in a long time, or for once in your life, followed your heart and not what your—"

"Harmony, please—" Ginger whispered.

Harmony walked around the desk and stood dangerously close to her. The room heated up around them. "Tell me you want me to go, and I'll never bother you again." Ginger looked away. Harmony grabbed her chin and slid her tongue in her mouth. Ginger received it, her body melting like putty. Harmony lifted her up onto the desk, kissing her roughly, passionately. She gripped a fistful of Ginger's soft hair, pulling her head back, kissing and sucking down her neck, and making her give in completely. The moans that escaped her mouth confirmed Ginger's desire for her. Because she had not been touched that way in so long, she instantly soaked the seat of her panties.

*BEEP!*

"Mrs. Grand. Demaci Senior is on line one."

Harmony released Ginger's hair, cursing under her breath.

"Hi, Daddy!" Ginger said excitedly, turning the phone on speaker.

"Hey, baby girl. How are you?"

"I'm fine. What have you been up to? Are we still on for lunch Friday?" Ginger asked. He gave a long sigh.

"Listen, baby girl. Something's come up, but I promise I'll make it up to you." Ginger mouthed every word. He spoke the same words she had been hearing since she was a child.

"Okay, Daddy. Tell mother I send my love," Ginger said, disconnecting the phone call. Harmony smiled at her. "What?"

"Why are you trying to push me away?" Harmony asked.

"Because, it's what I do best," Ginger said, seriously.

"Can I take you to lunch?" Harmony checked her watch. "My treat!"

"Sure. I know this nice place a few blocks up," Ginger suggested.

"Give me a chance." Harmony grabbed her hand.

Ginger smiled but said nothing. She was so unsure of everything at the moment.

# CHAPTER 21

Woo eyed Derek out the corner of his eye as he counted the bundled stacks of tax-free cash that lay on the table. He could see why it was against the law to sell dope. Derek sat across from him studying him intently. They both felt the tension. Harmony had laid down the law and told Derek to chill and all the tension needed to cease. They were a family. It was the only reason Woo was still breathing. Harmony said not to be at his throat, but he had to get it off his chest, or he was going to explode.

"I know you are fucking my little sister, and frankly, I—"

"Correction. I am not fuckin' your sister. I'm falling in love with her, and I don't need you threatening my life, because I have no intentions on hurting her. Nor do I have any ill motives when it comes to her. Plus, I don't take kindly to threats either, but honestly, I'm glad you know, so now we don't have to sneak around. If I'm what she wants, then I'm here for her. If not, I know how to respect her wishes, but until then, all the extra shit is for the birds."

Derek stood, shook Woo's hand, and said nothing. Woo looked up at him. He had lost count. "Twelve thousand and twenty," Derek said.

"Twelve thousand forty," Woo said, returning to the business at hand.

\* \* \* \* \* \*

"You are such a fuckin' liar, Peezy!" Samore barked through gritted teeth.

"Man, whatever, Samore! I'm sick and tired of you accusing me, and lower your voice before you wake up my son."

"You might want to wake him. You have not seen much of him." Samore scoffed.

213

*WHAP!*

Samore's back slammed into the hallway wall.

"Watch your mouth! And don't forget that *I'm* the man of this house. *I* pay all the bills. *I* take care of everything, so let me fuckin' breathe!" Peezy said, feeling guilty. He turned and stormed away, leaving her crying in the dark hallway. He was angry, but it was always easier to be angry than guilty. Aria had a hold on him. She had him out in the streets all times of the night and creeping in early in the morning. She had him right where she wanted him. He couldn't resist her, and they both knew it. He was risking his family, foolishly forgetting what was at stake. Peezy assumed that Samore would stick this out; she always did, but he was clueless that she was growing weary of his lies and infidelity.

Frustrated, Peezy climbed into his car and sped over to Harmony's. Something had come up and needed to be nipped in the bud. He finally arrived at Harmony's place but didn't remember much about the drive over there or when he first entered and took a seat. His mind was still filled with the incident back at home with Samore.

Peezy's nerves were getting the best of him; he could not stop his thoughts or eyes from drifting to Aria. Byou sat waiting with him and Aria in the beautiful home Harmony and Aria shared. Peezy was pretty sure that Byou had caught him staring at Aria more than once. Even he felt the tension in the room and could tell Byou didn't approve of his wandering eye. Peezy and Byou had been good friends for years, but his new status and attitude had changed their relationship. He just wasn't the same; Peezy wondered if all Byou could see in his eyes was guilt and an unhealthy hunger for power, and if so, had she figured out the reason why.

\* \* \* \* \* \*

Harmony pulled up in the circular driveway and hopped out looking fresh in a pair of khaki shorts and a white Polo. Her white leather Tom Ford kicks complemented her outfit. The thick rope chain dangled down her chest, her charm reading LOYALTY in big bold diamond cut letters. She walked into the room where Peezy, Byou, and Aria were already seated. Byou got up and embraced her as she wiped her feet on the rug. "Money! What's good?" She smiled and hugged her tight.

"It's all good," Harmony replied.

Derek and Devin walked in the room, and then so did Deon and Woo. "D!" Deon said.

"Hey, sis, I've missed you," Devin said. They embraced and took their respective seats.

Peezy stood. "I know that things have been busy, and we have not really had time to meet with each other," he said, feeling uneasy as he watched everyone embrace Harmony with love, he and Aria seeming like the oddballs. Jealousy jolted through Peezy from the praise and love Harmony was receiving from everyone. Where was his love? He established this shit. *I built this empire!* he thought. He saw Deon look over at Aria, then cut her eyes. Aria's gaze said it all: *I don't like you either, bitch.*

Harmony plopped down in her old La Z Boy chair after she acknowledged everyone, intentionally leaving Aria out, who watched and sipped from her glass.

Finally, Peezy cleared his throat. "Everybody has met Aria, and I know you and everyone else are wondering why I called this emergency meeting." Peezy smiled and clasped his hands. "We have a problem."

\* \* \* \* \* \*

Aria's Manolo's drummed on the lobby floor of the Heathman

Hotel. She looked left then right. *Where's this bitch at?* Her eyes fell on Deon and she admired her ensemble.

"What's up!" Deon said, trying to hide the coldness in her voice for Woo's sake. He had told her to be easy and trust that Aria was a soldier—that she wouldn't hesitate to pop off.

"Hey!" Aria said, embracing Deon. Her voice turned as icy as a glacier. "Listen, I don't like you, and I don't trust you. But for tonight only, will we be the best of friends. So let's hurry up and handle this business so I can get paid and won't have to be fake any longer than I have to," Aria whispered in Deon's ear, rocking from side to side. Deon pulled back and smiled.

"It's good to know the feelings are mutual, bitch. He is in room 249. The closest I could get was five doors down in room 251."

"Good. Here's your VIP pass, and I took the liberty of ordering our clothes. Neiman Marcus had them sent over," Aria said, looking down at her Cartier watch.

"We have two and a half hours to get to it," Deon said, linking arms with Aria.

\* \* \* \* \* \*

The club was lit and jammed packed as San Diego's elite celebrated the homecoming of Joshua, Biggs' nephew. Woo sat next to Squally and watched Joshua party with this homies. Squally shook his head. "I don't know why that nigga Joshua thinks Peezy is going to hand over his seat on the throne," Squally said as Woo sipped from his drink.

"I don't either," Woo agreed.

"He feels like Peezy should've never gained access to Biggs' position. He thinks only the flesh and blood of Biggs and Emma should run this city," he stated.

"Just because a man has a belief, doesn't mean it's always right."

"He called Peezy a soldier, a peon in other words. I did time with that nigga Joshua up state. He's cut throat," Squally said, sliding his hand under his chin.

"A lot has changed over the years though. Peezy is no peon," Woo responded.

"Joshua ain't either, but like I told Peezy. I know that nigga. What makes him sad, what makes him tick, and what his Achilles heel is."

"And what is that?" Woo asked.

"A bad bitch," Squally replied. Woo laughed.

"Well, that nigga is as good as dead," Woo said, thinking of Deon.

Joshua had been inquiring about the city and Biggs' whereabouts, and who the HNIC was. He felt as though Peezy, not being blood, needed to step down and hand over the keys to the city and all of Biggs' contacts. He wasn't the only one that felt that way, but the only one who was bold enough to say so. Peezy had no intention of doing that; he ran this city, and anybody that posed a threat would be immediately dispatched. Joshua knew that Peezy had manned these streets and fought plenty of wars for his uncle Biggs, and put any to rest at his command. He didn't feel obligated to acknowledge Peezy's position, but what Joshua didn't know was that Peezy wasn't the same thugged out, hot headed, recklessly trigger-happy little nigga he met ten years ago. During those six years, Biggs had taught Peezy everything he knew, and Peezy retained everything the streets had shown him, forming a deadly combination.

\* \* \* \* \* \*

Deon was wrapped in a white Alexander McQueen dress that left nothing unrevealed. She checked the mirror and added her golden wooded accessories. *Okay, the bitch has taste,* Deon thought, in reference to Aria's choice in clothes. She slipped the GHB liquid capsule between her breasts and stepped out of the bathroom.

"I'd rather have a thirty-eight," Deon said.

"You're the bait. I'm gay and don't want his filthy hands all over me."

Deon smirked and admired the crazy swag Aria was draped in. Her BeBe ensemble gripped her curves in the sexiest way. Aria tucked the caliber into her ankle holster, then ran her fingers through her curls. "Ready?"

After flashing her VIP pass, Deon smiled seductively at all the men that parted the crowd for them. They were seated in a booth directly within eyesight of Joshua and his goons. Aria ordered a bottle of Cristal in an attempt to get his attention. It worked.

"Ugh! This shit is nasty," Deon said, taking a sip from her glass. Aria laughed.

"Expand your horizon. This shit cost."

"So. Just 'cause it costs doesn't mean I have to like it," Deon snapped.

"Order something else then. Peezy put a tab at the bar for us." Deon ordered her a bottle of Patron with salt and limes. They sipped and observed Joshua. He mingled for a while, then made his way back to his booth, a swarm of women flowed with high hopes of giving him what he had been dreaming about for the past six years. His eyes danced in the direction of Aria and Deon's booth.

"He's noticed us!" Deon said, anxious to get rid of their problem.

"Good. Let's go dance," Aria suggested.

"Dance?" Deon said, confused.

"Yes, dance. Let's go shake our ass for him and entice him." Deon stood and smoothed her dress down, acknowledging her plan. Joshua's eyes followed them like Aria knew they would. He watched them as they swayed their hips back and forth. Deon gave him the eye a few times, but made sure not to look desperate. They both headed for the bathroom. On the way back to their booth, one of Joshua's goons stepped to them. *Damn, he is fine!* Aria thought. *I'ma fuck him, then blow his brains out.*

As soon as Aria was alone with Joshua's goon, Bun, she let him fuck her brains out, then filled his body with silent lead. She stepped into the hall, then looked down at her watch. "What the fuck!" Aria said under her breath, then knocked on Joshua's door.

* * * * * *

Deon didn't understand why the GHB hadn't knocked Joshua out yet. She forced herself not to cringe from Joshua's lips on her inner thighs. He pulled his gun from under his pillow after hearing the knocks on the door. "Who the fuck is that?" he asked, looking down at Deon. She shrugged.

"Whoever it is, get rid of them so you can finish eating this pussy." Joshua smiled. He opened the door. Aria stared back at him with lust in her eyes. "I fucked your homeboy's little dick ass to sleep. Can I come and join you guys?" Aria asked, stepping in and dropping her trench coat to the floor. Joshua turned around.

Deon smiled and said, "The more the merrier!" She stepped closer to Joshua and kissed him sensually, sliding her tongue in his mouth.

"Damn, lil mama!" he said, setting his gun on the table and picking her up. She winked at Deon who sat stunned at the role Aria was putting on. Aria kissed on his neck, distracting him enough for Deon to spike another drink.

"Come on, ma. Let me go first. You got your nut already," Deon said, faking a smile. Aria laughed.

"Pour up, so I can watch him bang ya back out," Aria said,

rubbing his length. Deon filled their glasses and toasted to his freedom. He was so excited by the two beautiful women that he had let his guard all the way down. Aria kissed all over his body, as Deon lay there rubbing her nipples.

"Come eat this pussy, baby," she said, knowing that he was beginning to feel the effects of the drug." Joshua tried to crawl toward her but felt weak.

"W-what th-the fuuuck. Y-yyou bitches dr-druuuged me," he slurred.

"We did, and Peezy sends his regards," Aria said, grabbing her gun from her trench coat and pulling the trigger.

# CHAPTER 22

Nearly three months had passed since Aria had heard Harmony's voice, and she felt the emptiness her absence left. Aria dialed Harmony's number again, only to receive voicemail. Enraged, she threw her iPhone across the empty office. Every now and then, Aria would come up to the room and sit and reminisce on the love they made and time they spent, but Harmony had emptied it and her closet, leaving nothing but the furniture. Aria pressed her fingers to her temple and closed her eyes. "Calm down," she told herself. Rejection tore Aria in two; her thoughts were becoming more irrational by the minute. *I am going to kill this bitch!* she snapped.

While Aria was out handling business for the team, Harmony was loading her things onto a truck. *How dare she?* Aria thought, retrieving her phone and slamming the door behind her. To make matters even worse, Peezy had not answered his phone in a few days. She was ill and alone. Aria poured her a glass of 100 Grand and turned on the stereo to silence the quietness. She sat on her plush sofa and powered up her iPad. Then she checked Betta's status and Mr. Pratts. She had to keep track of her foes. Panic set in when Mr. Pratt's whereabouts couldn't be found. She picked up the phone and called all around for him. Nothing. Finally she checked the county, who had sentenced him and saw his mug shot. He had aged tremendously over the past two years. He had no new charges under his name, which meant one thing. *I know these muthafuckas didn't.* Aria thought about him forcing himself on Harmony. The sound of Aria's phone ringing brought her out of her reverie. "Hello there," she said seductively.

"Hey, what's up?"

"I want to see you," Aria purred into the phone.

"I can't right now. I'm with Junior." Aria smiled. She missed the little boy, and because she and Harmony were not even on speaking terms, Peezy felt it would be inappropriate.

"Kiss him for me and tell him—" Her words were cut short by the sound of Samore's voice, then the call was disconnected. *So this nigga wants to be a family man now?* Aria thought, clutching the phone in her hand.

\* \* \* \* \* \*

Aria looked down at her cracked screen and pressed IGNORE. Peezy had been blowing her phone up for two days straight. She had business to tend to, and he was on her shit list, along with a few others. She looked up at the county jail and dialed Captain Busby, her inside man.

"Hey, baby. I'm coming inside now. I just pulled into the parking lot," she said, ending the call. Aria adjusted her beige pencil skirt and ran her French manicured fingers over her ruffled white blouse, then sighed. She was in complete turmoil and had not spoken to Harmony in about two and a half months. Aria missed her, and with her stuff gone from her house, she knew they were more than likely through. The fact that Peezy was making very little effort to spend time with her made her regret the feelings she had developed for him. He was going to regret them too. She was going to make sure of it.

Captain Busby met her in the lobby. She handed him a manila envelope filled with cash. She nodded her thanks, then rolled her briefcase into the small room he directed her to. She opened the door and waltzed in. Mr. Pratt's eyes bucked once recognition set in. He jerked on his chains. "You bitch! You set me up. You killed my wife!" Aria placed her hands on her hips slowly and smiled.

"I've missed you too, Frank, but quick question before we get started," Aria said, having a seat across from him and folding her hands. "How does it feel to be raped and beaten at someone else's leisure?" Mr. Pratt jerked toward her again. She laughed. "I made sure you were greeted by the welcome committee once you were dressed out and settled."

"I've been granted an appeal," he said matter-of-factly. "And when I get out, I'm going to kill you and Harmony."

"Correct. You have been granted an appeal, but I can assure you that you will not live to see that life sentence overturned. Pedophiles like you deserve to rot and die in prison," Aria spat.

"Fuck you!"

"The cowardice in you would not allow you to. On second thought, you're not even worthy of my presence. I'll leave the good deed of ending your pathetic life to someone who could use the money." Aria stood to her feet. "Oh, and how does that old saying go?" she asked, snapping her fingers. "Don't drop the soap."

"You fuckin' bitch!" Mr. Pratt yelled, jerking on his shackles and cuffs violently. Aria smiled at his helplessness, then shut the door behind her. She met Captain Busby in the hallway. "Spread the word. I got ten grand for whoever kills this bastard." He nodded and kissed her cheek good-bye.

\* \* \* \* \* \*

Summer was ending and the end of the year was approaching quickly. Six months ago, Harmony had no goals or dreams, just thoughts of being financially secure, but thanks to Ginger, she now had plans. Harmony sat across from Ginger and listened to her vent about work, her mom, and anything else that was bothering her. Whenever she was in her presence, Ginger's beauty captured her, demanding Harmony's undivided attention. The sweet energy that surrounded them made her irresistible. She inspired her on a deeper level, and whenever Harmony wasn't in the streets, she wanted to be nowhere but with her. She had finally moved out of Woo's house and into a penthouse in the heart of downtown. As much as she didn't want to admit it, she wanted to be close to Ginger. Since she removed Aria from her life, a major weight had been lifted off her shoulders. She knew that it was over and hoped that Aria would get the drift. Her intuition was never wrong; somebody else had Aria's mind and body, so her heart would soon follow. Harmony had tried to stick it out, tried to make things right between them. Only to be pushed further away, bruised her ego and hurt her to her core. The energy it took to try to fight the pain left her drained. She had no choice but to go. There was no love there. She felt it.

"Can I get you guys anything else?" the waiter asked.

"No, I'm fine. Harmony?" Ginger asked. She shook her head and smiled.

"What?" Ginger said.

"Nothing. I just noticed that you don't call me Money anymore." Ginger smirked.

"I prefer Harmony. It's just . . . more personal. I don't know. I want to know you, not this facade you have made up for the world to see." Harmony's eyebrows shot up.

"I don't have a facade made up. This is me. Yes, there is another side to me, but it takes time and trust, or disloyalty and disrespect to get to know that person."

"Not everyone is out to hurt you, Harmony." She smiled at Ginger. "That is what I have been trying to tell you." Ginger looked away. Harmony touched her face.

"We've both been hurt, so let's help each other heal," Harmony said, kissing her lips softly.

"It sounds real easy, but we both know it's much more complicated than that."

"What's not complicated when our emotions are involved?"

"Nothing." Harmony's phone buzzed.

"What's up, Woo? Uh yeah, but I am busy at the moment. Let me hit you back." Harmony slipped the phone into her pocket. She could feel Ginger's eyes on her. "Sorry about that." Ginger cleared her throat.

"Harmony, what do you want to do? You're still young, and the skies are still the limit, no matter where you come from. I don't know . . . something just tells me that you want more out of life than to reign in these streets." Harmony sat in silence for a moment. Ginger always had her thinking outside of the box, outside of her comfort zone, and far beyond the streets. This was something no one had done. It was always hustle and hustle hard.

"Well, I dropped out in my senior year and involuntarily started running the streets, and I have not looked back since."

"Well, I'm asking you to think about what you want to do, and in five years, where do you want to be, physically, mentally, and financially." Ginger kissed Harmony's lips. "I have to run. My lunch break is almost over, and I have to make copies and run a few more errands." Harmony stood and helped her into her jacket and wrapped her arms around Ginger.

"When will I see you again?"

"This is a busy week because we are getting ready for a trial, but I will make time, just call me. Bye," she said, kissing her hand and walking off.

"It's never bye. I'll see you later." Ginger smiled.

"I'll see you later."

* * * * * *

Peezy pulled up to Aria's house, furious. She had been ignoring his calls all week. He had to spend some time with Junior and

225

Samore. That was his family, his obligation. She needed to get that through her head; they weren't going anywhere. He came to let her know that even though he was fucking her, he still had a life outside of whatever it was they had, and if she didn't respect it, then just as he had come he would leave. Aria swayed downstairs wrapped in a green silk robe. His manhood throbbed at the sight of her curves and curly jet-black hair that bounced on her shoulders in a mass of curls.

"Why haven't you answered the phone?" he barked, ignoring the feeling rising in his loins.

"I figured you were enjoying being a family man, so I decided to let you do just that," Aria said slickly. Peezy stormed across the room and wrapped his hands around her neck. Aria pushed him off of her. He shoved her into the wall. She had so much control over him, he couldn't help but acknowledge the feelings that lurked beneath his denial. He had never let a random bitch make him even remotely mad, not enough to put his hands on her. There were feelings there and they both knew it and it enraged him.

"Man, I'm out. You trippin'!"

"Peezy!" Aria called. "Don't leave. Please. Harmony, sh-she packed up all her stuff and moved out."

"She what? Why? Why would she leave?" Aria looked at him and could see the fear in his eyes, which to her equaled control. "What did you tell her?" he asked, storming back across the living room.

"I didn't tell her anything," Aria said, scrunching up her face in disgust at his accusation. She would never tell Harmony about their betrayal, and would kill anybody who tried. Aria was going to use any and everything she could to trap Peezy, but telling Harmony was out of the question. "I came home and all of her stuff was gone." Aria couldn't hide it anymore. He could see the way she felt. It was clear. Everything in her demeanor screamed she was falling in love with him.

"Fuck!" he said. This put Peezy in an uncomfortable position. He couldn't just leave her high and dry when he was the reason behind their break up. Only he stood to lose everything, and Aria stood to lose nothing at all. He knew that what they had needed to cease. "Damn, I'm sorry."

"Don't be, 'cause I'm not," she lied. "Now you can have me all to yourself," Aria said softly. Seductively dropping her robe to the floor. Peezy swallowed. He could not resist her. His manhood rose to the occasion. She slid her hand into his sweat pants and dropped to her knees. Aria pulled his swelling length out and began kissing and sucking him viciously.

"Mmmph! Damn, Aria." She spat on his tool, jerked him slowly, then took him into her mouth again. His entire body stiffened, and his head dropped back. He grabbed her head and pumped slowly, making his inches disappear deep into her throat. Not once did Aria gag or choke. Letting her go was not going to be easy, and not only because he didn't want to, but because she didn't plan on letting him.

\* \* \* \* \* \*

Harmony had called Peezy and told him to meet her at some random address downtown. He sat outside the building feeling guilty, his heart beating rapidly. He had no idea why she wanted him to meet her here. He was fighting with his thoughts. How was he going to tell her that he was sleeping with Aria? He had been wrecking his brain on the drive over here, but came up with nothing.

Peezy killed the engine and dropped his head. He tried to think about how things had gotten so out of control; how he had got caught up with his sister's girlfriend. He climbed out of the car and entered the building. The doorman greeted him, checked him in, and showed him where the elevators were. Peezy boarded the elevator, then pressed PH he looked out at downtown through the elevator's windows and smiled. Harmony had come up, partially thanks to him, he thought selfishly. He needed her as much as she needed him. They fed off of each other. Where he was weak, she was strong and vice versa, but now that he had betrayed her and stolen the heart of the woman she loved, he wasn't sure where this would leave their relationship. The adage "bros over 'hos" would be cliché in this situation.

Peezy followed the music, surprised that this was the only door on the entire floor. Harmony answered to his knock with a smile. They had not really been spending much time together, due to the hectic schedules they both kept. Time seemed to elude them, aside from the two days a week they met to go over the business and update him on the activities.

"Hey, P!" He looked into her eyes. *She doesn't know,* he thought, diverting his eyes from hers. She caught it. "What's the matter, bruh?" she asked, sensing his mood almost immediately.

"What's good, P?" Byou said, walking into the foyer to greet him. She looked at Harmony, then at him, feeling the weird energy that was confirmed by Peezy's delayed greeting. "You good?" Byou asked.

"Umm yeah, me and Samore are going through it," he lied.

"Sorry to hear that," Harmony said. "Is that all?"

"I brought some good kush. Roll up, B," Peezy said, changing the subject. Byou halfheartedly smiled and took the bag from him, leading him into the penthouse.

"I invited you here because I wanted you to see my new spot."

"It's nice," Peezy said, taking in the sexy decor.

"But before you step off of my marble floor, please remove your shoes. I know they ran you a couple hundred dollars, but this is *my* first spot, and I want to do things my way. Feel me?" Peezy put his hands up in surrender.

"I got you. When were you going to tell me that you moved out?"

"I wanted to get right first. I crashed at Woo's for a while until I found me a nice cozy place to start over." Peezy's jaw tightened, obviously jealous of her and Woo's relationship. Everyone could see they were close. Harmony was always with him, and she confided in him. If she wasn't a striking resemblance of Peezy, you'd think Woo was her brother. *I don't like that nigga,* he thought to himself as the plush carpet greeted his feet. The vanilla bean marble and dark wood cabinets matched the chocolate leather decor.

"Whoever decorated this place went all out. I know you didn't do this," Peezy said playfully.

"Hahaha. I picked out the color scheme and Helena, my interior decorator did the rest. I told her she could do it big."

"And that she did," Woo said, coming down the hall and into the living room.

"'Sup," Peezy greeted him dryly and declined the beer he held out.

"So why did you move?" he asked bluntly. Harmony sighed.

"Things between me and Aria—it's—*she* has changed. Things have changed between us. She's not the same loving, attentive woman I fell in love with. I've never been the type to fuss and fight, which is all she seemed to want to do." Woo chuckled.

"My ex was the same way, or at least I thought she had changed, until I found out she was fucking with some off brand nigga from Watts." Peezy looked over at Woo, trying to read him, trying to see if he knew anything or meant something by the comment he didn't ask for.

"What's up, Peezy?" Derek asked as he too walked into the room and joined in on the conversation.

"I can't call it. Where is Deon and her other half?"

"Oh, they are on the roof. Yeah, ya sis got a pool up there. You can fit a hundred 'hos in it too," Derek said, clowning. Everybody laughed.

"So you done with her?" Peezy asked, ceasing the laughter.

"Why? You wanna smash?" Woo asked. Everybody burst into laughter. Harmony watched Peezy who didn't find the joke funny.

"Nah, I was just wondering, because I know how much you care about her."

"I did, but now I feel as though she doesn't. So I've washed my hands with her. I know that she probably has another bitch somewhere. Somebody has her heart and mind because they no longer belong to me, and I kind of require those things when I am with someone. Her disloyalty is what caused me to move out and move on. My tolerance for that type of shit stays at zero," she said, looking at him.

*If she doesn't know, she suspects something,* Peezy thought.

* * * * * *

Harmony decided to take Ginger's advice and finish out her senior year. She had plans. Peezy and the rest of the team agreed that it would be a smart move. So she sat in the library studying for her Social Studies test. Harmony had picked up where she left off, as if she had not been running the streets for the past two years. Her grade point average jumped to the top, leaving her counselor no choice but to place her in honors courses. Most students had worked extremely hard to get to where Harmony had seemingly jumped to. Her crazy swag and charisma had some of the girls in school questioning their sexuality, but Harmony was focused and Ginger had her attention and spare time. Her phone buzzed, breaking her concentration. She checked her phone and shook her head, deleting Aria's text. She had not gotten the picture yet. Harmony never answered any of her calls or responded to her text; it had been almost four months, and she still had not moved on. Now that Peezy had decided to let Aria put in work to get a little money, she thought that this was her shot to rekindle their flame. Not. Harmony thought it was a good idea. She never wanted to see her hurting for nothing or going without. Plus she didn't need to be getting her hands dirty in any kind of way, so Aria stepping up made things easier for everyone. Harmony was trying to reach heights most chicks in her position hadn't even thought of. Heights that nobody could snatch from under her.

# CHAPTER 23

The wind blew Harmony's white T-shirt against her skin. She stared out at the dark marina with so much on her mind. "I should've worn a jacket," she said to Peezy, who was awkwardly quiet. He seemed to always be tense and timid as of late, like there was always something on his mind. Harmony had never been married, but she wasn't a fool. It was more than his problematic marriage on his mind. She just wished he would let her in.

"He should be here in a minute. He is never late."

"Good because I am starving." The sound of gravel crunching under tires made them turn toward the black Navigator truck approaching them slowly. Peezy looked down at his Rolex and smirked. He and Harmony climbed into the backseat of the truck. The rich smell of Cuban cigars stained the air.

"Maurice, I have someone I would like you to meet." The man reached across the seat and shook Harmony's hand firmly.

"Nice to meet you. I've heard so much about you."

"Only good things, I hope," she said, smiling.

The man chuckled, then reached in his breast pocket. "I have." He looked back at Peezy, then pulled out a cigar and lit it. "I assume that I can speak freely, being that Philip has brought us together." Peezy and Harmony nodded. The driver handed him a manila envelope. "Here's half. I will give you the rest when his death certificate is printed and signed. I would go into details, but just know that this is personal. It's nothing like the betrayal of a friend. I want him dead by Friday. I want it clean and quiet." Peezy nodded.

"My sister will make sure it gets done." Maurice smiled. Harmony listened as Peezy gave him some updates about some things Harmony knew nothing about, and in return Maurice gave him all the details about the narcotics unit and what they had planned for the next month. They shook hands, and he thanked Peezy for keeping the violence down in the streets, then wished him well.

"Who was that, and why did you tell him that?" Harmony asked.

"That was the Mayor, and don't worry, I am going to take care of it."

"The Mayor? Seriously?"

"Yes, I'm serious. In our line of business you have to have people in high places indebted to you and deep in your pocket. I wanted him to meet you and now be in debt to you as well, just in case life happens."

"What do you mean if life happens?"

"Tomorrow is not promised, lil sis. You live by the streets, nine times out of ten you die in them."

\* \* \* \* \* \*

Peezy opened the door and slid out of his jacket. It was early, almost dinnertime, but strangely the house didn't smell of food. It was eerily quiet. When he rounded the corner, Samore was sitting on the couch with a drink in her hand. Even though Peezy had made sure not to stay out late and spent more time with her and Junior, she had withdrawn, becoming distant. It was out of her character. Normally she would be climbing up Peezy's body and into his arms. He missed that.

"Hey, baby!" he said, bending down to kiss her. Samore jerked her head away. He looked into her eyes and saw a trace of tears.

"Baby? Don't baby me, Peezy!" she said, throwing an envelope at his face.

"What's this? What's wrong?"

Samore scoffed. "*You're* wrong, and I'm dumb. I told you what that bitch said about taking you from me, and you just couldn't respect my wishes. I wouldn't even be as hurt if it was another bitch. Dammit, Peezy! All I ever did was love you. What did I do to deserve this shit? Nothing!" Samore yelled, storming down the hall and into their room, slamming the door behind her. Peezy picked up the envelope and sat down. His heartbeat picked up as pictures of him and Aria leaving her house, kissing, hugging, holding hands while shopping, and dining fell into his lap.

"Samore!" Peezy yelled, running down the hall. "Baby, please. Just listen—" Peezy's words got stuck in his throat. He didn't have an explanation. He was caught. He stormed into Junior's room. "Samore, where is my son?" he yelled. Samore said nothing. She had packed their stuff and taken him to her mother's house. She was done and couldn't do it anymore. Peezy beat and kicked on the door calling her name. She didn't respond. He knew there was no way in. After he had ran up in so many niggas' houses and tied up their family, he made it his business to protect his own. All the doors were thick oak wood. "Open the door, baby. Please. I'm sorry."

Peezy walked into the living room and paced back and forth. *Did you really think that you'd be able to hide it forever?* he asked himself, running his hand over his face. "Fuck!" He looked at the photos again. *Who took these? Had Samore called Harmony?* So many questions ran through his head. Peezy stormed back down the hall. "Samore. Baby, please talk to me. Baby, say something please." Her silence left him feeling ill. He grabbed his coat, then left out the door. Samore's silence scared him. He never meant to hurt her. He loved her. She had bore his only child. She was everything to him. Samore stayed down when no one else would or knew how. *Damn!* he thought as he swerved through traffic. He knew he had fucked up.

* * * * * *

235

Aria opened the door with a smile. She knew that Samore had received the photos of her and Peezy early this morning and she would be devastated. She had instructed Ragen, her private investigator, to drop them in the mailbox once Peezy left the house. And just as she suspected, he was at her door step, caught deeper in her web. "What's the matter?" she asked.

"This is," he said, shoving the photos in her hand. Aria pretended to flip through them. She had picked each one carefully. She suppressed the triumphant smile that wanted to stretch across her face.

"Who took these?" she asked angrily. Peezy was pacing the floor.

"I don't know. I guess Samore had someone following us. I know she is gone now. She wouldn't even talk to me. Damn!" he said. Aria looked at Peezy, anger surging through her. *That's what yo ass get for fucking playing with my feelings,* she thought.

"Does Harmony know?" she asked, trying to sound concerned. She knew Samore was weak and would run like a bruised animal.

"Man, I don't know. This shit is all fucked up. She took Junior and is probably going to be on some bullshit with my son." Aria went over to the bar and poured him a drink. *I told that 'ho I would take what I pleased, and if he thought that I was going to let him play me to the left, he had another think coming.* Aria handed Peezy a glass of Jack Daniels.

"Here, don't worry about that. We'll cross that bridge when we get there. Relax, gather your thoughts. I'm here for you." Peezy looked at her and smiled.

"I can't help but worry, babe," he said, chugging his glass. "Pour me another one, please." Peezy sat down. He wasn't sure where they would go from here, but he knew that it was going to take some time for Samore to forgive him. Peezy sipped from the glass. His eyes lingered on Aria. He decided that he wouldn't completely shut Aria out; he needed her and he knew it. Even though he tried to deny it,

Peezy knew she had become just as much a part of him as he had her. Aria stood in front of him, then slowly dropped to her knees and unbuckled his pants. She gave him her all, sucking and swallowing him with ease until he released his anger and frustration down her throat.

\* \* \* \* \* \*

Aria's Louboutins drummed on the lobby floor of the Embassy Suites hotel. She had not seen Harmony in almost four months, and the mere thought of seeing her face brought on a swarm of butterflies. Harmony had not been attending the meetings they had scheduled, or by the time she got there she was gone. It hurt to know that she was intentionally dodging her, and even more because she was confused about the feelings she had for her. When Peezy stepped to her for her expertise, she jumped at the invitation to be in Harmony's presence. Because she and Deon had executed their last job without a flaw, it impressed the team, and they figured it would be to their advantage to have them work together. In her arrogance she felt as if they needed her, when in actuality she was taking Harmony's place as a gunner.

When Aria walked in the room, everyone greeted her with a dry hello or head nod. She sighed when she looked around to see that Harmony was not in attendance. Woo lit a blunt and passed it to Deon. They never said it, but the chemistry between them was undeniable. Aria looked at Woo, and they smirked. *She is hot*, Aria thought. *But I still don't like the bitch.* She cut her eyes at Deon.

"Sorry I'm late," Harmony said, coming into the room with a fly Todds leather backpack slung across her shoulder. "What's up? Did I miss anything?"

"Heeey!" Deon said, standing to hug Harmony. They had become close. Whenever Harmony and Woo were together, she was never too far away. A bolt of jealousy shot through Aria as she watched them embrace.

"What's up, y'all!" she said, setting her back pack down. Harmony slapped her hands together, then rubbed them against each other. "First line of business. I'm going on a little vacay for two weeks, so I will need the books and stuff in order for me when I get back next Friday."

*To where? With who?* Aria thought, making a mental note to put Ragen on her.

"I got you," Derek said.

Peezy's jaw tightened. *She comin' up in here like she runnin' shit.* He was avoiding Aria's stare, who had noticed and felt the sudden tension rise toward Harmony.

"Secondly, them West Coast niggas are skimming off the top of everything."

"How?" Deon asked.

"I don't really know, but our numbers keep coming up short."

"Don't worry. Me and D are on it," Byou assured. Devin scrunched up his face.

"They have some real ego issues too. Real disrespectful dudes." Derek smirked.

Peezy sat silently as everyone gave their reports along with Aria, who sat with her long legs crossed, willing Harmony to look her way.

"Well," Peezy said, once everyone had spoken. "Aria is on standby if you guys need an extra hand, being that Harmony will be out of town. But I need you two for an assignment in the next week." Deon rolled her eyes.

"It doesn't take a rocket scientist to pull a trigger," Deon murmured.

Aria caught the look but not her actual words, but flipped her a bird anyway.

"The feeling's mutual," Deon barked. Aria dug into her Prada bag and pulled out some trail mix. Peezy dropped his head.

"Deon, I need you on this. I need you guys to get along. These are very dangerous people, and this job has to get done properly. It's going to be the first hit I do for this client, and I need him on my roster, feel me?"

"Gotcha," Deon said smartly.

"He is coming into town for a charity banquet. Get him drunk, drug him, and tie him up. I don't care, but I need him alive," Peezy said, looking at Aria, who saluted him. The room fell awkwardly silent. Normally after their meeting they'd catch up on each other's life, but Aria's presence changed the atmosphere.

Aria turned to look at Peezy, then stood to her feet. "Anything else?" she asked. Peezy looked across the room at Harmony. A flashback of him fucking Aria from the back seeped into his mind and plagued him with guilt. Aria's eyes were on him as Harmony looked at them. He cleared his throat. He couldn't read Harmony like he used to.

"Yeah, meeting adjourned," Harmony said. Aria's eyes shifted to Woo then Deon, who was mean mugging her.

"See you in a few, bestie," Aria said sarcastically, grabbing her bag and swaying out of the room.

Peezy closed his eyes because they would follow her ass out the door if he didn't. Deon smacked her lips. "Ugh! I don't like that bitch coming in here like this is the damn red carpet. Trying to be cute."

"Only for you, Money," Devin said, laughing.

"Man, I'm done with that lady," Harmony said.

"You better be, 'cause she don't mean you no good."

"That bitch is a grade-A psycho. I can see it in her eyes," Derek commented.

"Nah, she is a stone-cold killer," Byou said.

"Now I agree with that. Aria is a heartless bitch when it comes to her murder game, but I still got love for her, so take it easy on her. She takes some time to get used to," Harmony said in her defense.

"Says the one she shitted on," Deon said. Harmony smiled.

"I got this one, Deon. I'm over her; I've moved on."

"She hasn't." Everyone burst into laughter.

Aria stood at the door and wiped away a tear as she heard the team talking down about her.

"Deon! Ay, I'm gone. I'll see y'all in a few," Harmony said, leaving.

"Yeah and she might just be the one to save one of y'all ass while y'all ragging on her," Peezy said, disrupting their fun and walking out.

\* \* \* \* \* \*

"Nice car," Aria said, eyeing the new white Bentley coupe.

"Aria, what do you want?" Harmony asked, annoyed.

"I miss you. Are you ever going to forgive me?" she asked, following her.

"Forgive you for what?" Harmony responded. Aria grew quiet. They had never spoken in depth about why she left, but they both knew they were at a place where they were never coming back from. Only Aria's pride is what made her hold on, deceiving her all along. Although she loved Harmony, her heart now belonged to Peezy. *I'm not letting her go that easily,* she thought.

"My point exactly, but what's understood doesn't need to be explained," Harmony said coldly, popping her locks. Aria looked in the front seat at the chocolates and pink teddy bear and her heart filled with jealousy and desperation.

"Harmony, listen. I know that I shut down and stopped being who you fell in love with, but listen . . . I—"

"Aria!" Harmony yelled. "Stop it with the water works, okay? This time it is not going to work. I am not a yo-yo or some toy. You can't string me along, or pick me up when you get bored. I'm done. It is over. We're finished."

# CHAPTER 24

Aria's beaded Givenchy ensemble wrapped around her frame and sparkled in the light, catching everyone's eye, especially Mr. Cox's. He had requested her company after an hour of them eye fucking each other from across the room. She lifted her champagne glass to Deon, who sat across the room fuming. Aria had made sure to piss her off right before the banquet. She had plans, and Deon was never good at masking her emotions, which made her unapproachable. Aria needed to be the one to snag Mr. Cox for her plans to work. She had mingled with just about everyone, even the mayor and his family. Now she had her targets right where she needed them. Mr. Cox whispered in her ear. She giggled. Aria knew that once he touched her freshly shaved treasure, he wouldn't be able to resist her. She had planned to make him succumb to her seduction, so panties wouldn't be necessary. He stood and buttoned his jacket, then led the way up to his suite. Everyone was enjoying the banquet, but Aria had murder on her mind. Aria stripped him out of his expensive threads before the door could shut behind them. He surprisingly grew in size as she bit on his nipple and shoved him on the bed. He licked his lips.

"You are so beautiful," he said lasciviously, taking her full beauty in.

"Then fuck me!" she barked. Aria mounted him, letting her wetness touch his length.

"Wait. Let me g-get a condom," he said breathlessly, seeking out his suitcase. She reached inside her bra, walked up behind him, and stuck Mr. Cox in the neck with a sedative. She backed up as his body swayed back and forth. He stumbled forward and dropped onto the floor with a thud. Aria dragged his heavy body onto the couch and tied him up. *Mission accomplished*, she thought.

Aria stripped out of her dress down to pair of boy shorts and bra, then opened Mr. Cox's window and shimmied out onto the ledge to the room she rented for Deon. Then she texted her phone 911. Deon came into the dark room in a rush. Aria had been standing behind the door waiting on her. She hit her in the back of the head with her glock, sending Deon crashing to the floor. She bolted the door, then pounced on her like a feline. The pencil skirt Aria chose for her gave Deon little room to fight her off. She knocked Deon back down to the floor. "You were smart not to trust me."

*WHOP!*

"But foolish to think that I wouldn't see about your ass for trying to vote me out and plant seeds in Harmony's head to turn her against me."

"Harmony doesn't want your psychotic ass!" Deon said, pushing back and then head-butting her. The sharp blow blurred Aria's vision and sent the gun sliding across the hardwood floor. Deon crawled away.

"Psychotic? I will show you psychotic," Aria said, rushing her.

Deon kicked Aria in the chest and sent her flying back, then desperately crawled toward the gun. She was hurt and could feel herself slipping into unconsciousness. Aria was on her in seconds.

*WHOP!*

"I am enjoying this more than I thought I would."

*WHOP!*"

Deon rolled over and looked at Aria. "I'll see you in hell, bitch," she managed to say, before darkness overcame her. Aria dragged Deon's body into the bathroom and dumped her body into the tub. She then poured acid over her body. Deon's skin melted off her bones like a stick of butter bubbling into liquid. This made it easy to send her existence rushing down the drain and removing any trace of her presence. Aria shimmied back across to Mr. Cox's room where she got dressed, then dialed Peezy.

"Hey, I've done my part. He's tied up and out cold. The room number is 1402," she reported.

"Okay good," Peezy replied.

"Oh, and for future reference, I'd rather not go on a job with her if you can help it."

"It's business, baby." Peezy laughed.

"Okay, okay. Will I see you later?"

"Of course."

\* \* \* \* \* \*

Aria sat in the middle of her California king bed, anger surging through her. Peezy had not called or answered any of her texts. Her rational thinking was going out of the window as she began to blow up his phone.

"What!" he finally answered.

"Why in the fuck didn't you come over last night? I waited up for you; I'm still waiting."

"Well, keep waiting." Peezy hung up. He had other things to handle and Aria's constant calls and demanding texts to see him were becoming a bit much.

\* \* \* \* \* \*

"Just when things start coming together for us, here comes an unexpected blow," Peezy complained, upon learning that Deon was missing in action. Harmony stood beside him on the balcony, glancing at him as he kept flexing his jaw.

"Relax, we have no idea what is going on, so let's not speak on it. I have men searching high and low for her. Plus the police are doing all they can."

"You're right," he said, sighing. "How's school?"

"School is easier than I imagined it would be. I had planned on taking Ginger to the Cayman Islands, but now I don't think I should leave with something like this going on. It just doesn't feel right. Like I'm deserting my girl Deon."

"Is it serious?"

"I like her a lot, but I am taking it slow. We are both broken, and I know that hurt people hurt people, which is the last thing either one of us deserves."

"You're right. But listen, if you're feeling her like that, don't let her down because of this street shit. I'll hold it down as always."

"Yeah?"

"Yeah, man. I got you."

"How are Samore and Junior? I miss my nephew." Peezy closed his eyes, and Aria popped in his head.

"Samore changed her number and made it clear that she doesn't want to see me. We are going through it. She wants full custody of Junior."

"What! Why didn't you tell me?"

"It's difficult. You know sometimes you let your desires and pride block reality and what's really important. I was being selfish. I forgot how much I loved her until she was gone."

"Damn. I guess the old saying is true, huh?" Harmony patted Peezy on the back. "Let me go check on Woo. He is losing it," Harmony said, stepping back inside. She sat next to Woo, who lay still on the sofa. Tears fell down the sides of his face.

"It's like she was here one minute, then gone the next," he said. Harmony had never seen Woo show any emotion other than happiness or anger. "No good-bye, or I love you? She would not have left without saying at least that." Devin had locked himself in her condo, refusing to answer the door or his phone. The absence of Deon's quietness was spreading confusion and pain throughout the team. Harmony was at a loss for words. She wasn't the type of person to console someone, or say something stupid like "everything is going to be okay." The one person that had consoled her had betrayed her. All she could say was: "We will get to the bottom of this." And vowed to do all she could to make sure of it.

\* \* \* \* \* \*

Harmony watched Ginger strut across the deck of the yacht in the sexiest bikini she had ever seen. Her physique was flawless, and the honey blonde blow out flew behind her in the island wind. She smiled once she caught Harmony's stare. It felt good to get away from the stress of the streets, and Deon's sudden disappearance. Ginger needed an escape from the stress of her job and pressure her mother was putting on her to rise up and make Assistant DA. This past week she had been with Harmony, and life seemed easier. She could relax, take off her shoes, and be Ginger. It had been almost a year since they first met, and she had to admit that she was falling for her. Hard and fast. Although Harmony wasn't exempt, she promised herself she wouldn't let Ginger know that she was already crazy about her. She had foolishly wore her heart on her sleeve with Aria, a mistake she would never ever make twice.

"Let me help you with that," Harmony said, taking the sun tan lotion from her. The feelings that raced over Ginger's body whenever they touched was like heroin shooting into a first-time user's veins. Harmony breathed down Ginger's back, making it arch. Moans escaped her throat. She wanted Harmony so bad. A light ache began to throb between her thighs. Ginger tilted her head and closed her eyes. The soft kisses Harmony placed on her neck ignited a fire throughout her body that spread like a forest fire. Ginger was lost in Harmony's touch, soaking the seat of her bikini. The smell of her Polo cologne invaded her senses. She left a trail of fire across her back, then around to her lips, piercing the bottom one with her teeth. Ginger opened her eyes and stared deep into Harmony's eyes.

"I want you so bad," Ginger admitted.

"Me too, but I don't want to rush. I want you to be sure you're ready," she said, restraining herself.

"I'm sure, Harmony." Ginger grabbed her hand, stood to her feet, and led the way to their cabin suite. They said nothing as they undressed each other. Harmony laid her down gently, taking in her full C cups and silky butter-tanned skin. Her body was something like a goddess. Ginger's eyes fell low as Harmony kissed and sucked down her body. She lifted her long legs into the air, then dropped them into a split. Images of Aria tried to pop into her head, but she quickly removed her from her thoughts as Ginger enticed Harmony's hunger for her. She wanted to feel the ecstasy that she knew Harmony could provide. She grinned at Ginger. Harmony knew from the look in her eyes that from this moment things between them would be different. She promised herself that she would not get lost in this beautiful, intelligent, *married* woman's world. Before she could bury her head in her wetness, Ginger grabbed her face.

"Harmony, promise me you won't hurt me. Please," she asked.

"I promise," Harmony whispered.

Hours of lovemaking followed, their bodies were in sync, something Harmony had never experienced before. As they lay tangled in the sweat-filled sheets, both out of breath and satisfied, a comfortable silence filled the room.

"I thought you said that you weren't into women?" Harmony commented. Ginger chuckled.

"I'm not, or I wasn't. But that doesn't mean I have never been with one before. My college days were pretty wild," she said, smiling. Harmony kissed Ginger's shoulder. She was overwhelmed by this woman in every way. Everything about her was perfect.

Harmony had no idea that she was already lost in her world, and there was no turning back.

* * * * * *

Devin sat on Deon's plush sofa and rewound the tape from the night before the banquet for the thousandth time. Harmony had paid almost a hundred grand for the tape and had to call in a few favors. The police had no leads, and in his opinion, weren't really doing too much of anything. He watched Deon enter the room, and ten minutes later, Aria came out of Mr. Cox's room and knocked on the door. Then she pulled out her phone and tried to reach her just like she had said over and over. Devin paused the video. *She died in that room,* he thought, rewinding the last moment of her life again. The sound of the doorbell broke through his misery. He shuffled over to the door and looked through the peephole. It was Derek and Woo.

"Devin, open the door, man." Derek banged. Tears pricked his already bloodshot, swollen eyes. He had not spoken to anyone in almost three weeks, until Harmony came to drop off the tape this morning. Devin slid the chain from its holder and unlocked the bolts. Woo's eyes swelled with tears as memories of Deon swarmed him. The scent that wafted into his nose made his heart sink. *I can't do this.* He let the tears fall as he turned to walk away. Devin dropped his head. He knew how much Woo loved his sister, and approved of him taking her hand in marriage. Her not being here was wreaking havoc on them all. Derek avoided Devin's stare in an attempt to resist the tears he had yet to shed. He always had to be the strong one, always had been holding everyone up, but this load was too heavy to carry. Devin looked at him.

"She is gone, bruh." He sobbed. "I can feel it." Derek sighed and took his baby brother into his arms. Finally, he let the tears fall. "Something happened in that room and when I find out, I'm going to kill everybody who was involved." Devin and Deon had a connection. This, Derek knew. When Katrina hit, Deon knew that Devin hadn't drowned with the rest of their family. "He's alive. I can feel him," Deon had stressed. Derek went back a few days later and found Devin trapped, soaked, and badly dehydrated, but he was alive.

\* \* \* \* \* \*

Harmony planned a beautiful memorial service for Deon with so many flowers you could barely see the casket. She had done it all out for Deon, whom she had come to know and love like a sister. The service was very emotional and strictly for the team. Byou sat on the sidelines. She had gotten in her car and drove until she ran out of gas. Her heart was broken as she watched everyone mourn her beloved friend. She had gained a new love and respect for Harmony as she wept for Deon like she was family. Byou had lost everything in Katrina, and to see the last of her family be picked off by the ruthlessness of the streets, one by one, made her hurt like no other. She decided it was time she moved on. She had more than enough money saved to live a normal life, and right now that sounded like the smartest thing to do. The streets wouldn't claim her life like they had with so many of her loved ones. She would make her announcement. Byou was done.

\* \* \* \* \* \*

Aria was growing more and more impatient with Peezy, who seemed detached and distant. Something she made sure to take note of. He barely answered his phone, or had a thousand excuses when he did. Or sometimes he would flat out say he wasn't in the mood. Only when he wanted to come over and get his dick wet, was he the least bit cooperative. She knew his sudden change in attitude stemmed from his little family visits with Samore, whom he begged relentlessly for forgiveness. Aria also made a note to take care of her. But now Aria sat alone in her huge house stewing. *So what. I'm not good enough anymore. Does he think he can just use me up, then throw me away when he is done? I got something for his ass.* Her phone vibrated on the bar.

"Hello?" she answered.

"Where you at, ma?" he asked. Aria gripped her drink.

"I'm at home, Peezy. Why? What could you possibly want?"

"Girl, you know what I want. Go freshen up for a nigga. I'm on my way."

"Don't keep me waiting, nigga," she said, forcing the malice out of her voice. Aria gulped down her vodka, then headed upstairs to shower. She sprayed Versace on her pulse points and added a light layer of makeup, then wrapped a silk robe around her naked frame.

An hour later, Peezy came in with his spare key and up the steps where Aria lie in wait for him. In seconds he was undressed and all over her.

"Did you miss me?"

"Nigga, you know I've missed you, so stop asking stupid ass questions and get in this—"

"Don't ruin it with your smart mouth."

"Ruin it? Shut up, Peezy," she barked, pulling him onto the bed and swallowing him whole, forcing his girth to rise to the occasion. She slid down onto his manhood after she worked him over. Peezy had his hands behind his head while she rode him. *This nigga think he got it made, like he is some king or something*, Aria thought, her blood boiling to the top.

*WHAP!*

"You must think I'm some kind of toy or something?" Aria asked, slapping Peezy hard across the face.

"Bitch, what the f—"

*WHAP!*

"Nigga, shut the fuck up. You must have lost your damn mind," Aria said, grinding harder on his length, pinning him to the bed, making his toes curl. "I don't give a damn what you got going on in these streets, but besides Junior, I should be your number one priority!" she yelled, slapping Peezy across the face again.

*WHAP!*

The crazed look in her eyes made him leery of speaking his mind. "Did you forget that I was fine until you came along sticking your dick where it didn't belong, seducing me away from your sister?"

*WHAP!*

Peezy grabbed both of Aria's hands. "Stop hitting me, girl." She lifted a little, then dropped all her weight down onto his girth, making him moan in frustration.

"I refuse to let you play me, nigga. I'm not going anywhere, so get used to it. Make room on your busy ass schedule." Peezy grabbed Aria by her hair, then wrapped his hands around her throat.

"Bitch, don't nobody run me," he said, thrusting deep inside of her, pulling her close to his face. "The sooner you get that through your head, the better off you will be." Aria smiled at him, but her smile wasn't that of a sane woman. He was losing control, and he knew at that moment that he was in way over his head.

# CHAPTER 25

Because Aria seemed to be the only one who was emotionally stable, Peezy decided to send her along with his soldiers to make sure things got handled properly. Harmony refused to get her hands dirty anymore. Aria was ruthless and very much capable. She had almost forgotten how exciting it was to be in the midst of the action. Not to mention being the new enforcer and street reporter. She was graced with Harmony's presence more often, and whenever she was in the room like now, her heart beat drummed against her chest with anticipation. She was always dressed in some expensive threads with that fresh ass Caesar cut. The love that she thought she had lost for Harmony seemed stronger than ever.

Yeah, Peezy was still fucking her on a regular, but she knew he didn't love her, not the way Harmony had. She had multiple pictures of his weekends with Junior that included him and Samore arguing and him pleading with flowers that she refused. It sickened her to know that Peezy had played her into thinking that they would have something more special than what she and Harmony had. It angered her that she had allowed herself to get caught up and lose the best thing that had ever happened to her.

Whenever she was in the room with Harmony, she never once looked in her eyes or at her stunning beauty that had not too long ago left her floored and weak for her. She saw the passion marks on Harmony's neck. Jealousy surged through Aria as she thought about the pictures that Ragen, her PI, brought her from the little rendezvous she had with Ginger in the Cayman Islands. She could not believe that Harmony was fucking that snob, Ginger Demasci. The Mayor's daughter. Aria paused as her thoughts took control, causing her to stumble over her words and blink away the tears that surprisingly formed. Aria cleared her throat and finished her report, then quickly excused herself, her Jimmy Choo's pounding on the bar's cement floor.

\* \* \* \* \* \*

Peezy had been stewing on coming clean with Harmony for the past week. Aria's sporadic behavior, pop up visits, and threats were really putting him in a crazy position. He felt like she was intentionally torturing him. As much as he hated to admit it, he had feelings for Aria. He was emotionally divided, and the stress of his betrayal was eating away at him. Harmony ordered a double shot of Patron.

"You want something?"

"Yeah, a double shot of Jack," he said to the bartender. His phone buzzed.

> ***Aria:*** *Meet me @ my house in twenty minutes.*
> *Be late & I swear U will regret it.*

Peezy read the text from Aria, then looked at his watch. He sighed, thanked the bartender, and dropped the whiskey into his throat.

"You good?" Harmony asked, sensing his mood. Peezy sighed again.

"Yeah, I'm good. I gotta run though, but I am going to get up with you later, sis." He stood and dropped a twenty on the counter.

"Peezy!" Harmony called after him. "One day you will tell me what is really going on." Peezy dropped his head. A sure sign of guilt.

"Yeah, one day I will," he said and walked out the bar. He drove to Aria's house and stormed inside.

"Look, we have to end this," he said. Aria laughed in his face.

"End this? Yeah, *right*."

"No. For real, Aria."

"Okay. Well, I'll just tell Harmony myself what we have been doing every night and most mornings in her bed, in her house, since your bitch ass suddenly can't handle the guilt." Peezy pounced on Aria, smacking her hard in the face.

"You won't tell her anything."

"If I do then what?" Aria taunted, seemingly unfazed by the blow. "Or how about I tell her that you are the reason things between us didn't work out."

*WHAP!*

Aria took the blow, then laughed at him mockingly. "Save your energy, nigga. It can be better spent on you helping me get Harmony back." Peezy scoffed.

"My sister doesn't want you, girl. She has moved on." He tried to hurt her with his words as hers had hurt him.

"Nobody moves on from me. *I'm that bitch!*" Aria screamed, knocking everything off the bar. Peezy grabbed Aria's arms and restrained her. She kissed him as tears ran down her face. His body reacted to her touch in a way he so badly wished he could fight. Peezy lifted her onto the counter and ripped her dress off, kissing her back angrily. He flipped her onto her stomach and shoved himself forcefully into her wetness; he hated the effect she had on him. Aria, however, loved the fact that she had Peezy right where she needed him to be. Literally.

\* \* \* \* \* \*

Woo had just flown back in town from upstate visiting with Betta. He had sent his love to Harmony, but sparked major suspicion within Woo. Aria was the last person to see Deon alive, but what was her motive? He couldn't think of one, but would definitely check into it. His thoughts were heavy as he stood outside waiting on Harmony.

Ten minutes later, Harmony pulled up in her Bentley with Derek in the passenger seat. He put his things in the trunk, then climbed into the backseat. After they exchanged pleasantries, they rode in silence. After a few minutes had passed, Harmony pulled over at some mom and pop restaurant and they climbed out. Woo was the first to break the comfortable silence.

"Betta says he loves you and to keep your head in those books," Woo said.

"Damn I miss him." Harmony sighed.

"Ay, who's Betta?" Derek asked.

"My cousin. He's serving time upstate on some trumped up charges," Woo said.

"Damn. Ay, can't your lawyer chick help him out?" Derek asked.

"I don't know." Harmony shrugged. "But now that you mention it; I'ma holla at her." She missed Betta. He would always be her right hand.

"So what are you planning on doing for your birthday?" Derek asked. Harmony shrugged again.

"I'm focused on school right now, so I probably won't do much."

"Last year was crazy," Woo said, remembering the venue and attendance. Harmony smiled.

"I know."

"That only means you have to do it even bigger this year," Derek said.

"Don't worry. We will put something together for you."

"How is Devin?" Woo asked, thinking about his bloodshot, teary eyes before he left. Derek shook his head.

"He's getting better, just give him some time."

The waiter came and took their orders while Derek caught Woo up to speed. The fact that Peezy gave Aria so much power made him leery. There was more to their story than just business, and he made it his business to see about this new arrangement. Woo's gut never steered him wrong. Ever.

# CHAPTER 26

Aria awoke to Peezy standing over her with twelve dozen tulips. Her favorite. "Happy birthday, ma!" he said. She rubbed her eyes, squinting from the light shining in the window.

"Aw . . . thanks, Peezy. At least you care if nobody else does." Aria was beginning to feel so alone. She was becoming depressed after Harmony made it blatantly clear that she wanted nothing to do with her, period. The more she tried not to care, the more her guilt and betrayal ate away at her. Aria was very aware of her feelings for Peezy, but for some reason she couldn't let go of Harmony. Her pride was her biggest downfall. All of these mixed emotions had her confused and frustrated.

"Here," Peezy said, digging into his pocket and handing her a slim black velvet box.

"What's this?" Aria asked.

"Diamonds. Aren't they a girl's best friend?"

"I could use a friend right now." She smiled sadly, opening the gift.

"Peezy!" she cried. "Oh my goodness! It's so beautiful . . . thank you so much!" Aria held the yellow canary choker to her neck. Peezy looked down at her and smiled.

"There is more," he said, handing her a birthday card.

"You're really showing out, aren't you? A round trip plane ticket to Atlanta? It's the place to be right now."

"I know, and I wish I could go with you, but I can't. I have to handle some business, get my ducks in a row, and I can't do that if I am in Atlanta with you."

"Really?"

"I got a few things I need to straighten out."

"Let me know if you need me to straighten somebody for you," Aria said.

"Nah, I'm good. Go have fun." Peezy chuckled.

"You sure?" Aria said, crawling to the edge of the bed.

"Yeah, it's personal." Aria wrapped her arms around his neck and kissed him passionately. He didn't resist. Peezy felt what was happening between them, something he so badly wanted to stop.

"Come, let me express my gratitude before I go," she whispered against his ear. He smiled and felt his manhood rise eagerly for the pleasure she provided. He never intended to fall for his sister's girl, but with Aria, there really was no other choice. Her beauty, charm, and no nonsense attitude made even the strongest fall weak and become entangled in her web.

\* \* \* \* \* \*

Peezy dropped Aria off at the airport, then sped to meet Samore and his son. He wrapped his arms around Junior, whom he had not seen in more than a month. Samore watched in tears as they embraced. The joy that her son expressed at the sight of his father evoked guilt and weakness, then anger followed. *Why am I feeling guilty? He's the one who couldn't keep his dick in his pants,* she thought. Peezy reached out to hug Samore, who put her hands up in protest.

"Damn, it's like that? Don't act like you don't miss me." Samore smacked her lips.

"Yeah, I miss you, but you made it like this, nigga," she snapped.

"I did. I made it like this, Samore, and I am sorry. But I can't fix it if you won't let me."

"There's not a big enough diamond or flashy car that will make the hurt and humiliation go away," Samore said, helping Junior into the car.

"Samore?"

"Listen, Peezy. I'm not sure about a lot right now, and—" Peezy wrapped his arms around her.

"No, you listen. I'm sorry. I love you. I miss my family, and I want you to come home. Samore . . . Aria—she . . . she didn't mean nothing. It was just . . ."

"Just what? Something to do out in the streets? That's just it, Peezy. I am tired of waiting at home while you and your ego does as it pleases. I'm tired of the abuse, Peezy. I'm tired of everything. I'm done." Samore bent down, kissed Junior good-bye, then closed the door.

"Samore?" Peezy said softly, feeling defeated.

"Try not to keep him out late. He is going somewhere with my mother in the morning," she called over her shoulder. A pang of guilt shot through Peezy. He had hurt her, and this time he wasn't sure if they would ever recover.

\* \* \* \* \* \*

Aria sat in the luxury chair wrapped in a plush robe while she sipped her tonic and watched the Chinese woman give her a pedicure. Ricky was a stylist from Saks who came in smiling and chatting with her like they were old friends. He was tall, loud, and flamboyant. His cinnamon skin tone was flawless, and his ice blond temped mohawk matched his personality to the tee.

"Stand up and hold still, honey, so that I can get your measurements," he said, waving away the Chinese woman.

"My measurements?"

"Yes. I am about to give you a new style, honey. Compliments of your fine ass man!"

"I don't need a damn makeover," Aria said.

"I'm sure you don't, but there is not a thing wrong with upgrading."

"Okay, you have a point." Aria smiled. Peezy had went all out for her birthday. It was the little things he did to acknowledge what was becoming of their love affair. Ricky disappeared with a short good-bye and a promise of glamour. She was excited to see what he had in store for her.

The spa treatment was nice, but it still left her feeling like blah. As she sat in the back of the Lincoln Navigator, her mind was in turmoil and her ego was bruised. Aria knew that eventually she was going to have to pay for her selfish choices, but she never knew that being rejected by Harmony would make her feel so low. Her thoughts were interrupted by her cell phone. It was Ragen. She had put him on Peezy before she left for her flight. Something told her that it was more to this trip than a birthday gift. She hoped to be paranoid, but she wasn't. Peezy was out with Samore trying to win her back. "Okay. Thanks, Ragen. Please keep me updated," Aria said, hanging up. She squeezed her iPhone in her palm. *This nigga got another think coming, if he thinks for one second I'm going to be his side bitch secret forever!* "I need a drink," she said aloud, sighing in frustration.

"Would you like me to stop somewhere?" the brown-skinned, husky driver asked.

"Please."

Aria's red bottoms clicked on the tile floor of Jim's Bar and Grill. She took a seat at the bar and ordered a berry margarita and sipped it slowly. Her eyes caught the seductive stare of a beautiful woman sitting across the room. The left side of her head was riddled with honey blonde curls and the other cut into a low fade. Aria couldn't help but smile. This stranger was openly flirting with her, and it felt good, especially after the call she just received from Ragen. If she could somehow keep the feelings for Peezy at bay with a little distraction, things would probably be a little less frustrating. The woman slid off the barstool, her long, butter-toffee legs strutted across the room toward her. Aria could feel the mutual attraction as she took all of her in. Her complexion shimmered in the light. She looked like money. Her skin was flawless, and her lips poked out involuntarily.

"What's good, beautiful?" Aria smiled at her flirtatious nature. She looked down at the goddess's thick thighs and shook her head.

"Not much, gorgeous."

"I'm Ava, and I couldn't help but come over here and get a closer look at your beauty and hopefully have a drink with you. That is, if you don't mind." Aria smiled. "What are you drinking?"

"Long island," Aria replied. Ava looked at the bartender. "A long island and a glass of coconut Cîroc." The bartender nodded and started on the drinks.

"My name is Aria."

"Pretty. So what brings you to Atlanta?"

"It's my birthday, so I decided I'd surround myself with new people, places, and pamper myself in the hottest city in the States."

"Interesting, what do you have planned?"

"I'm going to hit up one of these clubs' VIP section tonight, but first I want to do a little shopping. Do you have any place in particular in mind?"

"Club Envy is definitely the place to be. I'd love to show you around while you're out here. Show you my secret hideouts."

"That sounds like a plan," Aria smiled seductively. She looked into Aria's eyes and sensed the chemistry. The pair chatted for a while until a phone call. She excused herself, leaving her number written on a napkin with instructions to hit her up tonight. The newness of her presence excited Aria. She was definitely going to call her.

\* \* \* \* \* \*

Peezy watched Junior play video games and enjoy himself at the arcade. His mind was going crazy. He was trying to sort through the mess he had gotten himself in. He wanted his family back, but wasn't sure how he was going to get away from Aria. Part of him wanted to stay, but the other wanted to be with Samore. Peezy allowed himself to blame his doggish ways on Aria and reasoned that she was irresistible; it was just easier that way. Aria's chocolate-brown face lit up his screen. He dropped his head at that moment. He could no longer deny that he was caught up. He had to make a decision—he couldn't have cake if he wanted pie too. *Damn!* he thought, sending Aria to voicemail.

\* \* \* \* \* \*

Aria threw up the peace sign as she snapped a few selfies. Ricky had come to her hotel suite with Aria's new, glamorous, I'm-that-bitch wardrobe. He had definitely upgraded her swag over the course of a few hours. The peach Ferragamo high-waist skinny's she wore, hugged her hour glass frame. The multi-colored half-shirt showed off her toned stomach and accentuated her perky breasts.

"You standing real tall in those Ferragamo pumps, honey. You think you can walk around in them all night?" he asked.

"Most definitely," she replied. Ricky snapped his fingers twice.

"I love it! Confidence. Work it, darling. Work it!" Aria strut her stuff back and forth as they burst into laughter. "Come on and have a seat so I can put on our face." Aria sat patiently while Ricky did her hair and makeup. Once she looked in the mirror at her reflection, she knew that she would be turning heads. Aria thought about Ava and smiled. "Go on and smile, honey, 'cause you got it."

"Oh, I am definitely going to catch myself a fish tonight." Ricky plugged his nose and fanned the air. Aria laughed. "Umm, I am going to need your card because I want to look like this every day," she said, snapping her fingers, mimicking Ricky. They both laughed and toasted to the night.

After finishing up their drinks, Aria saw Ricky out, then dialed Peezy's number. Voicemail. She poured herself a drink and called again. Each time he sent her to voicemail. Aria took a deep breath, trying to refrain from throwing her phone, something that had become a habit. Peezy had sent her to voicemail for the fifth time. *Fuck him!* Aria thought. *Fuck Harmony too. It's all about me tonight. It's my day, always has been.* Suddenly, Aria stopped and tried to wrap her mind around when it had ever been about anybody else or how they felt and how she felt about them. "Why the sudden change?" she asked aloud. She shook her head and vowed to get back to her old self. *It served me better anyway.* Aria pulled Ava's number out of her clutch and called her.

"Hello?" a soft, sultry voice answered.

"Hey, gorgeous. It's me. Aria."

"Oh. Hey, what's up, sexy? Where you at?"

"I'm en route to club Envy."

"Good. I'm almost ready. I'll meet you in VIP."

"Okay." Aria could hear Ava smiling on the other end of the phone.

"See you in a few," Aria said, then slid her phone into her clutch. Her phone buzzed with a text from Ragen. Pictures of Peezy and Samore together enraged her. *So this is why he sent me across the map?* Feelings of betrayal sunk in, and Aria felt nothing but hate for Peezy. *I got something for him.* So many thoughts swarmed her mind. "Aaaaahhhh!" she screamed, startling the driver.

"Ma'am, is everything okay back there?"

"Umm yes, I'm good." *Calm down, Aria. You got this.* She felt like catching a flight back to San Diego and murdering him on sight. He had ruined her relationship with Harmony and was trying to ride off into the sunset with this bitch, after he played with her emotions. *This nigga's got a death wish, but death would be too easy of a punishment for him.* The driver pulled up to Club Envy and opened the door. The cool breeze brought Aria out of her murderous thoughts. She smiled at the driver, who looked at her strangely.

"I'll call you when I am ready." He nodded, saying nothing.

Aria strode to the front of the line and handed the bouncer a few crisp hundreds. He opened up the red rope and let her in without question. She made her way toward VIP.

"Damn shawdy. What's good with you?" a woman said, stopping her in her tracks. "I got a few party favors, if you are looking to have a good time." Aria giggled at the sexy woman's dirty south accent. Her dark chocolate melted into the cream outfit she wore.

"My name's Aria, not shawdy," she said.

"And my name is Cream." Her name rolled off her lips like a sweet song. Aria was attracted to her sophisticated bad boy swag almost immediately. Cream's linen attire and Prada loafers reminded her of Harmony.

"What you got for me, Cream?" She smiled at Aria's flirty behavior and stroked her hand across her tempered fade briefly.

"I have ecstasy Molly, and—" *Fuck it. You only live once,* Aria thought. She had never done any drugs besides smoke marijuana, but she had heard the buzz about ecstasy.

"Let me get two e-pills," she said, cutting her off. "How much?"

"Thirty a pop." Aria purchased two and handed her a hundred dollar bill. Cream gave Aria her change and wished her a good night, knowing that she would make sure to run into her before the night was over.

"Thanks," Aria said, licking her lips seductively.

"Mmphh! That one is dangerously sexy and probably nothing but trouble," Stacks said, slapping Cream on her back. Aria smiled at Cream's friend's ability to point out a bad apple. Her phone buzzed. It was a text from Harmony. Her heart beat sped up momentarily.

> 10:40 p.m.
> **Harmony:** *Happy B-Day Aria. Be safe & enjoy*
> *your night. The one & only.*

Aria read between the lines and texted back.

> 10:42 p.m.
> **Aria:**  *I love U 2 Harmony. Hopefully 1 day*
> *U will 4give me. Forever Yours*

She sent a few photos of her flawless upgrade. Aria didn't receive a reply, but Harmony had pulled on her heart strings. "It's me, fuck them," Aria told herself.

The music was blasting throughout the club as the DJ spun hit after hit. Aria was seated in the back of the VIP section where she had a view of the entire club. In a semi-festive mood, she ordered a bottle of top shelf Patron. Remembering what Ava had ordered earlier that day, she requested a bottle of coconut Ciroc. Aria filled her glass.

"Let's toast to a good night, your birthday, and each other," Ava said, sliding in the booth next to her. "For me?" Ava said, picking up the bottle of Ciroc.

"Yes, I think it is appropriate." Aria smiled. "Where are your friends at?"

"Oh, I'm kind of anti-social. I prefer to ride solo. I can't betray myself."

"I definitely agree with that. I got some goodies on the way up. You want to pop?" Aria asked.

"Sure. Why not?" Ava smiled.

"I've never popped before, but I grabbed us some," Aria said.

"It's always good to pop and celebrate another year. Hell, another day!"

Aria reached in her bra and pulled out the pills. Ava held her palm out. A single purple pill sat in the palm of her hand. "These are the best ones." They poured themselves another drink and simultaneously swallowed the pill.

"To us," Ava said with a wide smile.

"To us," Aria said, grinning also.

"Come on, let's dance." She grabbed Aria's hand.

* * * * * *

Harmony hesitated at the thought of sending Aria a reply. Damn she looked good, but she could see the sadness in her eyes. True enough, she and Aria were through, but she still loved her, always would.

"You ready!" Ginger asked, stepping into Harmony's living room. She smiled back at Harmony's reaction to her curves that poked out of her teal mini dress. Harmony made her feel so safe and beautiful, loved and respected. Something her husband had never been capable of. Everything between her and Harmony was progressing so fast, quicker than either of them had realized or acknowledged. Guilt swam in Ginger's stomach as she replayed her words when her secretary questioned who Harmony was. Ginger wasn't sure how any of this was going to sit with her parents, but the way she felt about Harmony could not be dismissed.

"Yeah, babe. I'm ready," Harmony said, standing to her feet and sliding her phone into her pocket.

Harmony pulled into traffic and headed toward Los Angeles. They had planned a weekend at Ginger's time-share in Beverly Hills, with the promise of no phones, no computers, just them. It seemed as if the harder Harmony tried to hold out on her feelings, the harder she fell.

"Question," Ginger said. "Is your brother in the streets too?" Harmony cleared her throat.

"Why? Would it bother you if he was?"

"No. I was just wondering." Ginger saw so much potential in Harmony, but the battle couldn't be won with just her. The odds were stacked against her.

"Ginger, the streets are all me and Peezy know. They raised us; they are all we ever had," Harmony said sadly. Ginger sighed. She had money put up in a trust fund she had yet to touch, but now she highly doubted she had enough to tame Harmony's appetite. She could tell by her threads, this Bentley, and her penthouse apartment that she was used to money. "What's on your mind?" Harmony asked.

"Just thinking about you, about our future." Harmony smiled and grabbed Ginger's hand.

"What about me, about us, and our future?" she asked.

"I want it to be secure." Harmony already knew where this conversation was going. She forced herself not to roll her eyes. She had plans, big plans, but she needed a few more months in the streets to secure them. "Ginger, baby, listen. I'm not going to be in the streets forever, but before I get out of them, I'm going to make sure my ducks are in a row and that financially I'm good—we're good."

"Money isn't everything!" Ginger snapped.

"That's easy for you to say when you have no idea what it's like to struggle, or know what hunger pangs feel like. You have no idea, and probably will never know the significance of money," Harmony said harshly.

"Well, I—" Ginger could not say anything in her defense,

because she always had the finest things money can buy. Her father always made sure of it.

\* \* \* \* \* \*

Aria drowned herself with alcohol. The ecstasy had invaded her blood stream and every little touch or brush of wind felt euphoric. Especially the way Ava was grinding her body into her, lust dripping in her eyes. "Aria, I want you," Ava said softly in Aria's ear. Sharp chills crept up her body. At that moment she could see herself sleeping with Ava.

"How bad?" Aria whispered back. Ava smiled and slithered her tongue against her ear.

"I can't wait to show you how—"

"Really? Ava, you got this slut bitch all up on you?" Aria turned to the loud voice and hand that was grabbing her arm.

"Bitch, get your hands off me!" Aria barked.

"Or else what?" Ava stood in front of Aria, who pulled her .22 out of her clutch.

"I'm far from the one to challenge, bitch!" Aria said, pointing the gun in the woman's face.

"Whoa, whoa, calm down, lil mama," Cream said, stepping between the three women. Aria's murderous stare pierced her, her gun pointed directly in the woman's face.

"Ava, you and Miranda are trippin'. Y'all gotta bounce." Ava cut her eyes at Cream, then kissed Aria's cheek. "Happy birthday, ma. I'm definitely going to hit you up," she said, then walked off. Miranda quickly followed. Aria kept her gun trained on Miranda until she was out of sight.

Cream turned to Aria. "Please put that gun away." Aria slid back the safety, then put the gun into her clutch. "Thank you," Cream said sarcastically. She grabbed Aria's hand and led her upstairs.

"You smoke?"

"Yes," Aria said sweetly, as if she didn't just have a gun in someone's face.

"Good. Let's go celebrate ya b-day. My nigga owns this bitch." Aria smiled and followed Cream without objection. Cream opened the door to a mini apartment that hung over the club. The view was amazing. She could see every inch of the club out of the two-way mirrored floor-to-ceiling windows. The floors were black marble and buffed well enough to see your reflection in them. "Thirsty?"

"Yes, please. Can I have a bottle of water? I've had more than enough to drink."

"Can't handle your roll?" Cream laughed.

"I think I am doing a good job with this being my first time popping," she admitted. Aria sat down on the plush white leather La Z Boy and crossed her legs. She looked around at the place. It was elegant. The black and white theme suited the small space well. The huge fish tank gave it a homey feel.

Cream stepped into the small kitchen and retuned with a wooden box and some swishers. Her phone buzzed. She answered and explained her current situation with Aria to whoever was on the other end.

"What was your name again?"

"You never asked." Cream smirked. She loved a woman with an attitude. "Aria," she answered in a sexy tone.

"Aria," Cream repeated her name.

"Good boy." Aria laughed.

"Oh, I'm far from a good boy," Cream said, sitting across from her. Part of Aria wanted Cream to come and sit right next to her, but she knew she needed to suppress her want for her.

*Chill out!* Aria scolded herself. The sound of music pouring into the room interrupted their flirting. Cream stood to her feet and greeted a dread head who was just as sexy. "Stacks, meet Aria. Aria, this is my potna, Stack Bundles." Aria stood and shook her hand. A tall woman came in. Her black dress wrapped her curves.

"Aria, meet Envy. Envy, this is Aria," Stacks said, smiling. Aria's mouthed opened and her eyes widened instantly, recognizing the woman.

"So this is where you've been hiding at?" The two women embraced. Aria had not seen her cousin since she was arrested a few years ago for killing her girlfriend.

Cream and Stacks looked at each other, then at the two women, baffled.

"Y'all know each other?" Stacks asked, eyeing Aria.

"Yes, this is my baby cousin!"

"Damn, this is a small world, ain't it?" Cream said, seemingly irritated by the discovery. Envy knew Cream had it bad for her and wouldn't let her cousin get wrapped up into her fantasy.

"Well, we are going to step out and let you guys catch up," Stacks suggested. Envy cut her eyes at Cream.

"Good idea." Aria caught their exchange. She knew Envy was going to spill all the details. Cream closed the door behind them. Envy sat down with Aria then hugged her tightly.

"What's been going on with you?" Aria asked.

"Nothing. Getting to this money. What are you doing in Atlanta?"

"It's—"

"It's your birthday!" Envy said, looking at her phone. Aria smiled.

"Yes, it is my birthday, and I had to get away from my drama."

"What drama?"

"I have somehow managed to fall for my girlfriend's brother."

"Brother?" Envy knew that Aria had never really been into men.

After what Envy's father had done to Aria, she had been with women ever since. "And?"

"And he's still in love with his wife."

"Aria, pull yourself together and get real. You don't even like men!" They both laughed.

"I know. He reminds me time and time again why."

"So what's up with your finances?" Envy asked seriously.

"Financially, I'm straight, but you can never have enough money."

"Well, if ever you want to get to it, you can come down here. There will always be a spot for you." Aria nodded.

"So what's up with you and Stacks? That's you?"

"Nah, she's everybody's 'ho. I'm just the one she wants. I am truthfully getting tired of her ass."

"Well, whenever you get sick of her ass, you can come fly down to Cali and fuck with me."

"Oh, I most definitely will."

"I'm flying out to Cali in the morning."

"Don't go, just stay for the rest of the weekend," Envy pleaded. Aria could never deny her cousin, especially after she made sure she had a paid lawyer for her case. She would forever be indebted to her.

"Okay, but no later than Monday." Aria needed to eventually go handle Peezy and his lies.

# CHAPTER 27

Harmony looked around and smiled. Tonight marked her nineteenth birthday, but strangely she felt much older. The past year had so many highs and lows, but most of all, she was thankful to still be breathing. Her friends and family two-stepped and swayed to Young Thug's new hit with bottles in the air. She searched the crowd for Ginger. Their eyes locked as she snapped her fingers. Harmony felt butterflies rise in her chest at the sight of her. They were falling head first into something neither of them could get enough of. Their lust for each other had quickly escalated into love, and even though they never addressed Ginger's failing marriage, they both understood and nothing else needed to be explained. Ginger walked over to her and wrapped her arms around her neck.

"Happy birthday, baby!"

"Thank you. Are you enjoying yourself?" Harmony asked.

"I am. I'm glad to see you are loved by not only me." Ginger said, leaving Harmony on pause.

"Me too," Harmony finally said with a smile. Ginger had just expressed the way she felt in a subtle way, like she had always done.

Derek and Byou came over, handing them both a drink. Derek signaled the deejay, who made a shout out to Harmony and played her favorite song. She smiled. "Congrats on your birthday, but more so to you for being a thorough young nigga," Derek said.

"Aww, Derek. Thanks," Harmony said, hugging him. Her phone buzzed in the back of her linen pants.

12:16 a.m.

**Woo:** *TURN AROUND!*

Harmony turned and saw Woo and Peezy rolling out her cake. It was made like bundles of cash. It looked so real. She couldn't help but admire it.

"I love you," Woo said, embracing her.

Ginger handed Harmony one of many gifts. She opened the velvet box and smiled at the fourteen carat gold chain that held half of a heart pendant that was filled with Le Vian diamonds. Ginger reached inside her dress collar and pulled out the other half, then placed it together. It clicked. Harmony hugged her, then kissed her passionately as everybody began to sing happy birthday. And happy she was.

While everyone else seemed to be wearing smiles, the deadpan expression on Peezy's face unnerved Harmony. She wondered what he was upset about this time. Or was that simply envy plastered all over his face?

* * * * * *

Aria stood hidden in the crowd watching Harmony and Ginger enjoy what she still felt entitled to. Part of her was blown that Harmony had actually moved on, and she could tell by the way she looked at Ginger that she was head over heels for her. She needed to dig deeper and find a way to end their little love affair. Aria pulled out her phone and emailed Ragen. She smiled. He had probably gotten filthy rich off of her, but in her twisted mind, it was money well spent. Aria was far beyond pissed. She had thought she would be able to string Harmony's love-sick ass along, while she selfishly enjoyed her cake too, but feelings got involved and everything went haywire fast. Now she was fighting to keep control over the simplest things. Everything was falling apart, not to mention Woo and Devin wouldn't stop poking around Deon's disappearance. If they both knew what was good for them, they would leave well enough alone.

All of her plans were seeming to backfire, and she was losing her grip on it all. Suddenly she felt nauseous. Aria moved swiftly through the crowd and into the restroom. She fell into the stall and vomited. *Did the sight of them make me that sick?* she thought, wiping her mouth with tissue. When she came out of the stall, her eyes met Peezy's, stopping her in her tracks.

"What are you doing here?" he asked. Aria smiled.

"I came to wish her a happy birthday!" she said, slyly.

"Aria, don't play with me."

"What. I know you're not jealous because I'm still in love with her, are you?" Peezy balled up his face, but Aria called it. She thought that not only was Peezy jealous, he was afraid of what she was capable of. He knew she had too much power over his life.

"Bitch, please! You and I know you can't get enough of me." He turned his back and walked out of the ladies room. "Carry your ass home, Aria!" he yelled, disappearing into the sea of people.

\* \* \* \* \* \*

Woo had given up drinking; it only fueled his anger and depression, so he agreed to be the designated driver. He watched Harmony and Ginger cuddle in the backseat. It made him miss Deon like no other. He had so much on his mind, and the fact that it was envy and possibly betrayal within the family, brought discomfort. He always sensed the cold shoulder Peezy tried to give him, but figured it was just too much testosterone in the room. He had seen Aria in the crowd watching Harmony enjoy herself and saw Peezy follow her to the bathroom. He wasn't sure if Peezy was trying to protect Harmony, or if there was more to their weird interaction. Woo didn't want to cause any unnecessary rift between Peezy and his sister based off assumption and paranoia. Ever since Betta told him to be mindful of Aria, he had begun to pay her more attention, and he didn't like what he saw. Woo parked the car and helped Ginger out of the backseat. They said their good-byes, and he watched them disappear into the lobby of Harmony's place. A text from Devin came through.

3:17 a.m.
**Devin:** *I am about to pull up. Where are you?*

3:19 a.m.
**Woo:** *I'm on my way!*

They had come no closer in their efforts to find out what happened to Deon. Woo had moved out of the place they shared and moved way across town to Paradise Hills. The memories were just too much for him. They ate away at him with no mercy. Woo drove in silence, analyzing the details of Deon's disappearance and still could think of nothing. He pulled into his driveway and parked next to Devin's Escalade truck. They hopped out, Woo leading the way to the huge one-story flat Harmony helped Woo find.

"What's good?" Devin finally said, breaking the comfortable silence that always lied between them.

"A lot of good and bad lately."

"Tell me about it. Something's not right about that nigga Peezy, more than him envying your relationship with his sister," Devin said harshly.

"Like what?" Devin lit his cigarette and inhaled sharply.

"I can't quite put my finger on it. He just seems like he's hiding something, and when he's not throwing shade or being distant, it feels forced for Harmony's sake." Woo cleared his throat.

"Well, I'm not sure either, but I do have to agree—the vibe has definitely changed recently." He didn't want to share his assumption just yet. He had to be sure before he started planting seeds. "And that bitch, Aria. She still gives me the creeps. She was at the club tonight. I saw her one minute, then she just disappeared. I don't know . . . she is so cold toward us, like we are not even a part of this team. She comes to the meetings and reports, but exchanges only with Peezy, unless one of us asks her a direct question. Then she gets her next assignment and walks out. What is up with that chick?" he asked in deep thought. Woo shrugged.

"It's her way of letting us know that we are irrelevant to her, and in her sick, twisted mind, inferior. Deon told us she was a psycho." Devin laughed.

"I know. Deon couldn't stand her ass." Their eyes locked as the words left his mouth, as if they were having the same exact thought. And they were.

\* \* \* \* \* \*

Harmony kissed Ginger on her cheek. "So, are we on for dinner?" she asked, turning to leave.

"Yes. I'll meet you at your place. How's seven o'clock sound to you?" Harmony nodded.

"Seven is fine." She fought the urge to tell Ginger she loved her. *It's too soon.* She scolded, opening the door to leave. Her eyes fell on the Mayor, who stood a few feet away from her. Recognition flashed in his eyes, then fear and anger followed.

"What are you doing here?" he asked, his voice filled with suspicion. He had canceled their last meeting, something Harmony found extremely strange. Ginger's secretary stood to her feet.

"I'm sorry, sir. Do I know you?" Harmony asked innocently. Maurice looked around at all the eyes that were glued to them.

"Oh, please forgive me. I thought you were someone else," he said, convincingly. "I'm a little overprotective of my daughter." *Daughter?*

"It's okay. It was nice meeting you though. You enjoy your day, sir," she said politely, side stepping the big man. Harmony dug in her pockets searching for her phone, then dialed Peezy's number. "Guess who I ran into?"

"Who?"

"Mr. No Show."

"Where?"

"At Ginger's office. Peezy, he's her father." Peezy sat on the phone in silence. "He didn't look happy about seeing me there either."

"He'll be all right. He has no choice but to be," Peezy said arrogantly.

"Well, I'm about to head up north to see Betta and—"

"For what?"

"I always go see him, twice a month. I will be back later, and we can link up, grab a drink or something."

"Okay," Peezy said, attempting to mask his feelings, something he failed miserably at. Harmony shook her head, then hung up. She hopped in her coupe and climbed onto the interstate.

* * * * * *

Ginger lied through her pearly white teeth when her father came storming into her office demanding to know what that *dike* was doing in her office. She had told him about a favor someone called in, and she was the one with the connections to make sure it got done. He ate her story up. She hadn't actually lied only by omission. Her father would not have the least bit of understanding if she had told him that she was very much in love with that *dike* and was leaving her husband for her. Ginger's mother was going to lose her mind and give her the speech about making Assistant DA and fixing her marriage, and what about her grandchild, something she wanted to avoid at all costs. Only she couldn't help but wonder what Harmony would say if she knew that she had denied her so matter-of-factly to her father. Ginger went throughout her day with her secret heavy on her mind. She called her contact to make sure the business was handled because her father was more than likely going to go behind her to make sure she wasn't keeping anything from him. Ginger sighed as she looked out the window.

*Beep!*

"Mrs. Grand, your husband is on line one." Ginger rolled her eyes and pressed down on the button.

"Tell him I am in a meeting and I will call him back later," she said, although she never intended on doing such a thing. He had become more concerned about her whereabouts as of late, sending flowers and cards, but it was too late for any of that. She was in love with Harmony. She had spent the last four days at her suite and couldn't think of any other place she'd rather be in the entire world.

\* \* \* \* \* \*

Tears pooled in Betta's eyes as he read his court paper work. His sentence had been reduced to five years, and now he was only looking to serve maybe four more years. He didn't mind doing another four years in prison due to his foolishness, but to sit for another nine because some cold-hearted bitch realized she hadn't covered her tracks well enough, pained him every night. He sat speechless for a few minutes. All he could do was thank God.

# CHAPTER 28

Aria rode in the taxi quietly, anxious to get home. Peezy had some random excuse as to why he couldn't come and pick her up, but she already knew where he was, and because he continued to lie and creep with his wife, she had something for him, something that would crush their marriage once and for all. Her thoughts drifted back to her cousin Envy and all her mess. They were so similar, there was no way they didn't share the same DNA. They both were knee deep in some bullshit, only Aria had decided to end it. She had stopped by to visit with Ricky while she was in Atlanta, and he indeed hooked her up. She paid the taxi driver extra to help her unload the trunk with her fly gear.

Aria stepped inside and shuddered at the silence. It was a big change from her cousin's noisy, busy lifestyle. Aria made a few phone calls and got ready for the night. She had to do it big one last time before she ended things with Peezy for good. She lit candles and slid into the sexiest two-piece lingerie getup. The white lace laid against her skin with no other intention except to seduce. She knew Peezy would not be able to resist her.

Peezy came in smiling like he had not spent the last two nights over Samore's house. Aria held her smirk back as she undressed him and kissed him passionately all over his body.

"Did you miss me, baby?" she asked.

"Yes, baby. You know I did. Why did you stay gone so long?"

"I hoped your heart would grow fonder with my absence." She smiled.

"It did," he said, pulling her down onto the bed and kissing down her body. Peezy spread her legs and began kissing her pleasure as his manhood throbbed for her wetness. Aria slid back and climbed on top of his face, riding his tongue until she orgasmed. Then she pulled his length into her mouth, stroking and sucking him softly. "Tell me you love me," Aria whispered between slurps.

"I love you!" Peezy moaned.

"Tell me you're never leaving me."

"I'm never leaving. I swear I'm not," Peezy moaned louder, as Aria swallowed him deeper into her throat.

\* \* \* \* \* \*

Peezy lay next to Aria watching her sleep. He replayed the sex they had been having three days straight. He was in so deep he didn't know what to do. One thing he did know was that being a part of Junior's life trumped any and everything and Samore made it clear that if he was going to be a part of their life, Aria wouldn't be a part of his. Peezy sighed, then slid out of the covers and into his clothes. He didn't know how he would break the news to her, but he had no choice.

\* \* \* \* \* \*

Ginger hung up on her pleading husband. It was over. The divorce papers had been drawn up. All she needed was his signature, but she wasn't sure if he'd cooperate, seeing as how he had been blowing up her phone all day. He seemed desperate, making a last attempt to alter her decision, but she would have none of it. Ginger had made up her mind; she wanted to spend the rest of her life with Harmony. Only she would have to break the news to her parents, and she wasn't sure that was something she could do. Ginger sighed. She had an hour to make it to Harmony's place. She noticed that Harmony was slowly but surely weaning herself off the streets. She had been accepted into San Diego State, and even though she didn't speak on it, she knew Harmony had big plans for them. Ginger grabbed her Vera Wang jacket off the couch and headed out. A manila envelope sat in the middle of the foyer of the apartment she rented. Ginger bent down and flipped it over. It didn't look like it had anything to do with business, so she opened it. Ginger gasped as she looked through the photos of her and Harmony on various dates kissing in the Cayman Islands, hugging, holding hands, and shopping. A small note typed in bold ink read:

> Stay away from her or I'm going to tell daddy about your secret affair!
> Try me . . .

Ginger suddenly felt sick. As a rising DA, she knew not to take threats lightly. *Damn!* she thought, shredding each photo. Her phone rang. She sent Harmony to voicemail.

\* \* \* \* \* \*

Woo sat irritated with Peezy, who had told him in so many words to not call him for anything. That Aria was handling the traps the neighborhood Crip ran.

"But the only reason I called was because Aria wasn't answering the phone or returning my calls," Woo explained.

Peezy sat in the meeting and gave Woo the side eye. Now he sounded like he had a whole lot more on his chest than he had put on.

"Listen *Woo*," Peezy said, sarcastically. "Last time I checked, Aria told me that them niggas from 47 paid their taxes and that she handled everything else. Are you challenging her motives, or implying that she is skimming off the top?"

"Skimming?" Aria said, walking into the meeting late. "There is no reason for me to skim. I got more money put up than you niggas have seen in a lifetime. I don't have to take shit from you." Aria threw a Birkin bag filled with cash on the table. "I have somewhere to be. You can fill me in later."

The team sat irritated. Derek and Woo looked at each other knowingly. Derek shook his head. "So you are just going to let her leave before the meeting is over?"

"Umm, correct me if I am wrong, but Devin has not been to half the meetings in the past month!"

"Yeah, but we all know why," Woo said, defensively.

"Yeah, whatever," Aria said, heartlessly. "Get at me later, Peezy. I'm out." Aria strutted out the door. Derek stood to his feet.

"This shit is one big joke." He unzipped the bag and began counting the money, dividing everyone's cut. Peezy sat stunned at how his empire w as rapidly falling apart. He needed Harmony. Byou didn't even attend meetings anymore. She just handled her business, came and collected her paper, then left just as quietly as she had come.

"Y'all trippin' for no reason. A lot has happened over this past month and—" Woo shot to his feet, cutting Peezy off.

"Nigga, don't act like there isn't division amongst us." Peezy looked at Woo.

"What are you talking about?"

"Come on, Peezy. Don't act like you don't see it—feel it," Derek said.

"You probably can't see it because it starts with you!" Woo said.

In seconds, Peezy was across the room, his fist connecting with Woo's jaw. They exchanged blows. Derek was barely able to keep them apart.

"Enough!" Devin yelled, as insults flew across the room.

"Well, if there wasn't any division amongst us, there damn sure is now, and I can clearly see where everybody stands," Peezy said, grabbing his coat and slamming the door behind him.

\* \* \* \* \* \*

Devin sat in the hotel room where Deon breathed her last breath. Tears rolled down his face. "Please, Deon. Let me know something. I can't do this all by myself," Devin said. He sipped on the fifth of Jack Daniels and looked out the window. The breeze dried the tears as they fell down his face. He ignored his phone that had been buzzing nonstop. Devin looked out onto the ledge that sat outside of the window. He looked left then right, and a glimmer of something caught his eye. He climbed out the window and onto the ledge toward the shining object. He picked it up and gasped; it was a bracelet with heart-shaped karats on it. He crawled back to the room, his mind racing. He had to get back to his house so he could watch the tape. He was almost sure that this was the bracelet Aria had on that night. Devin had watched the tape so many times, it was etched in his mind. The mark's room had been just a few doors down and could be accessed from the ledge. He picked up his phone and called Woo.

"Meet me at my house. I think I found something to connect Aria to Deon's disappearance."

\* \* \* \* \* \*

Aria sat across the food court watching Samore play with Junior. She was highly upset that Samore and Peezy were trying to mend what she had once so easily dismantled. Peezy had ruined her life, and now Harmony wanted nothing to do with her. If she couldn't have Harmony back, he damn sure wasn't going to get his family back. Samore stood to her feet after buckling Junior in, then stepped away to get their food. *This is my only chance!* Aria pulled her fitted cap over her head and walked briskly over to Junior. She dropped the wrapped gift into Samore's shopping bag, and then blended in with the busy shoppers. She smirked at her success. Nobody played with Aria without paying for it. All the flowers and gifts Peezy had been showering Samore with, broke through her weak ass resolve. *They'll never be together if I have anything to do with it*, Aria thought. She knew that once Samore saw the tape of the many lovemaking sessions she and Peezy had, she'd probably want to slit her wrists.

Aria rushed home, packed up most of her things, and sped off to the condo she was leasing in Chula Vista. Peezy would come looking for her, and she didn't want to be a sitting duck when he did.

\* \* \* \* \* \*

Harmony was stoked to be finally graduating high school, and to be doing so at the top of her class gave her the confidence she needed to pursue a better life. It meant more than anybody knew. When she looked out into the crowd, all her loved ones were in attendance, all except Peezy. Ginger and her beautiful smile had been very distant lately. Harmony couldn't put her finger on it, but it was definitely going to be handled. The one thing that mattered now was that she was there on her day. Derek, Devin, and Byou stood taking picture after picture as she stood to receive her award. She smiled in an attempt to hide the pain of her brother not coming to celebrate her accomplishment.

When Woo expressed his feelings about Peezy and Aria, she had to shake the initial shock and ache that his possible betrayal left in her stomach. Today was her day. Peezy and Aria would have to wait. As if the thought of Aria made her appear, she came into view, smiling and blowing a single kiss. Harmony cut her eyes, and then stood to throw her hat with her class. When she looked up, Aria was gone. Harmony took note of her flawlessness, then turned her mind to her loved ones.

"Congrats, my ninja," Byou said, smiling with love. She handed her a card and balloons. Harmony smiled.

"Thanks so much y'all for supporting me through this."

"Aw, we owe it to you, sis. You took us in like we were family," Devin said behind his jet-black Ray Bans. They all hugged Harmony and said good-bye, with plans to link up later.

"So what's been going on with you?" Harmony asked Ginger, once they were alone. She shrugged.

"I've just been real busy with this case," Ginger lied.

"And what else is new?" Ginger turned to Harmony.

"My father doesn't want me seeing you anymore. He said you are dangerous and—"

"Ginger, I would never hurt you," Harmony said, her tone hurtful, making Ginger's lie harder to tell. "Please don't do this to me. I-I love you." Ginger dropped her head.

"Harmony, I'm sorry, but I can't." Ginger cried, walking off. Harmony stood there in the middle of the school parking lot, heartbroken.

\* \* \* \* \* \*

Aria and Envy laughed at the petty hustler trying to spit his weak game. "We only fuck with ballers," Aria said, walking off.

"Damn it feels good to be back in Cali. I can't remember the last time I was out here," Envy said, smiling.

"Well, to be honest. I'm ready to leave Cali. It has brought me nothing but heartache. I was hoping you still had that position open for me?" Aria said sadly, knowing there was nothing left out here for her. Peezy had been blowing up her phone sending threatening messages, and Woo had been snooping around her house.

"Of course you know you're welcome to anything I have."

"I am so grateful for that," she said honestly. They placed their bags in the trunk of Aria's new Audi 745 and pulled off into traffic. As they rode in silence, Aria boasted about her crib and all she was about to leave behind. She pulled into the garage and killed the engine. "I just need to grab a few things, but I can show you my place before we get out of here. Envy looked around at her baby cousin's house. She had definitely been living good. Aria showed her every room, even Junior's old play room, her gun collection, and office. Envy stopped her in the hall.

"Okay, what are you running from?"

"Running?" Aria asked, nervously.

"Yeah, you're doing really well for yourself. Why are you leaving all this behind?"

"It's complicated. I—" Envy realized that her baby cousin was just like her—running from something.

The doorbell rang. Aria excused herself, but before she could reach the bottom of the steps, Woo had damn near broken down the front door. "So where have you been hiding at?" Woo asked calmly.

"Hiding?" Aria chuckled. "Nigga, please! I don't hide, but enough with the small talk. We ain't never been cool anyway. What's up?" Aria responded.

"Missing something?" Woo held up the bracelet.

"So you come bearing gifts?" Aria kept a straight face. Yet panic set off inside of her. She had not been able to find that bracelet for months. *How did he get that?*

"Bitch, don't play dumb. I know you had something to do with Deon's murder."

"Murder?" Aria smiled and walked over to the bar, then poured herself a drink. "No body, no murder," she said stoically. Woo rushed toward her.

"What is that supposed to mean?" he yelled, leaving little space between them.

"Exactly what it sounds like," Aria replied, dousing Woo with a glass full of acid, then reaching for her silenced .38. His screams pierced throughout the house as the acid ate away at his flesh, leaving Aria no choice.

*Pfft.*

She put a bullet through his head, silencing him forever. She bent down and picked up her bracelet pocketing it. "I was looking all over for this." Envy came down the steps.

"Aria, what's going on?" She had a pistol in her hand. Aria smiled.

"Nothing. I got this. Look under the bed and grab them black duffle bags, then put 'em in the trunk of my car in the garage. I also need my lap top. Take it out of my office and wait for me in the car. Envy looked down at Woo's body, then ran back up the stairs. Aria dragged Woo's heavy body down the hall and into the bathroom where she kept a small supply of acid. After struggling to get his dead weight situated in the bathtub, she unscrewed the top off both containers and poured acid all over his body. Smoke and fumes lit up the air as Woo's body dissolved into nothing.

* * * * * *

After days of Ginger ignoring Harmony's calls, she was left with no other option but to confront her. She took a few deep calming breaths in an attempt to relax her growing anger. She was deeply in love with Ginger, and ever since her graduation, for some reason she had been dodging her. Stedfast in her decision to get to the bottom of things, Harmony walked into Ginger's office demanding her whereabouts.

The mildly shocked receptionist stood up. "Umm, Mrs. Grand is in a mee—" Harmony kept walking and barged into Ginger's office, interrupting the meeting.

"Harmony!" Ginger looked shocked to see her. Harmony stood her ground, gazing right into Ginger's eyes.

"Either we can talk here, or in private. It doesn't matter to me, but you will hear what I—" Ginger grabbed Harmony's hand.

"Umm, please excuse me." Everybody fled out of the office quickly and quietly.

"What the fuck is going on? Why are you avoiding me, dodging me every time I call? I know you love me, Ginger. Tell me what is going on. One minute you want to spend eternity with me, then the next you won't even take my calls." Tears pooled in Harmony's eyes. "Tell me what I did? Is it the streets? I've let them go. You know I would never hurt you, Ginger. Tell me what it is?" Ginger reached in her desk and pulled out the threatening letters and more pictures of her and Harmony.

"Somebody is threatening me. I can't afford for my father to find out, or my boss. I'm trying to make Assistant DA, and I just have so much going on in my life right now that I didn't know what to do. I am not stupid enough to take threats lightly. I—"

"Aria," Harmony said, her face turning red.

"Who?"

"It's my ex-girlfriend," Harmony said. "Don't worry, ma. I'm going to take care of it. She spun on her heels and stormed out of the office. Harmony sped to Aria's place as she called her repeatedly. No answer.

* * * * * *

Envy packed the duffle bags into the trunk and loaded up her gun collection. She figured it would come in handy. They went through the house gathering up a few things.

"Here. Take these to the car," Aria said, tossing a few bags down the steps. *One last thing and I'm outta here,* she thought, going to check on Woo's body, making sure the acid had eaten him alive. She couldn't afford to leave any loose ends.

"Going somewhere?" The sound of Peezy's voice stopped her in her tracks.

"No. You wouldn't care if I was," Aria replied.

"I just have one question. Why?"

"Because you ruined my fucking life! So I thought I'd return the favor."

"Ruined your life? Bitch, my sister had been done with your disloyal ass. You're the one who couldn't play your position and got all attached like we were ever really going to be together," Peezy said, laughing. Aria pointed her gun at him and let off a shot, sending him to his knees. "You bitch!"

"Fuck you! You played on my emotions, lied, and then thought that I was just going to let you leave me while you lived happily after ever with that weak ass bitch." Aria laughed, sending another shot through Peezy's arm.

"Aria!" Harmony's voice evoked an emotion she couldn't handle at that moment. "Let him go. It's over," Harmony said.

"Fuck him!" Aria shouted, letting off another round into his stomach. Harmony looked at Peezy. She wanted to hate him for betraying her, but seeing blood leak from his stomach made her want to protect him.

"Aria. Baby, please just leave. It's over."

"She ain't going nowhere. She has a few questions to answer," Devin said, stepping into the living room with his gun trained on Aria. She switched her aim from Peezy to Devin.

"Wait, wait. What is going on in here?" Harmony asked.

"Tell him, Aria. Tell him how you killed my sister," Devin said. Aria laughed.

"I don't know what you're talking about. Harmony, tell him to put the gun down or else—"

"Or else what are you going to do? Shoot me too?"

"Everybody just put their guns down!" Harmony yelled.

Devin let off the first shot, then Aria. Both of them tearing through one another's flesh. Aria crashed into the china cabinet.

"Nooo!" Harmony looked at Devin whose stare seemed far off. Before he could regain his composure, his brains splattered onto the wall, and he fell to the ground. Envy appeared in the living room with her gun trained on Harmony.

"I'm going to tell you one time and one time only. Put your fucking hands where I can see them."

"Envy, no! Don't shoot her!" Aria managed to yell.

"Are you okay?" Envy asked.

"Yes, just get me to my truck. I'll be fine."

"Who are you?" Harmony asked.

"No one."

"Harmony, I'm so sorry," Peezy said, choking and coughing.

"Let's go!" Aria said. Harmony looked up at them as they backed pedaled out the living room. Envy's gun trained on Harmony.

"Aria!" she yelled. "You have twenty-four hours to disappear. I don't ever want to catch you in my city ever again," she said, helping Peezy to his feet.

* * * * * *

*BEEP! BEEP! BEEP!*

The sounds from the monitor woke Peezy from his sleep. He attempted to sit up, but was snatched back down by the pain that shot throughout his body, crippling him. His eyes bucked open as reality set in, and his last memories replayed in his mind. Peezy looked around the hospital room, and his eyes landed on his sister Harmony, who lay next to him in the reclining chair. He shut his eyes, trying to remember everything that happened. Suddenly his room door opened, and Aria came strutting in with a sly grin on her face. She walked over to Harmony's sleeping body and pumped her heart with two bullets. Then she turned the gun on him. "No, no, Aria, wait! Let me explain."

"What's understood doesn't need to be explained."

*Boom!*

Peezy jumped out of his sleep, grabbing his chest.

"Peezy, calm down. It was just a dream," Harmony said, sitting up in the reclining chair.

"Right . . . a dream."

# Author's Bio

Belle Ahosi was born and raised in San Diego, California. Writing is her passion, but also her therapy as it has always given her a way to vent her feelings. While growing up, Belle was once taught that emotions turn you into a fool. So she decided to let her emotions bleed through the ink between the lines on paper, and through her characters.

While at Fulton County jail, she participated in a program called New Beginning. The entire class was given an assignment to write something creative, so she wrote a short story and was immediately drawn to writing. Creating and shaping stories helped her escape from her own misery. Belle believes that writing gives her a purpose. Never did she think she would become a novelist, although she has always been ambitious and dreamed big. For Belle, dreams feel different once they actually happen. She hopes to give her readers what so many other authors have given her. An escape from temporary madness.

Belle is the mother of two children, Isaiah Amir and Elijah Malik, who are her greatest accomplishments. Currently, she is serving time at Pulaski State Prison in Georgia.

*Beautifully Ruthless* is her first novel.

MURDER *Breeds* MAY·HEM

*A Hood Love Story*

PIERCE J. ANFIELD

WHEN WHAT *God* HAS... *ain't* GOOD ENOUGH

A NOVEL BY
FALICIA BLAKELY

*Beautifully* RUTHLESS

*A Novel By*
BELLE AHOSI

www.ingramcontent.com/pod-product-compliance
Lightning Source LLC
Chambersburg PA
CBHW021320250626
47155CB00002B/567